Crossing the Friend Zone

KELLY EADON

FOREVER
YOURS

New York Boston

Copyright © 2017 by Kelly Eadon
Excerpt from *The Wedding Date* copyright © 2016 by Kelly Eadon
Cover design by Elizabeth Turner. Cover images © Shutterstock. Cover copyright © 2017 by Hachette Book Group, Inc.

Forever Yours
Hachette Book Group
1290 Avenue of the Americas, New York, NY 10104
forever-romance.com
twitter.com/foreverromance

First published as an ebook and as a print on demand: March 2017

Forever Yours is an imprint of Grand Central Publishing. The Forever Yours name and logo are trademarks of Hachette Book Group, Inc.

The publisher is not responsible for websites (or their content) that are not owned by the publisher.

The Hachette Speakers Bureau provides a wide range of authors for speaking events. To find out more, go to www.hachettespeakersbureau.com or call (866) 376-6591.

ISBNs: 978-1-4555-9402-3 (ebook), 978-1-4555-9401-6 (print on demand)

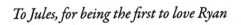

To Jules, for being the first to love Ryan

ACKNOWLEDGMENTS

First and foremost, thank you to my husband, Dan, for being my biggest fan and supporter. I'm lucky to have you.

Thank you to Jules Dixon for seeing Ryan's potential and encouraging me to explore his happily ever after. Thank you to Ellen Butler for your enthusiasm and showing me all the ways of marketing.

To my editor, Michele Bidelspach, for your faith and guidance. To my agent, Dawn Dowdle, for creating a fantastic and supportive community for us authors.

And last but not least, thanks to my Lemerk family for showing me true, lasting friendship.

CHAPTER ONE

Ryan Lawhill straightened his bow tie one last time, then raised his fist and knocked on the apartment door.

A few seconds later, it swung open. Ainsley Slone stood on the other side, her blonde hair twisted at the nape of her neck and her slim body encased in a sparking green gown. He fought to keep his eyes on her face. Ainsley was a friend, period. Even if she weren't so completely his opposite, the merest hint of anything else could fracture their friend group. He might not be good at relationships, but friendships were sacred.

That meant he was staring directly into her blue eyes, which he couldn't help noticing were underlined with dark circles and rimmed by red lids.

His chest ached. For the briefest of seconds, he was overcome with the urge to wrap her in his arms and crush her to him. He hated for anyone to be unhappy, ever. Even though they weren't the closest of friends, he had an obligation. Kate and James, Beth and Griffin, Ainsley and Ryan. They were a group of six now, and as the only two of their friends left uncoupled he and Ainsley were inevitably going to be spending more time together.

Then her gaze dropped to his blue Converse and her eyes narrowed. "You cannot wear those to a black-tie party."

And just like that, the feeling passed. He was wearing a tuxedo, which he'd rented especially for their friends Kate and James's engagement party. That meant he could wear whatever shoes he wanted. Plus, his Converse were sharp.

He rolled his eyes. "They match my bow tie. Besides, is that any way to talk to your knight in shining armor? Your just-for-the-night prince charming?"

Kate had been very clear about his assignment for the evening: protect Ainsley from party guests who wanted to gossip about her newly single status or rehash her breakup. Ainsley's boyfriend, Scott, had boarded a plane and moved to Hong Kong only forty-eight hours ago. Without her. It was a fresh wound, and the Fallston crowd could be ruthless when they sensed blood in the water.

Which was another reason he'd worn the Converse. He'd give those uptight society types something else to talk about.

One side of her mouth quirked upward. "If you're my prince charming, even just for one night, my fairy godmother and I need to have a serious talk."

He lifted one hand to his heart and staggered back, feigning a mortal wound.

Then he glanced at her from the corner of his eye and caught her smiling. *Success!* Ainsley's smile had always been beautiful. It was her crazy uptight rules and expectations that needed work.

He straightened up and held out his arm. "Your chariot awaits, milady. She's a hell of a lot better than a magic pumpkin, too, if I do say so myself."

She hooked her arm through his. "On that point, I'd agree with you."

He grinned. His Mustang was sexy. Everybody knew it.

He punched the button for the elevator. They stood for a moment, waiting in silence, and he let his gaze travel through the hallway. Over the plush carpet with intricate diamond patterns. Up to the detailed crown molding and the custom-framed paintings on the wall.

He didn't want to know how much her rent was. And for what? To live in the Point? In a luxury building where every unit looked exactly the same?

No, thank you.

The elevator pinged its arrival, the doors opening slowly, and when he glanced back at Ainsley he saw tears crowding the corners of her eyes.

Shit. Hell. Damn.

His stomach clenched. He didn't do crying women. They triggered his urge to flee far, far away. He thought of it as a biological instinct, something he'd probably inherited from his father.

He gritted his teeth and tugged gently on her arm, leading her into the elevator. Should he say something or just pretend he didn't notice the tears? When she was safely inside, he pushed the button for the lobby.

"We don't have to go, you know." He blurted the words.

She dropped her chin and stared at her sparkly gold sandals. "We do have to go."

His spine tensed. "No, we don't. Kate didn't even want this party. If you'd rather go somewhere else or do something else, she'd understand completely."

And she would. Kate was cool like that, a true friend. It was why he'd offered to escort Ainsley tonight. Kate deserved to enjoy her party without worrying about everyone else.

He racked his brains. "I bet if I looked it up on my phone, I could find a club with male strippers."

Strip clubs always cheered people after a breakup, didn't they? Not that he'd ever gotten serious enough with a woman to find out firsthand. He knew better than that. Maybe if he showed Ainsley the joys of single life, she might loosen up a bit.

She made a strangled noise in the back of her throat, then giggled. "I feel obligated to inform you, for the sake of all women, that we prefer our therapy in the form of chocolate and shopping. Although sometimes Magic Mike does hit the spot."

He shrugged. Hey, at least he'd tried. He had other ways of cheering a woman up, he just wasn't about to try any of them on Ainsley.

She frowned. "And we do have to go. I promised Kate. Besides, my parents will be there. Along with everyone I grew up with and everyone I know. If I avoid it, they'll only talk more. I have to hold my head high and just get through it."

He swallowed a sigh. He'd never get that scene. Where was

the fun in constantly worrying about what other people thought of you?

He reached for her hand and squeezed it. After all, he'd promised Kate. Surely he could get Ainsley through one night. "All right then. If we're actually going to do this, we need to come up with a special code word. Something that signals the need for immediate escape and rescue."

She raised an eyebrow at him. "For you or for me?"

He slanted her a look, sure there'd be half a dozen women at the party he'd hooked up with over the past year. But he could handle them. He wasn't the one who needed a bodyguard.

She wrinkled her nose. "I suppose 'strippers' would be an inappropriate safe word for the occasion."

His pulse sped. *Safe word?* He liked the sound of that, but he had to keep his mind focused and on task.

A strand of blonde hair fell across her face and he reached to tuck it behind her ear. Her eyes flicked up to meet his and suddenly his throat went dry. He would not think about what it would be like to kiss her, he wouldn't dare consider what she looked like without that formfitting dress. Kate trusted him and he couldn't violate that trust. Not to mention that the cardinal rule of his dating life was to keep things casual. Dating your best friend's best friend could never be casual.

He swallowed hard. This was just witty banter between friends. "Why not? I have faith that you could work that into a conversation. In fact, I'd love to see you do it."

Her eyes flashed, but he couldn't read the emotion in them. Was it amusement? Annoyance? "I bet you would."

The elevator pinged as it reached the ground floor, and the doors slid open.

* * *

For the briefest of seconds, as she'd looked up into his deep blue eyes and her heart thudded, she's understood. She'd finally seen a flash of whatever compelled women to fall into his bed without the hint of anything more. Not that she was the type of woman who'd fall for Ryan Lawhill's routine.

Then he'd given her that wolfish grin. "Personally, I'd love to see how the ladies who live in the Point react to the mention of strippers. Or does excessive plastic surgery prevent them from having facial expressions?"

Just like that, the feeling passed and she was back to the flicker of annoyance he frequently inspired in her. He could make fun of her world as much as he wanted, but what people thought did matter. Belmont was a small town, Fallston was a small private school, and the Point was an exclusive neighborhood. She couldn't help it. She'd always cared what they thought of her and she probably always would. Why did he have to judge her?

With a huff, she strode out of the elevator ahead of him.

He could pretend all he wanted, but he needed her just as much as she needed him. Ryan had slept with half of the twenty-something women who lived in the Point. She'd protect him from scorned, disappointed lovers, and his presence as her date would allow her to save face. Ryan was good at pretending he didn't care, but she knew there had to be something more underneath the surface. Everyone had their own personal battle. Hers was Scott and the breakup. She couldn't help but wonder what Ryan's was.

She squared her shoulders, ignoring the sadness that had lodged itself in her stomach weeks ago and refused to budge. So what if she was almost thirty and still unmarried? So what if Scott had dumped her, leaving her to start all over? If anything, Kate and James were proof that love struck when you least expected it. They'd reconnected only six months ago and were already engaged, thanks partially to her matchmaking abilities. Surely she could manage something similar for herself. Her eyes blurred, but she sucked in a deep breath and released it slowly. She wasn't going to beat the disappointment and sadness, not yet, but she didn't have to put her emotions on display for everyone to see. As her father said, that was a true sign of weakness.

Behind her, the rubber soles of Ryan's sneakers squeaked on the marble floor. "How do you walk so fast in those damn heels? If you're not careful, you'll break your neck."

She spun on her heel. The shoes put her a few inches short of eye level with him. Which was part of the reason she wore them. It gave her a sense of confidence and power to be almost, but not quite, as tall as her date. She'd read the tip in a magazine in middle school and had put it to good use ever since.

His eyes sparkled mischievously. "So, safe words. Did we choose one yet?"

Her cheeks flamed and she glanced over her shoulder to see if the uniformed doorman was listening. *Safe word*. Had she really said that? Talk about a Freudian slip.

She took a step in his direction and poked him in the chest with one manicured fingernail. "The safe word is *commitment*. Because I want to see you work that into a conversation."

With that, she stalked out into the damp spring night, pulling her wrap tightly against her bare shoulders. Maybe he'd unsettled her for a minute, but she was every bit as good at projecting an image as he was. Tonight she'd prove it.

CHAPTER TWO

Ainsley was seated in the Mustang's passenger seat, trying to block out Ryan's loud rock music and visualize her plan for the evening when her black silk clutch vibrated. She popped it open and pulled out her phone. That and a lip stain were the only two things she'd managed to wedge inside.

Kate's name flashed across the screen, bringing with it a wave of panic. She'd wanted to spend the afternoon with Kate, helping her get ready for the party, but instead her friend had convinced her to just arrive an hour early and help with any last-minute details.

"Hello?"

"Houston, we have a problem." Kate's voice was a terse whisper.

"What kind of problem?" She tried to use her calm, event planner voice but sounded high-pitched even to her own ears. Whatever it was, she had to fix it. Kate deserved for tonight to be perfect.

Kate inhaled sharply. "The dress doesn't fit."

Ainsley squeezed the phone so hard her knuckles ached. What did she mean, it didn't fit? Kate had tried it on only a few days ago, when they'd picked her jewelry for the evening.

"Of course it fits. You will make it fit."

There was a burst of hysterical laughter on the other end of the line. "I can't! My boobs are falling out."

At that, her mind switched fully into business mode. It was simply impossible. The satin gown had a high, draped neck and a plunging back. The only place Kate's boobs could go was inside the dress.

"Send me a picture." There had to be an easy fix.

Kate's voice rose. "Of my boobs? I think not."

Ainsley made her voice soothing and calm. "A picture of the dress, not your boobs."

Ryan's head swiveled in her direction. Of course the mention of boobs had caught his attention. With one hand, she pushed the side of his face until he faced the road again. The last thing they needed was a car accident.

Kate muttered an expletive. "I don't know how to get a picture of the dress without my boobs. That's the problem, the boobs won't go in the dress."

Silently she cursed herself. She should have been there to help Kate get ready. She'd shown up at 4:00 p.m., but Kate had sent her straight home with strict instructions to take a nap. Even her favorite concealer could no longer hide the dark circles under her eyes.

"Don't panic." She'd helped pull off more than a hundred weddings and other events. This was her area of expertise.

She knew Kate was just nervous about the party. The only way to talk James's mother out of a 500-person wedding had been to concede to a 500-person engagement party.

"OK." Kate's voice quavered.

"Put the phone on speaker and set it down. Then unzip the dress. Step out of the dress."

A few seconds passed.

"Now I'm naked, and I'm definitely not going to the party naked."

Ainsley chuckled. "I would never let you go to your own party naked. Now, hook your index fingers under the two straps and hold the dress up."

The dress they'd chosen was silky and draped intricately so it hugged her curves. Kate could have easily slipped an arm through the wrong hole, causing the whole thing to hang funny.

There was a rustling sound. "OK."

"On one side the neckline will be high, and on the other the neckline will be low. Very, very low."

"Yeah..."

"The high side covers your boobs. It goes in front. The low side doesn't cover your boobs, it goes in back. And I put double-sided dress tape in the front pocket of your garment bag so you can make absolutely sure everything that is supposed to be covered stays covered."

It was an industry trick she'd picked up years ago.

There was a *whoosh* as Kate let out a breath, followed by hysterical giggling. "Holy shit, I'm such an idiot."

Relief flooded her and she allowed herself to smile. "No,

you're nervous, and someone should have been there to help you put on your dress. Except you ordered that someone to take a nap."

"Yeah, I did. Speaking of, did you finally get some sleep?"

She bit her tongue. No need to tell Kate she'd lain awake on her bed staring at the ceiling, going over the same damn questions. Why had Scott boarded that plane without her? Why didn't he want her?

Her stomach twisted and she blinked back tears.

Not tonight. She was done wallowing.

"Uh-huh. Yeah. Ryan and I are already on our way over, so I'll see you soon. In your gorgeous dress, with your boobs in their proper place."

Kate sighed. "Thanks to you, I won't be naked. If you weren't already a bridesmaid and my friend, I'd hire you to event plan the shit out of my wedding."

Her chest grew tight and she forced a laugh. That was her, the wedding planner who'd never actually have a wedding. At this rate she should pull a Carrie Bradshaw and register for a crap ton of expensive shoes.

She tried to ignore the sadness squeezing her chest. After all, who didn't like expensive shoes?

* * *

Ten minutes later, Ryan tossed his car keys to the valet. He glanced up at the massive, well-lit house and grinned. Someday, when his music management company really took off, he'd buy a house like this, with fancy columns out front and floor-to-ceiling bay windows that spanned the entire first floor.

Only his house wouldn't be in the Point. And he'd throw parties full of musicians and artists and other creative types. Not stuffy uptight financial brokers and insurance salespeople.

He bent next to the open passenger-side door and extended his arm to Ainsley. She rested her palm on his tuxedo sleeve and rose from the Mustang's bucket seat in one fluid motion. How did she do that? With her pointy heels and her long dress?

He shook his head. Women. She'd totter around on those shoes all night, but he bet she couldn't hike five miles in boots without complaining of blisters.

"You're here!" Kate flew out the front door, then skidded to a halt when she reached the top of the stairs.

Some women, he corrected himself. Kate in high heels resembled a baby elephant on stilts. James, who was clad in a tuxedo, stepped out beside her and rested a hand on the small of her back. He bent to whisper something in her ear and she beamed back up at him.

Ainsley's hand on his arm tensed. *Shit.* It didn't matter how much she loved Kate and James, tonight was going to be hard for her. Even he could see that.

Which was why she had him. He cupped his left hand around his mouth and yelled. "Katie! Glad to see you figured out the boob situation. It sounded perilous, although I have to say, that would have made for one hell of an engagement party."

Next to him, Ainsley giggled and the pressure of her hand on his arm lessened. *Good.*

Kate fixed him with a look, but the corners of her mouth twitched upward. "You're a pervert, Ryan Lawhill."

He waggled an eyebrow, and Ainsley dissolved into another round of laughter. *Mission accomplished.* Good thing Kate knew him well enough to understand exactly what he was doing.

He and Ainsley climbed the stairs. When they reached the top, James pulled him into a backslapping hug, while Kate embraced Ainsley. Then he and Ainsley swapped places and he gave Kate a quick squeeze.

"You look great," he said.

And she did. The dress had obviously been one of Ainsley's picks. It was long and dramatic, the fabric draping in ways that confounded him.

Good thing he wasn't the one who had to get her out of it. Women's clothing should be sexy when worn and easy to remove. Was that so much to ask for?

Kate arched a brow. "Careful now, it sounds like you're finally coming to terms with your bridesmaid duties. And Ainsley has already claimed the role of bridesmaid style adviser."

He scowled, annoyance surging. "For the last time, I'm not a bridesmaid. I'm a bridesman."

He grimaced. That sounded worse. "And I still haven't said yes."

Kate patted him on the shoulder as the four of them walked into the house. "Of course you'll say yes. Because you love me and you want me to be happy and you're one of my closest friends in the whole entire world."

He sighed in resignation. Yup. She was right. The exact title shouldn't bother him, but he couldn't help it. How was he supposed to score a bridesmaid when he was one too? No, Kate had to think of a better word for it.

A sudden idea came to him. He knew exactly how to prove his point. "So when I get married you'll be a groomsman? And wear whatever I tell you?"

Her eyes sparked. "Absofreakinglutely. When you decide to settle down, I will cram my ninety-year-old body into the tuxedo of your choice and use my walker to stand beside you at the altar."

He threw his head back and laughed. She had him there. He could be a bridesmaid if that's what she needed, but he had to make sure there weren't any catches first. And they still had to call it something else.

James raised one hand, in a pledge. "Ryan, I swear that if you choose to be a bridesman I will not let them put you in a pink tuxedo. Or purple."

Ainsley shrugged. "You didn't say anything about baby blue. I think a nice, light baby blue would be just the thing to bring out Ryan's eyes."

She reached to pinch his cheek, but he caught her wrist and took a step toward her.

He'd meant to say something playful and funny, something to make her laugh the way he planned to keep her laughing throughout the party. But she couldn't mask the lingering vulnerability in her eyes and it caught him off guard. He found himself waiting a beat too long before he could think of something to say.

"Black tuxedo only. Promise me, Ainsley."

Her lips parted, sending a wave of heat through him. He took an abrupt step backward.

What the hell was wrong with him? The moment had been weird, oddly intimate. Which was the exact opposite of what could, and should, happen between him and Ainsley.

He looked up to see Kate and James's attention fixed on them.

He quickly plastered a smile on his face. Whatever had happened, he hoped they hadn't noticed. The best thing he could do was to distract them immediately. "I will accept my position as bridesman on three conditions. One, we find a new name for it, because I'm not letting anyone call me that shit. Two, I wear what the groomsmen wear. And three, I get to help plan the bachelorette party, but I'm going to the bachelor party. Because I've already started my research into strip clubs with male dancers, but I'm not paying to see naked men."

James's mouth dropped open and Kate's face paled. Bingo. Problem solved.

He pivoted on his heel and walked away, in pursuit of the bar. Let them chew on that for a while.

CHAPTER THREE

Ainsley gripped her clutch tighter and threaded her way through the crowd. Kate and James had been swallowed up by well-wishers an hour ago. Ryan had gone in search of their friends Beth and Griffin while she'd freshened her lipstick in the bathroom. With any luck she'd be able to spend the rest of the night with the three of them, avoiding notice.

Just then a waiter with a tray bumped into her, sending her off balance. She reached for the nearest support and found herself gripping a man's tuxedo-clad arm.

Immediately, she snatched her hand back. "I'm so sorry."

When she lifted her gaze her stomach sank, a feeling of dread spreading through her. She found herself looking into a pair of ice-blue eyes whose shade matched her own perfectly.

"Ainsley." Her father gave her a curt nod.

"Father." Ainsley pecked him on the cheek.

Of all people, why did it have to be him? Of course she'd known they'd run into each other, had prepared herself for it, but nobody was more likely to scrutinize her crumbling façade than her father.

Her mother was standing beside him and pulled Ainsley into a hug. "You look gorgeous, sweetheart. Just gorgeous."

She returned the hug diligently despite her growing nervousness. Although her mom was loving and supportive, she also didn't do anything to temper her father.

Someone cleared his throat from behind her.

Then Ryan appeared in her peripheral vision, his open hand extended. "Ainsley's parents! Great to meet you."

Her father's gaze raked over him from head to toe. When he reached Ryan's blue Converse his upper lip curled slightly, but he took Ryan's outstretched hand and gave it one firm pump.

Ainsley cringed inwardly. No doubt Ryan's footwear would feature prominently in her dad's later critique.

She shifted in her heels and tugged at one of her diamond earrings. Her father fixed her with a stare and she dropped her hand back to her side.

Where were Kate and James? Or Beth and Griffin? Anyone who could save them from her father's human icicle impression. She'd spent her life trying to pursue the things her parents wanted for her, but all her momentum seemed to have flown away with Scott. Suddenly their ambitions for her felt hopeless and exhausting.

"Nice party, huh?" Ryan grinned.

There was a long, painful pause.

"Yes, just lovely." Her mother's voice was quiet as she sneaked a glance at Ainsley's father.

"I wonder when we'll have a reason to throw a party like this?" Her father fixed Ainsley with a cool stare.

Her tongue stuck to the roof of her mouth. Damn, she needed a drink. She'd always had to summon her brightest, smiliest persona around her parents, but recently the task felt impossible.

"There's always the Fourth of July. You can arrange a private fireworks display. I've planned a few parties that had them and the guests are always impressed." There. So she did have some of her old social charms left.

The muscles at the corners of her mother's mouth twitched. *See?* She nearly jabbed Ryan in the side. *Plastic surgery doesn't freeze your face.* Her mother knew as well as anyone what a pain her father could be.

Ryan placed his hand on the small of her back. "Well, it was lovely to meet you both. I feel I'd be remiss in my duties if I didn't get my date a glass of champagne, and I'm sure you can't blame me when I say I'm reluctant to let Ainsley out of my sight. She's especially stunning this evening."

Her heart stuttered. Then he winked, and using the subtle pressure of his palm angled her body in the direction of the nearest bar. "I hope we'll have a chance to get to know each other better later."

She only had time to shoot her parents a quick smile before they were gliding across the room toward the display of champagne flutes filled with bubbling liquid. Relief swelled inside of her. He'd saved her from her parents, and he'd even made the whole thing look convincing. Sure, he wasn't the type of man they wanted for her, but at least she didn't like a totally pathetic dateless loser.

Ryan snagged two from the table and placed one firmly in her hand. "Bottoms up."

He downed his glass in one long swallow.

She examined the flute. Why not? She followed suit, tipping the glass back and letting the cool liquid tickle her throat.

Ryan took the empty glass from her hand and replaced it with a full one. "Since I'm the designated driver, you definitely need another one of these. So, do you have brothers or sisters?"

She sipped this glass more slowly. "One sister."

Younger. And engaged, of course. Suddenly the champagne tasted bitter. She wanted this, the party and the engagement and everything that came with it, so badly it made her chest ache.

It took effort to swallow the champagne. "Why?"

She and Ryan didn't talk about personal stuff. Ryan had never seemed like that kind of guy.

He shrugged. "Your dad strikes me as the kind of man who'd eat his young. You know, like a hamster or something. It's good to know you're not the only one who survived."

She burst into laughter, waves of mirth rolling over her. Her lingering uneasiness dissipated. Leave it to Ryan to make her see her father in a whole different light.

When she finally caught her breath, she looked into his blue eyes. Not cold like her father's but clear and confident. Somehow warm.

Her grip on the champagne flute relaxed. Maybe her fairy godmother did know what she was doing, at least for tonight.

* * *

He kept his palm firmly on the small of Ainsley's back. *So far so good.* The party was like a game of Pacman. Ainsley's father was a ghost, and they needed to avoid him or risk being eaten.

He spotted Beth's short, curly hair on the edge of the crowd and propelled Ainsley in her direction. If Ainsley's father was a ghost, Beth was an extra life, and he was determined to win.

A smile spread across Beth's face as they approached. Finally he allowed his arm to drop from Ainsley's back and flexed his hand. *Safe.* For now, at least.

Beth flung her arms around Ainsley's neck. He turned to Beth's boyfriend, Griffin, and clapped him on the back.

"Good to see you, man. I was starting to worry this was going to be an all Fallston crowd." He eyed Griffin's few days' worth of stubble and shaggy hair appreciatively. Then he looked to Griffin's feet, encased in an impossibly shiny pair of dress shoes.

Griffin grimaced. "Brand-new shoes. Beth insisted. The bottoms are slippery and I feel like a goddamn penguin. Where have you guys been? We've been searching the crowd for at least an hour. The babysitter said she can't stay long with Mabel."

One of the many benefits of being single. People could

judge his footwear all they wanted, but nobody could make him wear clown shoes. And he never had to plan around a babysitter.

Griffin's eyes narrowed as he looked at something past Ryan's shoulder. "Hey, didn't you date her? The redhead? I could have sworn you brought her into the coffee shop once or twice."

Redhead who'd gone to Fallston? Probably Allison. Or Ivy. It could also be Jessica.

"Tall or short?"

Griffin snorted. "Dude, I don't know. Medium. She's wearing a black dress and she's with a guy in a tux and they're headed over here."

Well, that narrowed it down. He shrugged. If they were really headed in his direction, he'd figure it out soon enough.

"Ryan?" A breathy voice floated from over his shoulder.

His brain pinged in recognition.

"Ivy!" He turned and lifted her into a bear hug, sweeping her feet off the floor.

She giggled as he set her back down.

"I want you to meet my fiancé, Bryson." She motioned at the dark-haired man standing next to her. Sure enough, the guy was clad in tuxedo, black bow tie, and requisite shiny black shoes. *Poor sucker.*

With a grin, he pumped Bryson's hand. "Good to meet you, man. Congratulations on your engagement, that's great news."

Bryson's eyes raked over him before his mouth relaxed into a smile. "I hear you run your own music management company?"

Ryan unbuttoned his tuxedo jacket with one hand. Damn thing was going to suffocate him before the night was over. "Yeah. You like music?"

Ivy placed a hand on her fiancé's arm. "We do. We're looking for a band for the wedding, if you have any suggestions."

He almost choked. Him? Suggestions for a wedding? Surely they were kidding.

He motioned toward Ainsley. "I'm not the guy for that kind of thing, but I bet Ainsley would know a few good ones."

The woman could party-plan the hell out of anything. Even a funeral.

At the sound of her name, Ainsley turned to face them. "What am I doing?"

Ivy's cheeks flushed slightly. "Helping us choose a band. For the wedding."

Out of the corner of his eye, he caught Ainsley's shoulders tense. *Shit.* He'd led her right into that one.

He grabbed her hand and squeezed. "Because you're the queen of event planning."

His heart thumped in his rib cage. *Great job, idiot.* Kate was going to kick his ass later.

She smiled tightly and nodded at Ivy. "Send me an email and I'll get a list of groups together for you."

Ivy beamed. "Oh, you're the best, Ainsley. I should have asked you straightaway, I just thought…"

She trailed off, her cheeks reddening.

He slipped an arm around Ainsley's waist and winked at Ivy. "Everyone feels bad asking for free expert advice. We're just lucky Ainsley is so gracious about sharing her knowledge."

Ivy angled her head to one side, her brows furrowing as she examined them.

Good. If anyone could start a new rumor, it was Ivy. Nobody would be surprised when things between him and Ainsley fizzled out. He had a reputation and he'd worked hard to build it. This way the people of Fallston would be distracted from the Scott and Ainsley breakup long enough for that to blow over. In fact, he was kind of annoyed he hadn't thought of it sooner. It was such a simple solution to Ainsley's problem.

He tilted his head in the direction of Ainsley's ear and adopted a stage whisper. "Let's get the hell out of here."

Her eyes shifted to his face and went wide. "Now? The party practically just started!"

"Absolutely." Kate and James were busy with their guests, so they wouldn't be missed. Beth and Griffin couldn't stay long. And he'd finally thought of a way to cheer Ainsley up.

Ivy's gaze darted between them, curiosity in her eyes.

A flush crept up Ainsley's cheeks. "Um, right. OK. We should go."

Finally. An abrupt departure would guarantee the rumor gained traction. He was a little surprised she'd decided to go along with it, but he decided not to question his good luck. Maybe she was escaping her parents, maybe she wanted to get away from the stuffy Fallston crowd, or maybe she'd caught on to his plan. Whatever the reason, he was ready to get his night started.

CHAPTER FOUR

Ainsley tried to keep the confusion from her expression. Where were they going, and why? She'd seen the way Ivy looked at them and knew what she must have thought, but she'd found she didn't care. After the encounter with her father, she was too damn tired of pretending to be happy.

"Why are we leaving?" she finally asked.

"I'm taking you somewhere fun. We're all dressed up, why not?"

She glanced back over her shoulder. "Are you sure Kate won't mind?"

After all, she'd promised her support tonight. What kind of friend would she be if she bailed?

"Absolutely, one hundred percent positive. She has James and they're busy making sure his parents are happy. I can't think of any reason you and I need to waste our night too."

The confidence in his voice swayed her. Kate was a good friend, she wouldn't mind. Plus, Ainsley couldn't take another second in that crowded party, watching people watching her.

Which reminded her of something else. Ivy. She'd seemed genuinely pleased to see Ryan and vice versa. Yet Ainsley knew for a fact they'd been dating each other a few months back. How was that possible?

"How many women at that party have you hooked up with?" She'd figured that was the reason he'd agreed to be her date, so she could act as a buffer between him and any former flames.

"A gentleman never tells."

She huffed. Typical. "But you did hook up with Ivy. I remember that. Why was she so nice to you?"

He frowned as he turned out of the Abells' long driveway. "Why wouldn't she be?"

She puffed her cheeks out in exasperation. Really? Was he that incapable of forming a legitimate emotional attachment?

Freaking men. And they said women were the ones who caused drama.

"Because you hooked up with her and then you dropped her. The way you've dropped every woman you've ever dated." Her tone was matter-of-fact. She'd known Ryan long enough to understand his dating habits. Why beat around the bush?

He gave a dry chuckle. "I don't drop anyone. I'm a fun guy. Women hang out with me to have fun, and when the fun runs its course we all move on."

She bit the inside of her cheek. No way was it that simple. Surely there were hurt feelings, whether he admitted it or not.

He glanced at her quickly. "It's all about expectations. Keep them low, and nobody is hurt or disappointed. I could teach you, you know."

Her mouth fell open. "Teach me?"

He chuckled. "How to have fun." He paused. "And not *that* kind of fun. Get your mind out of the gutter."

Her jaw clenched. Between the two of them, she wasn't the one with her mind in the gutter. "I *am* fun."

Although she also didn't have a lot of time to waste if she was going to get her life back on track, find the One and get married and have kids before her skin got too wrinkly and all her eggs dried up.

"Sure you are. But I'm the head Minister of Fun. I'm the funnest guy you've ever met. Admit it, you know I am." His voice was playful.

She frowned. "The Minister of Fun? What are you talking about?"

He groaned. "Like Harry Potter. Please tell me you've read *Harry Potter*."

She bit her lip. Wasn't that a kid's book?

He sighed loudly and shook his head. "Well, then that's your second assignment: Read *Harry Potter*. The whole series, front to back, cover to cover."

Sure, whatever. He could order her all he wanted, but he couldn't force her to comply.

Then his words sank in, causing the back of her neck to prickle. "Wait, what do you mean, second assignment?"

He blew by the exit for her street and merged onto the ramp for the freeway. "I offered to teach you to have fun. You claim you know how to have fun. I'm about to prove to you how wrong you are, and the first phase starts now."

* * *

For the first challenge he was going to show her a real night on the town at one of the city's hottest clubs. He told himself it was all in the name of competition, to force her to admit that he was at least partially right about the superiority of his chosen lifestyle. Sometimes the way they looked at him, Ainsley and Kate and James and Beth and Griffin, he was sure they pitied him. As if they thought he was lacking something in his life.

In reality, his father had done him a favor. He'd shown Ryan at an early age how disposable love could be. That had made him free, had allowed him to live his life without worrying so much about what other people needed from him. Now it was time to pay it forward. If anyone could use a little of the Lawhill life philosophy, it was Ainsley.

He turned onto a side street and pulled into a parking space outside a long, brick warehouse. Pink and blue neon lights flashed across the sidewalk as low thumping emanated from inside.

Then he watched, gleeful, as Ainsley's jaw dropped. "You have to be kidding me."

"Believe me, you'll know when I'm kidding. Now come on." He grinned, unable to keep the triumph out of his voice. Not that he was trying that hard.

He unbuckled his seat belt.

"I, um, I'm not dressed for clubbing. At all." She waved a hand over her sequined gown.

He looked her directly in the eye, determined to convince

her. For some reason he didn't understand, it was suddenly essential that Ainsley buy into this. "Of course you are. Trust me. Sometimes it's good to get out of your comfort zone."

She bit her lip and lowered her eyes to her lap.

He turned to her and reached across the center console to grip both of her shoulders, his fingertips digging into her soft skin. "Are you happy? Right now, at this exact second, are you happy?"

He waited, almost regretting the words. What if Ainsley wasn't as strong as he was? What if she really couldn't do this?

She blinked back tears, her gaze still fixed on her lap. "You know I'm not."

His throat tightened. Exactly. Much as it pained him, his plan could never work until she admitted that. "Then why not let me try? I think if you give my foolproof fuck-the-world-and-do-what-you-want plan a try, you'll be happier. And if you're not, what do you lose?"

She slanted him a look. "Is this a trick to get in my pants?"

He blinked hard, then burst into laughter. "If I wanted to get into your pants, I'd have been there a long time ago."

She clenched her jaw. "Wrong. If I wanted you to get in my pants, you'd have been there a long time ago."

A flash of heat surged through him, a sharp pang of longing. *Whatever you say, Ainsley.* If he was honest with himself, there was part of him that wanted her. But that would be in direct violation of how he lived his life. It would be too messy, too complicated. Ainsley wasn't capable of just sex, and he wasn't capable of anything more. The whole point was that he wanted to teach Ainsley to be like him, so she could protect herself from getting hurt in the future.

He grinned. "Well, OK then. I agree not to seduce you, and you agree to loosen up and have some fun. You'll do whatever I suggest for the next…let's say three weeks."

Her hand shot out. "Fine. Deal."

He shook it, his heart pounding faster. Three weeks should be long enough to teach her how to relax and have fun, without any complications. That was all this was. He was just helping out a friend. If he could convert Ainsley, then surely his friends would have to admit that his approach to relationships had merit.

She shifted her eyes in an obvious effort to look away, and she frowned, her attention fixed on a parking sign near the front windshield. "Just so you know, you're in a VIP only parking area."

"Yup." He climbed out of the car and stretched his legs.

When he rounded the hood, she'd already exited the passenger side.

He let his eyes rake over her body, taking in the curve of her waist, the sliver of tanned leg peeking out from the slit of her dress. His breath caught in his chest. It was a good thing she'd been in a relationship when they met, or he would have been tempted to make a move and they never would have become friends. Unlike sex, a friendship was permanent.

"You aren't scared you're going to be towed?" She planted a hand on her hip.

He nearly rolled his eyes but instead locked the car and dropped the keys into his pocket. "Not a bit."

"Are you going to tell me why?"

He strode toward the door to Club 812. Ainsley knew that he managed bands for a living, but she didn't know all the ins and outs of his business. "I promised not to seduce you, so I probably shouldn't tell you that I'm a partial owner."

Her high heels clicked on the pavement as she hurried to catch up. "You're what?"

He turned to face her. "I own part of the club."

She came to an abrupt stop and surprise registered on her face. "I didn't know that. Why didn't I know that?"

He shrugged and tucked her hand into the crook of his arm. "Truthfully, I own a very, very small portion of the club. It's more a way to promote my bands and to network than anything else. But it sounds sexy, doesn't it?"

Over time he'd found that it was easier to keep things light with his friends, to laugh and make jokes. If he started talking too much about his life, he'd have to get into details. Like how his dad had left when he was two, died when he was ten, and left him a good chunk of money to pay for college, start a business, and invest in the club. Revealing personal information led to questions, and he didn't want to answer questions.

Instead he winked at Ainsley and led her through the glass front doors.

* * *

The bouncer gave them a cursory nod as Ryan held the door for her. When he swept her pashmina off of her shoulders the pressure of his strong fingers launched a tingle that spread down her spine, catching her by surprise.

She clenched her eyes closed. *Get it together.* She could not be attracted to Ryan. Of all people, she knew better.

Although she did now understand how he did it. He brought women to the club where he had VIP status, in his Mustang, and charmed them right into his bed. *Smooth.*

Only he wasn't trying to seduce her. He'd promised. And that wasn't the way things were between the two of them. He felt bad for her and wanted to distract her, so he was doing what he knew how to do. For her part, she figured there wasn't any harm in agreeing to his deal. At the very least it might help keep her mind off Scott for a while.

"Would you like a drink?" He motioned to a bar behind a series of velvet ropes.

She eyed the stage, where a man in a suit crooned into the microphone. Two female backup singers stood behind him and he was flanked by two trumpet players and a guy with a saxophone.

She found herself tapping her foot in time with the rhythm. The music reminded her of something. Her brain pinged. It sounded like the soundtrack from *Saturday Night Fever*, which she'd been obsessed with for a few months during the sixth grade. Only…hipper. Fresher. More modern.

"I'd like to dance." She pushed her way through the crowd and onto the dance floor, leaving him to follow. She'd show him just how fun she could be.

By the time he caught up with her, she'd already found a spot in the crowd and was twisting her hips and shoulders in time with the music. She removed the pins holding her hair up and shook it out. It felt good to literally let loose for once.

He grinned at her before he gave a slow, delicious hip roll and began to move in time with the music.

Her mouth went dry as a pang of lust shot through her. *Shit. No wonder this worked on women.*

She quickly averted her gaze and pretended to scan the crowd, eager to distract herself. Still, she was painfully aware of Ryan's body and the heat radiating from him as he danced a few steps away from her.

Suddenly a strong hand snaked around her waist from behind. Her breath caught and she sidestepped in panic, twisting her head to get a better look. The hand fumbled to maintain its grip as her eyes shot to his face.

A shiver of fear traveled down her spine. Unfamiliar brown eyes, a sparse goatee, hair slicked back from his forehead. Who the hell was he?

He jerked her closer, bringing her body flush with his. "Come on, baby. I see the way you're dressed. I know why you're here. So let's dance."

Anger flared inside of her and she pushed away from his chest with both hands. This guy's tactics, on the other hand, did not work on women.

Behind her, Ryan cleared his throat loudly. The man's hands dropped from her waist and she found herself instinctively stepping away until Ryan's broad shoulders cocooned her back. She released a long, shaky breath, relieved to have found safety.

The stranger arched an eyebrow. "Hey, Ryan. She with you?"

She fought the urge to say something scathing and chose

Ryan's protection instead. He loosely rested a hand on her waist, the heat of his fingertips burning through the fabric of her dress.

"Of course she's with me." His chest vibrated against her back. As much as she longed to punch them both for this male mating ritual, to make sure Ryan knew that she didn't need protection, she decided against it. What was the harm in letting him play alpha male for a minute? Truth be told, there was a part of her that liked it.

The man's eyebrows furrowed. "Oh, sorry then. I just saw you guys and it didn't seem like, you know…"

Ryan stepped closer, until she could feel every inch of him pressed against her back. His breath was warm against her hair.

Her heart raced, even as she sighed with relief. Funny that it was Ryan of all people who'd managed to make her feel safe. She was vaguely aware of another feeling, the slight hint of longing and attraction, but brushed it aside. They would always be just friends.

"Easy mistake to make, Rick. Can't say I blame you." Ryan's voice was tight.

Rick gave a sharp nod. "Well, OK then, sorry for interrupting."

Ryan didn't move away from her, even as Rick retreated through the crowd. Anticipation coursed through her. Maybe the attraction wasn't entirely one-sided. Not that either of them was going to do anything about it.

"Guess you're stuck dancing with me," he whispered in her ear.

Her skin tingled, but she stepped away from him. Before

she turned, she worked to make her expression neutral. Hormones were one thing and feelings were another. Ryan only knew how to trade in the physical and that was a road to disaster, for them and all their other friends. She knew better than to let that happen.

She met his icy-blue eyes and gave a shrug. "Then I guess you're stuck dancing with me."

No doubt there were a dozen other women at the club he could be seducing with his dance skills, but apparently he'd decided to stick by her side and deter presumptuous weirdos. He was a good friend. Just a friend. She'd tell herself that a million times until it sank in, because anything else was impossible. Ryan was a player, and he was going to teach her to act like a player. That was their deal, wasn't it? Maybe this was all part of the tutorial. She really should start paying attention.

He folded his fingers around her hand and pulled her into his chest. His other hand came to rest on her lower back. See? She could do this. Physical closeness, even attraction, with nothing more behind it. She was just as capable of feeling nothing as he was.

As they danced, his hand inched lower until it hovered just below the curve of her hip.

She leaned into him, forcing herself to forget everything but the music. What was going on in his head? Probably nothing. Which meant there should be nothing in hers as well. That must be the lesson he was trying to teach her.

It's just dancing. They were here to have a little fun, to get her mind off of things. A hardness pulsed against her pelvis and she sucked in a breath.

Figures. This was, after all, Ryan. In his world everything came back to sex eventually. His dick controlled his brain and he never bothered to pretend otherwise.

Slowly she angled her body to create a little more distance between them. There was only so much self-deception a person could engage in, and Ryan was testing her limits. She knew what he was about, and crossing that line wasn't good. For either of them.

CHAPTER FIVE

Ryan shifted the Mustang into gear and sped away from Ainsley's apartment complex. He hesitated at the stop sign for only a second before he turned left for Belmont Bluffs Road. He'd take the scenic way tonight, roll down the windows, and let the salty sea breeze ruffle his hair. Maybe that would bring him back to his senses.

His spine prickled as he recalled Rick's arm wrapped possessively around Ainsley's waist and the panic on her face.

Asshole. So what if Ainsley hadn't been there with him in the sense that Rick had meant? How did Rick know that? It took balls, and stupidity, to walk up and yank a beautiful woman out of another man's arms. Rick was lucky it was him. Another guy might have punched him in the face.

He was doubly lucky he'd only insulted Ryan's general sense of pride and that there wasn't anything between him and Ainsley.

The muscles in his neck tensed. That was it. That had to be it. So what if the lingering scent of her perfume in the car made his brain fuzzy? So what if his blood had pounded when she pressed her ass against him in her attempt to escape Rick? So what if the way she rotated her hips had been enough to make him hard?

He was a man. She was attractive. That was biology. As soon as she opened her mouth to nag or fixed him with one of her critical stares, every inkling of attraction drained from his body.

He gritted his teeth and punched a button on the sound system. When he found the right song he cranked up the volume, letting the heavy guitar riffs and shouted lyrics pound through his veins.

His phone chimed through the speakers with a text message alert.

He twisted the knob, lowering the volume. "Read text message," he instructed the car.

A robotic woman's voice chimed over the speaker system. "Reading text message from Melanie. Rick said you were at the club with a blond. Does this mean you aren't coming over tonight? I promise to lick you all over before I make you come so hard you forget your name."

He slammed on the brakes and pulled over to the side, his sides shaking with laughter. The monotone robot voice was distinctly unsexy. Although…his mind drifted back to the memory of Ainsley's tight ass pressed against him.

Fuck. He dropped his head to the steering wheel. This wasn't how tonight was supposed to go.

His phone chimed again and he yanked it free from the car charger.

Claire: Can you come over or are you busy?

A grin spread across his face. He was never too busy for her.

Claire: Gremlin and I want you to make us grilled cheese.

Below the message was a photograph of a tan pit bull with her head resting on her paws.

Ryan: On my way.

When it came to love there were very few people who held a place in his heart. Claire and Gremlin topped that list, even though Gremlin wasn't a person. He had plenty of other nights to see Melanie. Some things were more important than fun, and family was one of them.

Claire: Hurry up, please. We're starving.

He shook his head and shifted the car back into drive. His baby sister knew good and well how to cook, but they'd developed a routine of two a.m. grilled cheeses one summer in college when he'd lived at home. It was a tradition he would always treasure. He hoped that even when she was fifty and married with kids she'd still call him in the middle of the night for their grilled cheese chats.

It only took him a few minutes before he reached the house. He pulled into the driveway, cut off the headlights, and shoved the keys into his pocket. He was careful to tread lightly as he twisted the doorknob and let himself into the hall.

Gremlin immediately launched at his feet, wagging and wiggling herself into a frenzy.

She flopped onto her back and rolled, her jowls flopping.

He bent to rub her belly. "Hi, girl. Who's the prettiest?"

He gave her one last pat and glanced down the hall.

"Claire? Where are you?" he whispered.

"In the kitchen," she hissed.

He tiptoed down the hall, Gremlin wiggling her way after him.

Claire immediately jumped off the kitchen stool and yanked him over to the stove, not even pausing for one of her bear hugs. She'd already laid out cheese, bread, and butter on the counter.

He narrowed his eyes. Had she really brought him here just to make grilled cheese? Usually they also had late-night chats where he got to dole out brotherly advice, something he loved in spite of himself. He didn't talk about emotions, unless he was talking to his mom or his sister, and even then he was careful to keep it in check.

He shrugged, set the griddle on the stovetop, and began to butter the bread slices. She'd confide in him when she was ready.

"So what were you up to tonight?" He kept his eyes on his work.

There was a long pause.

Aha. He knew there was something she'd wanted to talk about. His sister was pretty much the only woman he purposely got to open up to him. That list sometimes included Kate and, on rare occasions, Beth.

She ran a hand through her long blonde hair and pouted. "Dad won't let me go on the senior class trip."

"That sucks." That was his primary role as brother, to take her side and offer a sympathetic ear.

She sighed loudly. "He says nothing good happens on those trips. He says you were arrested and he had to fly to the Bahamas to bail you out."

He flinched, embarrassed Hank had told Claire about that debacle. Yup, that had happened. His stepdad had been pissed, naturally.

"It was just a trespassing, no big deal. No conviction. Hank got it all worked out." He and his friends had snuck their way onto a private nude beach. Mostly because he'd wanted a peek at a naked European woman.

Instead, he'd gotten arrested in a foreign country. Claire had been young at the time, and he'd sort of hoped she'd never find out. He wanted her to respect him and love him in spite of his many flaws.

She huffed. "Yeah, well, now I'm not allowed to go. So thanks a lot for that."

He left the sandwiches sizzling on the griddle and turned to face her. She was pissed, and rightfully so. "I'm sorry, Claire."

Regret burned in his stomach. It was unfair of their parents to hold his mistakes against Claire.

She crossed her arms over her chest. "Can you talk to him, please?"

All of a sudden other memories from that trip hit him. Memories of the beach, a bottle of rum, and naked women. The idea of Claire drinking and having sex made him want to hurl.

"Maybe your dad is right." He braced himself. She was going to be pissed, but shouldn't he look out for her best interests?

Her eyebrows knitted. "Nope. You don't get to play that card with me. I can't even begin to count all of the stupid things you've done. You've probably done more stupid things tonight than I've done in my entire life."

She was right about that. He'd actually allowed himself to

get hard while dancing with Ainsley, and it had taken all of his willpower not to kiss her. Even though he knew it would be stupid and they'd both regret it later.

Stupid.

"So?" She tapped a finger on the counter.

The sizzling from the griddle grew louder. He turned back to the stove, flipped the sandwiches onto two plates, and used the spatula to cut them in half. Then he slid onto the stool next to Claire.

This was one of those important brotherly advice moments, and he wanted to think it through, be sure not to screw it up.

"You are more responsible than me. A lot more responsible. I'll talk to Hank. But you have to swear, if I do, that you'll be careful. Don't drink anything a stranger gives you, use the buddy system, don't try to pet the sharks, lock your hotel room at night. Um…"

He trailed off. There was more, but he, of all people, shouldn't give his sister advice on sex. Especially not when he wanted to tell her to stay a virgin until she was forty. His stomach clenched. Or maybe sixty. Was it too late to get her into a convent?

She placed her hand over his and squeezed. "I'll be careful, I promise. I've spent my life learning from your mistakes."

He made a face at her, then took a large bite of grilled cheese and chewed, but he found it hard to swallow. She was right, of course. He liked to think that she looked up to him, admired him a little bit, but maybe he was fooling himself. Was that why he'd been so determined to enter this bet with Ainsley? Surely his friends and family could see that he was happy this way. He'd never make the mistake his dad did, of fooling himself into believing he was fit for commitment. If he decided to pick up and leave Belmont, he wouldn't leave a wife and kid behind. If he had a heart attack at thirty-five, at least he wouldn't be abandoning a son he barely knew.

Nope. He lived his life honestly, never pretended to be anyone else, and only offered what he knew he could give. With Claire, though, he really did try to do the right thing, to be a good brother.

She rested her chin on her hand and looked at him. "Speaking of life mistakes, where were you tonight, all dressed up in that tuxedo?"

"Kate's engagement party." He crammed the rest of his sandwich into his mouth and focused on chewing. He had to remind himself that this was their routine, the joking and the chiding. Of course Claire loved him and looked up to him—he was her older brother.

Her gray eyes zeroed in on his face. "And who was your date?"

He chuckled and shook his head. The advice thing was a one-way street. No way was he going to give her more reasons to pry into his personal life.

* * *

Ainsley punched the pillow and rolled onto her side. Four thirty a.m. It was a lost cause. She wouldn't be sleeping tonight.

She pushed back the covers, flicked on the lamp, and trudged to the living room. Might as well get her laptop and find some other insomniacs to chat with.

She flopped onto the sofa and pulled the computer onto her lap. Then she opened the lid and clicked the third bookmark. She'd found the Matters of the Heart website when she was dating Scott. Originally she'd frequented the Brides to Be page, delving into all subjects wedding planning. She'd been a sort of guru on those pages, full of useful advice and tips the other women hadn't discovered yet. Back then she'd been addicted to the euphoria she felt when helping people plan their perfect day.

Then Scott had announced the move to Hong Kong, and she'd found herself on the board labeled SOS Abroad. There she'd given far less advice, choosing instead to read others' stories and making mental notes of what she should and should not do herself. Now?

Well, now she had to find her place again. She'd figured she'd dump the site entirely. Coming back and admitting she was a failure seemed too painful, but there wasn't anyone else she could talk to in the middle of the night. No, it was better to hash out her problems anonymously online with other people who would understand.

She scanned until she found Breaking Up Is Hard to Do and clicked. Sadness washed over her. Leave it to the internet to make the whole thing sting even more.

The title for one thread caught her attention: Ready to get back out there. She opened it.

The author was someone named Glowbugdoodle. She quickly read the post:

My fiancé and I broke up two weeks ago. In the last few days I've been spending a lot of time with a guy friend. He's funny, he makes me laugh, and last night he kissed me. It was one of the best kisses of my life. The chemistry between us is intense. I think now that I'm single, I'm finally noticing it for the first time, finally letting myself be open to the attraction. Maybe it's always existed, I don't really know. The problem is, all of my other friends tell me not to jump into something. They say he has a reputation, that he dates around a lot. But a lot of men are like that, aren't they? Until they find the right person? What if the reason nothing worked out for him with anyone else is because things were supposed to work out with us?

Ainsley snorted. *Poor thing.* The author sounded completely, utterly delusional.

Her skin tingled as she remembered the way Ryan's gaze had seared her, the feel of his palms skimming over her hips as they danced. Heat flooded her belly.

She swallowed hard. It would have been easy to kiss him. Easy to cross the few inches between them as they'd danced, easy to press her mouth to his, easy to taste him.

She clenched her hands into fists. Easy, sure. But not right. Men like Ryan oozed sex appeal.

He was charming and she was lonely, that was all there was to it.

She sighed. Kissing Ryan would have been stupid. The same way Glowbugdoodle sounded like she was on the verge of doing something really stupid. Sometimes people made the wrong decisions when they were heartbroken and disappointed. Of all people she could understand that. For the first time in weeks, she found herself typing advice.

I completely understand where you're coming from, but dating him would be a mistake and you know it. Pinning your hopes on him would be a mistake. In the end you'll wind up crushed and disappointed, beating yourself up because you knew better.

She took a deep breath. Exactly like she was beating herself up now over Scott. The last few months it was obvious he'd lost interest in her, and yet she'd only clung to him and her visions of their future harder. It was pathetic.

He has a reputation for a reason and no woman possesses a vagina magical enough to convert a commitment-phobe into marriage material. How long would you waste trying to change him? Boyfriends aren't supposed to be projects.

Take a step back and imagine what you want for yourself. Where do you want to be in one year? Two years? Three years? Make a list of the type of man who will help you meet those goals and find him.

She clicked post. Then another thought came to her. She opened another reply box.

None of this is to say you shouldn't sleep with him as long as you can keep your emotions in check. We all need a little fun sometimes.

After all, none of them was trying to be Mother Teresa.

She opened another search box on her browser and typed in "world's best vibrator." If she was going to follow her own advice and dedicate herself to finding the right man, she'd need all the help she could get.

CHAPTER SIX

Ainsley's eyes fluttered open and she reached to massage the crick in her neck. That was when she caught sight of the clock. Ten fifteen a.m.

She shot up from the chair, knocking her laptop onto the floor in the process. She caught a glimpse of herself in the mirror and froze.

Shit. She was supposed to be at work in twenty minutes, to go through a menu tasting with a bride. And her hair was a giant, matted nest.

That's when it hit her. She'd been asleep. For several glorious hours, she'd slept. It was the first block of continuous sleep she'd gotten in months, since Scott had first announced he was moving to Hong Kong. She was nearly ecstatic, relieved to have caught some genuine sleep, until she remembered she was late.

She ran into the bedroom, pulled her phone off the charger, and typed a message for the front desk clerk at the hotel.

Ainsley: I'm going to be a little late for my tasting with the bride and her mother. Make an excuse for me, please? I promise I'll make it up to you.

This morning she had Mrs. Meyer and her daughter Brigitte, who'd graduated from Fallston the year before her. And had managed to snag a husband right before she turned thirty. It was an accomplishment Ainsley couldn't help but notice would probably elude her.

The phone pinged.

Rory: You? Late? Is the world ending?

Very funny. She grabbed a comb and went to work dragging it through her hair. With a whole lot of hair spray she could make this sleep-rumpled thing work. Messy buns were in.

Twenty minutes later she was striding into the lobby of the Meridien.

Her boss and the hotel's general manager, Brett Mackley, grabbed her elbow the minute she stepped inside. His bald head shone in the numerous mirrored surfaces as he dragged her to a corner.

"You're late." He crossed his arms over his chest, causing his blue button-down shirt to strain over his middle-aged paunch.

She pressed her lips together in annoyance, then, recalling the bright red lipstick she'd so carefully applied, stopped herself. "I overslept. It won't happen again."

"I'll have to write you up."

Anger flared inside her. Write her up? She'd never been late. She was a model employee, showing up early, staying late, and doing everything in her power to make sure the Meridien threw events worthy of the poshest Point residents.

She'd never messed up. Ever. It was her job to be perfect, and to make sure their guests experienced perfection.

Her vision blurred and she blinked, trying to summon all of her inner strength. "Please recall that I have never been late before in the three years I've worked here."

His eyes narrowed and he took a step closer. "We all have our problems at home, Ainsley. The key is to not bring them into the workplace. If your situation renders you unable to support brides, to give them your full enthusiasm and dedication, then perhaps you need to rethink things."

She reeled back, feeling as if she'd been punched in the stomach. Was he threatening to fire her? She'd never failed at anything in her life. Well, unless you counted getting married.

"Just get it together. And go meet with the bride. Now. Her parents are important, and we don't want to keep them waiting. They need to have the full Meridien experience." He plopped a meaty hand on her shoulder, which she shrugged off.

She did not want to be touched right now. Not by him, and not by anybody else.

She sucked in a deep breath, but it did nothing to release the tightness in her chest. The black-and-white lobby tiles loomed in front of her vision as if they might rise up and swallow her.

She raised her eyes to meet his gaze. "I'm good at my job and I work my ass off. The least you can do is give me a little slack."

Brett pinned her with a look. "Our brides don't care about your personal life. They care about their own weddings. So get out there and make it perfect."

He stalked away, leaving her staring after him. She pinched the bridge of her nose and tried to breathe. *You don't need his sympathy.* She didn't need anyone's sympathy. She'd put on her big-girl panties and trudge her way through this.

She had no other choice.

She straightened and followed Brett back through the lobby and past the front desk. Rory, who'd only graduated from college a few months ago, stared at her wide-eyed. She forced herself to wink and continued to the main dining room.

Fake it till you make it. Her parents had raised her to believe that everything was about presentation and perception. If she seemed poised and in control, surely Brigitte and Mrs. Meyers and the other staff members would buy it.

She paused at the double doors leading to the dining room and took a deep breath. Then she plastered a smile on her face. She could do this. Hell, she'd been doing this for years. Brides loved her, and because of her they loved the Meridien.

She slipped through the doors, then glided through the empty dining room to the only table that was occupied. She paused when she reached it and gave her most dazzling smile as she held out her hand.

"I'm so sorry I'm late. There was a little snafu with the dry-cleaning delivery in my building."

The bride, a petite brunette, smiled. "Please, don't worry about it. We were just enjoying some coffee."

Good. Rory must have thought to bring them the full coffee service while they killed time. She made a mental note to thank Rory.

Mrs. Meyers gave a tight smile and glanced pointedly at the

diamond-studded watch on her wrist. "Well, now that you're here, let's get down to business."

"Yes, let's."

A server peeked his head out from the kitchen and Ainsley gave him a nod. She withdrew a stack of sample menus from her bag, where she'd placed them on Friday before she left work.

A lump lodged in her throat. She'd prepared carefully for this meeting, knowing it wouldn't be easy. Up until the minute Scott had set foot on that plane, she'd been planning their own wedding in her head. The writing had been on the wall as soon as Scott accepted the job in Hong Kong. She'd just tried to ignore it, had denied the truth until the bitter end.

And now that it was over? She was exhausted. A little bit relieved, which didn't make any sense at all. Humiliated, of course. Mrs. Meyers and Brigitte would know exactly what had happened. But she was also resigned. She'd always been good at event planning, even if her parents did view it as a placeholder until she got married and could spend her days being a wife. Work wasn't much of a distraction anymore, given her situation, but she had to make the best of it. Brett was right. These brides were counting on her, and they deserved the wedding of their dreams. Even as hers drifted further out of reach.

She plastered a smile on her face. "In our initial consultation, Mrs. Meyers, you expressed an interest in providing your guests with a fine dining experience."

In other words, she'd read the cues and discerned that Mrs. Meyers wanted her guests to know she'd paid a premium for their meals.

Ainsley's eyes flicked to the bride. She hoped that was what

Brigitte wanted. From her own experience, she knew that a person's expectations didn't always line up with her parents'.

She continued carefully, watching Brigitte as she spoke. "Your options for first courses are steak tartare, lobster bisque, and foie gras."

A thought suddenly came to her. Something she'd seen online while scrolling through the latest bridal websites.

"Or, if you wanted to go with something a little more unusual, we could have a sushi station featuring signature rolls designed by Brigitte and her fiancé."

If it were her wedding, that's exactly what she would have wanted. The thought brought a fresh ache, but she was determined not to let the pain stop her. All those ideas she'd saved for herself? She couldn't let them go to waste. Other brides deserved to use them.

She forced herself to switch into professional mode. Brett would kill her for suggesting something other than their standard options, of course, but he'd live.

Mentally she calculated. It would cost the hotel less in terms of labor, because they could make all of the sushi in advance. But they could charge more under the guise that it was a unique dining experience.

Or some shit like that. She'd think of the right way to convince Brett later. After all, who said all of the Meridien's weddings had to be stuffy and uptight?

Brigitte's eyes lit. "Oh, Mom, I like that. I've never even seen that at a wedding before."

Ainsley experienced a glimmer of real satisfaction. That's why she'd loved the idea too.

Mrs. Meyers frowned. "What about both? A plated appetizer and a sushi station?"

It wasn't what she'd envisioned, but this wasn't about her. From a business perspective, Brett would love it, as it was technically two first courses, which meant they could jack up the price. The chef would kill her, as it would double his work.

"Absolutely. We can do that." She wrote it on her pad.

The waiter entered the dining room, and with a flourish set three plates in front of Mrs. Meyers and her daughter.

From now on she'd have to approach her job differently. These were other people's weddings she was planning, not her own. All thoughts of her own wedding needed to be placed on hold indefinitely.

In that moment she was glad that Ryan had convinced her to agree to his plan. He was right, she needed a distraction from her life.

* * *

Something warm and wet tickled his face. Ryan lifted an arm and rolled over. Through his fog he tried to remember back to last night. Who was in his bed with him? And why was her tongue so large?

He sat up with a start. Gremlin. Of course. He'd crashed in his old bedroom at his mom's. He loved the fact that his parents kept it set up for him in case he ever wanted to stay over, which wasn't infrequent. Truth be told, he often felt more at home in their house than he did in his own. His loft was sparse and minimal, mostly because he didn't spend a lot of time there. Why would he? When he wasn't dating or out for a night on the town it was far preferable to sleep in his old bedroom, in the same house as his family.

Gremlin licked him again. With a grimace, he wriggled out of the sheets and got to his feet.

Gremlin stared at him, her tail thumping and her tongue lolling out of her mouth.

"You're gross. Don't kiss me." He pointed a finger in her direction. Then he caved, bending down to squeeze her in his arms. Who was he kidding? He loved the goofy mutt. As much as he wanted a dog of his own, the commitment was too daunting. So he settled for Gremlin and her sloppy adoration.

A delicious smell wafted through the cracked door. *Blueberry pancakes.* His mom's specialty. *Home sweet home.* As much as he loved his independence, there was nothing like waking up to homemade pancakes.

"But thank you for waking me up." He pulled the door wide and let Gremlin go bounding out in front of him.

At the bottom of the stairs he encountered a stocky gray pit bull with its head tilted to one side. He couldn't read the dog's expression. Did she think he was an intruder? Or did she recognize him as part of the family? She must have been crated when he'd arrived at the house the night before, another of his mom's foster dogs.

He paused. "Hey, Mom?" he yelled.

"Yes, honey?" she called back.

"Who's the new dog, and does she like men?" Unfortunately, some of her fosters came from rough situations and were nervous around strangers.

"Hippo is a lovebug, feel free to give her a smush!"

He descended the rest of the stairs and held his hand out to the dog. Without sniffing, Hippo licked his hand and began to wag. He bent and gave her a hug too. She wiggled against him, bathing his face with kisses. Yup, he loved his parents' house. It was the one place in the world he felt completely accepted and understood, even if his family members did live to tease him.

He padded into the kitchen, both pit bulls bringing up the rear.

"Hi, Mom." He gave her a kiss on the cheek before he slid onto a stool at the breakfast bar, settling easily into his normal spot at the counter. He'd been sitting here for twenty years, ever since his mom had married Hank.

"Hi, honey. Claire said you were here. Late-night grilled cheese session?"

He snagged the French press on the counter and poured himself some coffee. His mom had always encouraged his close relationship with Claire. He'd been waiting in the hospital the day Claire was born, and he'd been the first person to hold her, other than Mom and Hank of course.

"Yup."

"What were you up to before that?"

He could feel her eyes on him. *Good old Mom.* She'd never stop worrying over him. Although, to be fair, he usually gave her good cause.

"Kate and James's engagement party. Don't worry, it was very tame. Ainsley and I went by the club afterward."

She flipped pancakes onto a plate and slid it in front of him. "Thank goodness for that."

She gave a teasing smile.

He had to hand it to his mom. How she'd raised him all those years, alone for six of them, amazed him. Through it all she'd always made sure he felt supported and surrounded by love.

"Speaking of my past adventures, Claire wants to go to the Bahamas." He shoved a forkful of pancake into his mouth. *Delicious.* He'd decided to broach the subject with his mom first, then work on Hank later.

She poured herself a cup of coffee and took the stool next to him. "I know she does. Hank is wary about it. For good reason."

She arched an eyebrow.

He sighed. He shared their concerns, of course. If anything, he knew better than the two of them how much trouble there was to be had in the Bahamas. But he'd promised his sister. "Claire isn't me. She's responsible, she makes good decisions, she can take care of herself."

"I know she is, we just don't want to see her get hurt." She ruffled his hair with one hand.

The words hung in the air. She'd always loved him for who he was, but he knew he worried her.

He reached over and squeezed her hand. "At least I've always kept you entertained." It was a halfhearted attempt at a joke, something to lighten the somber mood.

She rolled her eyes. "Oh yes. I was very entertained that time you were two and decided you'd take the bus by yourself to the beach."

He shrugged. "I try."

It had happened only weeks after his dad left. In retrospect, he was pretty sure he'd been going to look for his father, but he was glad his mom had never pushed deeper on the subject.

She placed her hand over his and squeezed. "I wouldn't change anything about you. Well, except…"

She trailed off. They both knew she had dreams for him. Dreams involving a house and a wife and kids. But she'd accepted that those things weren't on his radar. Or at least they both pretended she'd accepted it. She knew as well as anyone that he couldn't wind up like his father, even though they never talked about it. That would be too painful for both of them.

He scraped the last bites of pancake off his plate and popped them into his mouth, chewed, then swallowed.

"Stop worrying about me, Mom." He slid off the stool, planted a kiss on her cheek, and deposited his plate in the sink.

She took another swig of coffee. "That's never going to happen. I've seen what you're capable of."

Good. They were back to joking.

He gave her one last hug and snatched his keys off the counter. They'd see each other at least two more times that week. He never could go more than a few days without visiting his mom.

"I love you, Mom."

"I love you too." She watched him as he strode out the door.

CHAPTER SEVEN

Kate splashed some more wine into a glass and pushed it across the table to her. "So how was your day? Truthfully."

Ainsley glanced at Beth, whose eyes were also full of concern, and her resolve crumbled.

Her chest and throat grew tight as she let the tears flow.

"It's OK to be sad." Beth rubbed her back.

Kate lowered her head next to Ainsley's on the table and whispered. "We love you."

A lump formed in her throat, and she devolved into a series of hiccupping sobs. Why was it so hard to be strong?

She forced herself to lift her head. "Do you ever look at your life and think it's nothing like what you expected? Not what you pictured for your future self when you were eight or twelve or sixteen, or hell, even twenty?"

Kate nodded. "All the time. In fact, six months ago, I was completely miserable about the fact that I couldn't find a job prosecuting and I'd had to move back to Belmont."

She reached for Ainsley's hand and squeezed. "But then we reconnected." She grinned. "And you helped me reconnect with James."

Ainsley found herself smiling back. She hadn't done much. She'd just invented their fake relationship and wrangled them into playing along, until it inevitably turned real.

But that was different. Without a relationship, she felt completely lost. It was something she couldn't bring herself to admit to her friends.

She turned to Beth. "What about you? Is your life what you expected?"

Beth's eyes widened. "Definitely not. And I still don't know who or what I want to be when I grow up."

She swallowed a laugh. Beth had a dreamy boyfriend. His five-year-old daughter loved her, and she had a number of successful small businesses. Her life might not be perfect, but it was perfect for her.

Beth cocked an eyebrow. "That's the thing about life, right? You don't know what it's going to bring you. You just have to be open to it."

Ainsley flinched. Sometimes Beth was like the inside of a fortune cookie. It wasn't Scott himself that she missed, he'd already barely been around for months before the breakup. What she missed was the sense of belonging, knowing that she was half of a pair. Without that part of her identity, she felt adrift.

Kate nodded. "Beth's right. Things were very crappy for me before. You'll get through this, and you'll be happy again, but you have to give yourself the time to heal."

Ainsley took a gulp of wine. Kate and Beth couldn't understand the way being in a relationship had become such an ingrained part of her identity. She hadn't been single since middle school. Each time one relationship ended another took its place.

But she couldn't bring herself to say it out loud. Instead, she decided to move to easier territory. "Ryan tells me I need to learn to be fun."

The corner of Kate's mouth ticked up. "And what did you say?"

Beth rested her elbows on the table and leaned forward, her eyes dancing with curiosity.

"I told him I am fun."

"And what did he say?" Kate asked.

"He told me to prove it. That he could teach me how to be fun. So…" She fingered the stem of her wineglass and watched the light reflect through the golden liquid. "We made a bet, or a challenge, I think he called it. For three weeks I have to follow the Ryan Lawhill guide to living live without giving any shits. Think I can do it?"

Beth's mouth fell open.

"Seriously?" Kate's eyes widened.

Unease crept along her spine. "Well…" She shrugged. "It isn't like I have anything better to do these days." She needed to do something to move on, and Ryan's plan was as good as any.

Beth snorted. "Oh, man. This is going to be like an unscripted reality TV show, the two of you are a never-ending battle of wills."

She swallowed and focused on the table. Beth was right. She and Ryan liked to butt heads and annoy each other, but last night he'd kept things interesting. He'd even been almost comforting.

She suppressed a shudder. She knew better. Ryan wasn't the comforting type. He was, however, an excellent distraction. And right know she needed anything that got her out of her condo and out of her head.

She looked up and found Kate staring at her intently. "What's the bet? What does Ryan get out of this?"

She'd been asking herself the same question all day, and part of her wondered if Ryan was lonely too now that all their friends were coupled off. Not that he'd ever admit it.

"Why does Ryan do anything he does? I think he mostly wants to prove that he can corrupt me." The minute the word was out of her mouth she regretted it. *Corrupt* made things sound sexual, which they weren't. At least not yet, although she hadn't been able to help thinking about that too.

Kate pressed her lips together for a few more seconds. "I know that you know this and I don't need to say it, but I love you and I'd be a bad friend if I kept my mouth shut. You know how Ryan is. He's fun and he's a good friend and he means well, but he isn't capable of being serious. Don't get attached or entangled or develop feelings for him or something. Don't expect him to be more than a friend. He's more complicated than he seems on the surface."

Kate flushed.

Ainsley managed a laugh and squared her shoulders. After all, Kate was only looking out for her. "Of course I know that."

And she really, truly did. Ryan was not a relationship kind of guy. But what if he was something else? What if he was the one before the one? She'd never really thought of it before this afternoon, when she'd logged back in to Matters of the Heart.

Among the replies to last night's post was one by Ms. Relationship728.

What happened to all his previous flings? Could he be the one before the one? You know, the guy who's great for sex and helps you solidify the idea of what you want in a partner? The guy that reminds you that you're a desirable catch, so that you go back into the dating world full of confidence and snag the perfect guy? Don't get your feelings or hopes caught up in him, but like ASplanner said, a fling could be exactly what you need.

ASplanner was her of course, but she'd hardly noticed the affirmation of her advice. *The one before the one.* Once the idea had been planted in her mind, she couldn't shake it free. After all, Ryan had dated Ivy and now, less than six months later, she was engaged. This realization had prompted her to go online and search through the Fallston women Ryan had dated over the six months she'd known him. All seven were now in serious relationships, two of them engaged.

What if he was the one before the one? What if his deal between them wasn't about her learning to be like him, but about him helping her achieve her goals? Surely Ryan, of all people, couldn't object to her seizing the opportunity.

She forced the thought from her mind and reached for the stack of magazines in the center of the table. It was silly to believe in that kind of thing. The one before the one was a dating myth bought into by desperate women. Besides, this was Ryan they were talking about. And her. The two of them were friends and only friends, anything else would be crazy.

She leaned across the table and squeezed Kate's hand. "You

don't need to worry about me when it comes to Ryan, I promise. I can't think of any man who is less my type. Like Beth said, we're constantly going out of our way to annoy each other."

Kate flashed a relieved smile.

"Now let's stop talking about my sad life and get back to your wedding vision board."

The term "vision board" was Beth's, of course, as well as the mess of craft supplies that cluttered the other end of the table.

Soon enough they'd be doing this for Beth.

She swallowed the lump in her throat and tried to focus on being in the moment. With her friends. After all, that's what Beth would tell her to do, and Beth was one of the happiest people she'd ever met.

Fake it 'til you make it.

Her life was so good in so many ways. With any luck, Ryan's little experiment would help her get in touch with her happiness. After all, she didn't have to be like him in order to learn something from him. That was all there was, and ever would be, between them.

* * *

Ryan gripped the metal bat in his hand and watched James through the mesh of the batting cage. He'd been partially dreading and partially looking forward to tonight's guys' night out. He had to tell them about the deal with Ainsley. They'd worry about her, of course, but he knew what he was doing. He had all of this under control. Besides, they were busy with their lives and their relationships, which meant he should be the one to step up to the plate, so to speak, and cheer Ainsley up.

James swung and there was a clang of metal as he connected with the ball and sent it rocketing in the other direction.

"So what happened to you and Ainsley the other night at the engagement party? Beth and I never saw you again." Griffin stood next to him.

Inside the batting cage, James choked up on the bat and widened his stance. "Yeah, what did happen to you guys? You were there, and all of a sudden you weren't. Was she OK? Kate was worried."

Clink. James hit the next ball. He'd known the question was coming and had prepared for it. In his opinion he'd done a pretty good job of keeping Ainsley's mind off of her breakup.

"I promised Kate I'd protect Ainsley from the Fallston crowd and keep her distracted, so we went to Club 812 and danced for a while."

James cocked an eyebrow but stayed focused on the pitching machine. "You took Ainsley to Club 812?"

He had to admit, he had a hard time believing it himself. Ainsley had never struck him as the clubbing type.

"Yup. We made a deal." Might as well break it to them now.

Griffin turned to look at him, his features etched with curiosity. "What kind of deal?"

"Don't worry, nothing illegal." He chuckled, and thumped his friend on the shoulder. Then again it wouldn't hurt to keep them guessing a few seconds longer. Otherwise, where was the fun?

Inside the batting cage, James snorted, then swung and connected with another ball. "Maybe I'm crazy, but I don't find that reassuring. You've managed to stretch the boundaries of legal many times before."

He gave a small huff of exaggerated indignation. He was doing this for Ainsley, to help her through a hard time. Their friends needed to relax and trust him.

"I'm going to teach her how to be more like me. To stop caring so much what other people think and to just do things she wants to do, things that make her happy."

"Huh." Griffin gave a small nod. "That's actually a pretty good idea."

Duh. Of course it was. Although he hadn't expected the rest of them to fully appreciate it.

The batting machine whirred to a stop, and James stepped out from the cage. "So what exactly does this plan entail?"

James held the bat out to Griffin, who accepted it before he stepped into the cage. To Ryan's surprise he looked intrigued and not the least bit judgmental.

Ryan shrugged.

"To get her to try new things, keep her on her toes, make her get outside of her comfort zone."

There was no plan, that was the whole point. Ainsley needed to learn to stop organizing every aspect of her life so she could learn to live in the moment.

James's eyes gleamed. "Does that mean we get a say? In how to help Ainsley loosen up a little?"

He laughed. He should have guessed. James and Ainsley had been friends forever, which meant James probably had a few good ideas up his sleeve. Still, he was pleased they thought this was a good idea. It was important that his friends trust him.

"Sure. What did you have in mind?" Paintball and waterskiing were both top contenders. And a trip to Syd's hamburger place. He didn't think he'd ever seen Ainsley eat something that didn't require a fork and knife.

James sighed, his eyes on Griffin in the batting cage. "I don't know, but it would be good to see her happy in her own skin. I wish she could see herself the way we see her."

He nodded. It was a lofty goal, but he was determined to try. A little challenge had never scared him.

Inside the batting cage, there was a clink as Griffin connected with the ball.

"I just thought I'd get her drunk a few times and make her go rock climbing, take her to some shows, keep her out past her bedtime."

James smirked. "I can get behind that." He frowned and paused for a moment. "Just be careful with her, OK? Ainsley's fragile right now."

He swallowed. This was the part of the conversation he'd dreaded. Did they really think he'd go out of his way to hurt her? Besides, he had a feeling Ainsley was not as fragile as they thought. Sure, she was going through a hard time, but the woman had an iron will.

Inside the batting cage, the machine clicked off, indicating the end of Griffin's turn.

Ryan clapped one hand on James's shoulder. Before he took his turn, it was important that he address this, head-on. His own reputation preceded him, but he had no intention of hurting Ainsley. There were certain boundaries even he knew to respect.

"Ainsley and I are just friends. Besides, I don't think you need to worry about her. Ainsley can hold her own."

He should know. He was often the one on the other end of her sharp tongue. Not that he didn't deserve it. Truth be told, he did get a kick out of instigating her. The flush that came over her cheeks when she was frustrated or annoyed was just too irresistible.

Griffin stepped out of the cage and shoulde-bumped him. "Then who should we worry about? You? What if Ainsley starts to rub off on you?"

He snorted. Spending time with Ainsley was hardly going to turn him into a relationship person. "That's not going to happen and you guys know it. I'm like…"

His mind went blank and he struggled to think of an apt analogy.

"You're rubber and she's glue? Whatever she says bounces off you and sticks to her?" Griffin joked.

He blinked incredulously at his friend. "You spend way too much time with little kids, man. I'm like Iron Man or some shit. I'm impenetrable. You know, resistant."

James shook his head and jokingly pushed him into the batting cage. "Yeah, sure. Whatever. Your turn, Ironman. I can't listen to you babble on about this crap anymore."

He lifted his bat in a salute as he sauntered inside to take his place at the plate. They'd see. He did not intend to let Ainsley Slone affect him in any way. Plenty of women had tried, and failed, to change him. The Lawhill fear of commitment was strong, and he was going to help Ainsley see its benefits.

CHAPTER EIGHT

Ainsley crossed one leg over the other and sat up straight on Griffin's sofa. Where the hell was Ryan? They'd agreed to meet at Griffin and Beth's at 6:00 p.m. He was five minutes late, and Beth and Griffin had to pick Mabel up from her mom's apartment by eight. She knew she was supposed to be implementing his relaxed life plan, but his lateness still annoyed her. Then again, maybe it was a test of how well she was adhering to his lessons.

Across from her, Kate gestured animatedly as James looked on with a bemused smile.

"The guy is on the stand and he's in the middle of testifying," Kate was saying. "Well, he gets to the part where his ex-girlfriend broke into his house and stole the cheese, but he tells the judge he wasn't there when it happened. So of course I asked him how he knew it was the ex-girlfriend that had broken in." Her face was red, and she had to take a deep breath before she could continue without laughing.

"Under oath, in court, he looks me in the eye and says, 'Well, ma'am, because she's just a bitch like that.'"

Kate dissolved into laughter, joined by Beth, Griffin, and James.

Ainsley worked to muster a smile. It *was* a funny story, she was just distracted. If none of the rest of them were irritated, why should she be? She needed to work on being less of a planner and more with going with the flow. Ryan was right about that.

Still, where was he?

Out of nowhere, "Let It Go," from the movie *Frozen*, blasted through the room.

She glanced around wildly, then watched as Griffin lifted his phone to his ear. She stifled a giggle. Mabel must have picked his ring tone.

Across from her, both Kate and James were red faced as they tried to suppress their own laughter. It was a ridiculous ring tone for a grown man, but that's why Griffin was such a good father. He didn't care about that kind of thing, all he cared about was making his daughter happy.

"Hello?" Griffin answered.

As she thought about the ring tone, her heart twisted. Griffin was exactly the kind of father she wanted for her own children, if she was ever lucky enough to have them. Her dad had never been like that, which was why he was needling her about a wedding. He cared more about throwing an event and impressing his business colleagues than the identity of his daughter's potential groom.

Her eyes burned. That was exactly what she didn't want for

her own kids. But how was she supposed to find someone like Griffin? With Scott officially out of the picture, she was finally realizing how wrong for her he'd really been, and all that did was put her goals further out of reach. For once she saw clearly all of the attributes she wanted in a partner, which only made her realize that that kind of man probably didn't exist. Or at least, if he did, her odds of finding him were slim.

She forced herself to focus on Griffin's end of the conversation. Tonight wasn't about her goals and plans. She was supposed to be getting out of her own head and practicing living in the moment, the way Ryan had instructed, although the task would be a lot easier if Ryan were actually here to help her put his plan into action.

Griffin's mouth fell open. "You're kidding me!"

He made a few sounds of agreement, nodding as he listened. Not that whoever was on the other end could see him. Ainsley started to become nervous. Whatever this call was about, it sounded serious. She just hoped Mabel was OK.

"Wow."

A few seconds' pause. Her anxiety grew. *Exactly the opposite of what Ryan prescribed.*

"Wow," he said more emphatically. "That's really screwed up, Ryan. I'm so sorry. We'll head straight over. The police should be there by then and maybe Kate will have some ideas."

Her heartbeat sped as she reached a full-fledged panic. Police? What had Ryan gotten himself into now? Was he OK? Was the public at large OK? How had he managed to get himself arrested?

Another thought nagged at the corner of her mind. Maybe

he wasn't the best person to hand her life over to, even if it was only for three weeks. His decision-making had always been questionable, as evidenced by whatever had prompted the phone call to Griffin.

Griffin hung up the phone, his eyes wide. "Someone smashed in Ryan's car windshield."

Kate shot forward on her seat, perching on the edge. "You're kidding me! He loves that car, who would do something like that?"

Ainsley gripped the arm of the sofa. Who *would* do that? Ryan could be irritating, but smashing his windshield was just plain mean.

Griffin stood and extended a hand to Beth. "I told him we'd meet him, so we should get going. He sounds like he needs a friend right now."

Ainsley nodded and stood. He did need a friend, and this time she could be there for him. Although he'd said their deal was for her benefit, the more she thought about it the more convinced she became that he needed a distraction too. All of their friends were busier now and the least she could do was play along with his plan. The next three weeks might not be a good idea, but Ryan was sure to keep them interesting.

* * *

Ryan crossed his arms over his chest and swallowed the lump in his throat. Who would do this to his car? Who could be so cruel, so unfeeling? The pain of looking at his smashed windshield was so acute he wanted to cry.

He'd left it outside Club 812 overnight and caught a ride with a hot dark-haired girl clad in a pair of leather pants. She'd been covered in tattoos and he'd spent the night admiring all of them. And the morning. And part of the afternoon. Which is why he hadn't gone to the club to pick up his car until just before he was supposed to meet his friends for dinner.

He scowled, his jaw clenching in anger. It was probably some punk kids. With any luck their fingerprints would be all over the brick that sat in the middle of the driver-side seat. He'd make sure the police nailed them.

The uniformed police officer hung up his cell phone. "An officer trained as a fingerprint technician is going to be here in a few minutes. Once she arrives we'll let her process everything and then we can call a tow truck."

His gut clenched with disappointment and apprehension. A tow truck. His poor Mustang deserved so much better than this. And how was he supposed to get around for the next few days?

He decided to focus on the anger and channel it instead. "Any suspects? You know, kids who are known to run around the neighborhood smashing out windows for fun?"

The officer frowned, his expression doubtful. "It's always possible, but we don't have any reports of other cars being vandalized last night. Usually they smash out a side window and steal something, but I guess a less experienced thief might go for the front windshield."

Ryan's lungs constricted with fear. Steal something? There was only one thing in his car worth stealing. He took a determined step toward the car and peered inside, careful not to touch the exterior in case of prints.

The tightness in his chest eased. His custom sound system was still there, along with the docking station for his phone.

But if they hadn't taken that, why had they broken in? Confusion set in. None of this made sense.

Another police car pulled up and rolled to a stop in front of his Mustang.

His heart thumped faster as he watched the female officer climb from her car and reach into the backseat for a bag. He'd never imagined those polyester uniform pants could do such great things for a woman's ass, but hers was round and perfect. He ran a hand over his hair to give it that purposely rumpled look, his eyes still glued to her backside.

What had he been telling Ainsley the other night? That she needed to get out of her comfort zone and try new things? Well, he'd never slept with a police officer. Maybe something good would come of this whole thing. He'd make lemonade out of lemons, or however that saying went.

When the officer turned to face him, he held out his hand and flashed her his most charming smile. "I'm Ryan Lawhill. Thanks for coming out to investigate whoever attacked my poor car."

Women loved his car. Between the Mustang and his smile, he figured he had a good chance at scoring a number. And if not? He'd pull at that old line about being a partial owner of 812. Things were definitely looking up.

She put her hand in his and squeezed, so hard he nearly

gasped aloud. Then she gave it a quick pump and dropped it, turning toward the other uniformed officer.

"Brick through the window?" Her tone was clipped.

He nodded. "Yup." The handshake had caught him off guard, and he wasn't sure how to proceed. She was all business, despite the blatant sex appeal of his car. Or maybe the broken windshield had diminished that.

He went back to mentally cursing the culprits.

The female officer shrugged, set down her bag, and pulled out a pair of rubber gloves. She pulled them over her hands with a snap. "Sounds personal. Let's get the brick. I'd bet there's a note attached to it somehow. I'll fingerprint them both."

Confusion flashed through him. Personal? All thought of flirtation fled his head. Why would someone target his car on purpose? He always went out of his way to be friendly to everyone. Besides, this was Club 812. These were his people, he was loved here.

He was so caught up in his own thoughts that he didn't notice the low hum of a car engine or even the slam of car doors until a woman yelled, "Ryan? Everything OK?"

He turned in the direction of the voice and saw his friends approaching. Their arrival made him feel the slightest bit better.

"Oh, Ryan." Kate wrapped her arms around his neck and gave him a squeeze. "I'm so sorry. I know how much you love your car."

He swallowed hard and nodded as he released her. His poor car. Beth and Ainsley gave him quick hugs while Ryan and

James settled for claps on the back. He was glad they appreciated the gravity of the situation.

"So what exactly happened?" James asked.

He shrugged. "Someone threw a brick through the front windshield. Fingerprint tech is working on it now, and once she finds a match Kate's going to go after the guy for me."

He'd seen the gleam in her eye when she really sank her teeth into a case. He couldn't think of anyone better to help him, and his car, than Kate.

She lifted her hands, palms out, and took a step back. "No way, mister. For starters, I don't handle those kinds of cases. And second, you're my friend. That would be a conflict of interest."

He stepped toward her and reached for her hand. Didn't she know how important this was? His Mustang deserved justice.

"But, Kate. You're balls to the wall. Everybody knows it. I need you to be the one to handle my case."

Next to him Ainsley snickered. "Did you just tell Kate she was 'balls to the wall'?"

He turned and scowled at her. He, and his car, deserved the best prosecutor. This wasn't the time to joke.

Just then, the female officer stepped out of the Mustang. Ryan dropped Kate's hand and turned his full attention to her, along with another million-watt smile. Despite what the officer had said earlier, he was certain this couldn't be personal. The fingerprints would help prove that.

She held a wrinkled piece of paper, pinched between two latex-covered fingers. "I don't know who you pissed off, but I'm guessing she was here last night too. At the club."

He froze, his feet rooted to the spot. What was she talking about? Women loved him.

The technician fixed him with a knowing gaze. "It says, and I quote, 'How dare you pick her over me you giant man slut. I hope your dick falls off and rots.'"

Behind him there was a snort, followed by mixed laughter. He clenched his eyes shut in indignation. Great. Now his friends were laughing at his suffering.

The tech raised an eyebrow. "Anyone special come to mind?"

"Yeah, about forty of them." Griffin's voice rumbled from behind him.

He took a step toward the tech and lowered his voice as he placed a hand on her shoulder. Something had to be salvaged from this shitty incident. A date with the police officer wouldn't erase his pain, but it might help. "They're just kidding."

She narrowed her eyes at him.

Mentally he groped for a good cover story, then quickly gave up. The possibility of getting laid by a hot police officer was not worth lying to the police. Even he wasn't that stupid. Besides, he'd always prided himself on his honesty, which was why he couldn't entirely believe in the authenticity of the crazy note. All the women he dated knew exactly what they were getting into with him.

He dropped his hand from her shoulder. "Actually, they're not joking. There are about forty candidates."

Getting her phone number was a lot less important than finding the person who'd attacked his Mustang. The muscles in his shoulders knotted. Now that he was sure he'd struck out, he needed to get out of here and enjoy a few cold beers. Maybe something harder, since he sure as hell wouldn't be driving.

Kate stepped up beside him. "We'll get you a list of possible suspects by Monday, Officer Laruffa. Until then, we'll just get out of your hair and let you do your job."

Only then did the female officer smile. "Ms. Massie. Absolutely. I'll fast-track the fingerprint analysis for you."

"Thank you. We appreciate that." Then Kate gripped his elbow and steered him back in the direction of their friends and Beth's van. "Let's get you out of here. The first round is on me."

He gave in and let her lead him.

CHAPTER NINE

He frowned into his beer as his friends chatted around him. His shoulders were knotted with tension. Who could have done that to his car? It simply didn't make sense.

The other night he'd been telling Ainsley the truth. He had an implicit agreement with the women he dated. It was all just fun. He'd never led anyone to expect more, and they'd never indicated they wanted more. Until now, everyone had seemed to accept that. So what had gone wrong? No one had seemed angry at him, nobody had said anything. Obviously someone had taken exception to his choice of company last night, but he couldn't imagine who.

There was a dull thud in his temple and the nagging sensation of regret. Somewhere along the line he'd slipped up. Someone had gotten through his normally good honesty radar. Somehow, despite all of his best intentions, he'd hurt someone. Which was exactly what he'd always tried to avoid.

He sighed and leaned back in his chair.

Beth rested a hand on his forearm. "I'm really sorry about your car. If you want to borrow Martha after I make muffin deliveries this week, you can. I'm usually finished up by nine a.m."

Emotion built in his throat. He had the best friends in the world. Sure, they liked to poke fun at him, but when it came down to it, they had his back.

He quashed the feeling. It wouldn't do to get all sappy, it would only encourage his friends to pry into his emotions and shit. "I'm not driving your creepy white van around town. People will think I'm a rapist."

Griffin chuckled and sloshed more beer from the pitcher into Ryan's glass. "Glad to see you're feeling like your normal self again. After tonight, though, I have to say that it might not be a bad thing if Ainsley rubs off on you during the course of your little arrangement. Although that might put the windshield replacement company out of business."

His shoulders relaxed. This was more like it. Now his friends could stop worrying and they could all get back to making fun of each other. The way they were supposed to. Although he completely refused to let Ainsley turn him into a relationship person. This was a temporary setback. Somewhere there'd been a misunderstanding, and as soon as he could discover the source he would make things right.

Kate pulled a face. "I think you just broke my brain. I'm having a hard time imagining Ainsley trolling the town for penis while Ryan wears high heels and advises people on wedding colors."

Ainsley nearly choked on her white wine. Then a sly grin crossed her face. "I feel the need to make it clear that I could troll the town for penis if I wanted to. I just choose to implement a rigorous screening process before I take someone into my bed."

There it was. The opening. Now was the time to impart to her the details of his dating strategy, which was normally flawless. It was time for some tough love.

"That's your first mistake. You don't take them to your bed, you let them take you to theirs." He took another swig of beer.

Her nose wrinkled. "But how do I know if they've washed their sheets? What if they haven't cleaned the bathroom? Men aren't good at cleaning bathrooms, you know."

He rolled his eyes. Same old Ainsley, worrying about silly details. Clearly he had his work cut out for him. "You don't. And it doesn't matter. You're there for sex, not for a five-star lodging experience."

She pressed her lips together into a tight line but he could tell she wasn't actually mad. It was all part of the back-and-forth, how they interacted with each other. They had fun when they verbally sparred like this.

"So, Ainsley. What's this rigorous screening process? I'm curious." James popped a French fry into his mouth.

Ryan had been wondering this too.

She tilted her chin upward as if she knew they would judge her answer, but she was determined to give it anyway. "It's a three date system. By the end of three dates, I know whether or not I'm going to sleep with someone."

"Three dates? What exactly are you looking for on these three dates?" His voice was incredulous, and this time it wasn't for show. That was madness. She definitely needed to relax a little.

She gave him a smug smile and lifted one finger in the air. "On the first date I see whether we click and also whether he's willing to pay. I look at his shoes, the car he drives, and assess for general life stability. Of course at that point I've already Google-stalked him to ensure he has a secure job and his connections are good."

She raised a second finger. "Date two is about manners and also a test of whether he's a…" She glanced at him. "Whether he reminds me of Ryan."

For a second the comment stung, but then he reminded himself she was just trying to push his buttons. It was what they did, and there was no reason to let it bother him.

"You know," she continued, "whether he tries to take things too physical too fast. Kissing is fine, but trying to slide your hand up my skirt? No thanks."

Blood rushed below the belt as he imagined running his hand up Ainsley's smooth, tanned thigh. Then he mentally slapped himself. What was wrong with him? She was in the process of outlining how she would never date someone like him.

"On the second date he also has to offer to drive, pick me up from my house, and walk me to and from the door, but without trying to come inside."

His hands clenched in annoyance. This was some crazy nonsense. Some of her ideas might have validity, he was willing to concede that, but all her rules just meant most men were destined for failure. Even if she didn't want to subscribe to his dating philosophy, which he still thought she should, she was ruling out completely decent men for practically no reason. Other than it made her feel more in control.

"Date three," she lifted the third finger, "I'll let him come back to my house for coffee. He has to hesitate before agreeing to come up, extra points if he asks if I'm sure I'm comfortable. We have to talk for at least five minutes so I know sex isn't the only reason he's there."

He barked out a laugh. "But sex is the only reason he's there."

James slanted him a glance and he snapped his mouth shut. Fine. Let James and Griffin pretend they were better than that. No man was, not really. They were programmed to think about sex all the time. Why not be honest about what you wanted? Why pretend and read into signals and hold people up to unspoken standards? He was more convinced than ever that her dating strategy was flawed, but he knew that picking it apart now would only embarrass her. No, he'd have to use the Lawhill life challenge in order to help her understand the error of her ways.

"Like I said," Beth interjected, "this really should be a reality TV show. I'd watch it over *Help, My Brother's Mother's Cousin Is a Purple Hamster* or *Extreme Snow Boccie* or *The Real Housewives of Spike's Trailer Park*, or whatever is popular right now."

Griffin smirked and placed his hand on top of hers. "Your cultural references are…weird. But I still love you."

She shrugged. "I'm not the one who comes up with TV programming. I'm just saying. *Ainsley and Ryan, Battle of the Dating Strategies*, would be pretty amusing."

It annoyed him to hear his dating methods and Ainsley's

compared in the same sentence. So his approach had led to a smashed car windshield. Overall, he'd categorize his dating life as highly successful, and he was fairly certain that Ainsley couldn't say the same. Not that he was going to rub her nose in it, he was just going to help her see the error of her ways.

Which reminded him. "There is no Battle of the Dating Strategies. This is Ainsley learns Ryan's fail-proof not giving a shit approach to life. It's a one-way street. I plan on learning nothing."

"As usual," Kate joked under her breath.

He winked at her. Exactly. He changed for no one. It had taken him a long time to perfect his habits and a damaged windshield wasn't about to change that. Besides, in the grand scheme of things, one angry woman out of a few hundred wasn't that bad. No matter what, his success rate was still high.

Ainsley blushed. "And it's not about sex or even dating. It's just about trying something new. My dating strategy is perfectly fine, thank you very much, I just need to loosen up and mix up my life a little bit."

He resisted the urge to roll his eyes. Her dating strategy was not fine, but it wasn't beyond his powers to fix. He just had to get her to the point where she wanted to change. That started with teaching her how to relax and have fun in general. He had to get her out of her comfort zone.

"Speaking of which"—he set his empty beer mug on the table—"what are we up to now? I need a designated driver and a lot more to drink. I'm traumatized, you know. From what happened to my car."

He had only three weeks to show Ainsley how great single

life could be. Now more than ever he had to convert her and prove to their friends, as well as himself, that he knew exactly what he was doing. The Mustang incident was just a blip in an otherwise impeccable record.

* * *

Ryan lifted two fingers to the bartender, indicating another round of shots. From over his shoulder she shook her head and mouthed "wine." If she was going to drive his ass home tonight, she needed to keep her wits about her. Because he definitely wasn't in any condition to drive. It was obvious to her that Ryan was drowning his sorrows although he'd claimed this was introducing her to the joys of cheap, seedy bars. At least the bartender was on her side and had been pouring her drinks slowly and had even chatted with her for a few minutes about the wine list. Not that she was really interested in the wine list at a place like this, but she'd figured she should make some attempt to flirt, given the mission of the next few weeks.

After dinner, Beth and Griffin had gone to get Mabel, and Kate and James had headed home, leaving just her and Ryan to drink at the dive bar of his choice. Someplace called, ironically, Diver's. While Ryan drank away his sorrows, she'd been mulling over an idea Griffin had sparked during dinner. Why was she the only one trying something new? Ryan's playboy antics had gotten his car window smashed. Griffin was right. It would be good for Ryan to learn something from her too.

Too bad she had no idea how she was supposed to impart the benefits of commitment. He didn't have to become a serial monogamist like her, but an actual relationship would do him some good.

The bartender approached. He set down the shot in front of Ryan, then winked at her as he handed her the glass of white wine. Their fingers brushed against one another. He was handsome enough, in that hipster kind of way. He wore a PBR T-shirt and thick-rimmed black glasses, with his brown hair spiked a little in front.

She smiled back and carefully took a sip of wine, the cool chardonnay washing over her tongue.

When the bartender headed over to another customer, Ryan grabbed her elbow. "You should go home with him."

Then he grabbed his shot and downed it in one swallow. She flinched but held her tongue. After all, it was his liver to poison.

"Ummm, I don't think so." She'd promised to try his techniques, but she wasn't ready to throw herself into the deep end yet. She hadn't yet decided how much she wanted to commit to Ryan's plan. She was trying it out, just for fun. Testing the waters.

Besides, wasn't hanging out in this dive bar good enough for her second night of Ryan's mission? Baby steps.

"And why not?" His voice was overly loud, even for the noisy bar.

She expelled a long breath. Whom she slept with, or didn't sleep with, was none of his business.

He leaned closer. "Come on, tell me. After all, aren't I supposed to be your life guru or shaman or spiritual leader or whatever?"

She couldn't help it. She giggled, which made his grin grow wider. She should have known better than to encourage him.

"He's not my type."

Ryan shook his head vigorously, then wobbled on his feet. Yup, he was definitely drunk. "Ryan doesn't have a type besides 'hot' and 'woman.' That means Ainsley the protégée doesn't have a type either."

She laughed harder. "Trust me, I am not your protégée."

That would be taking things entirely too far.

He looked her in the eye. "Proposition the bartender before I do it for you."

Her mouth fell open. And how exactly did he plan to do that? She was pretty sure his usual tricks didn't work on men.

Actually, that might be a fun experiment. She gritted her teeth. He was drunk and he'd hardly remember in the morning. What was the harm in trying?

"Fine. Tell me how women catch your interest and I'll put their methods to practice."

A grin spread across his face, like on a kid's on Christmas morning. Or like Ryan's in a room full of naked women. It was the happiest she'd seen him all night, which almost made this worth it.

"Catch his eye and smile," he said, slurring.

As the bartender's gaze traveled across the bar, she caught his brown eyes and held them. She smiled and a second later he smiled back. She experienced a small flicker of triumph.

It had been ages since she'd met a guy in a bar, and certainly never in a hole-in-the-wall like this one.

"Now look away. Slowly lower your eyes to your wine."

She followed his instructions. Of course Ryan could walk her through the process drunk. He could probably do it in his sleep too.

"And lick your lips. Not like you're licking barbecue off your mouth but sexy."

"I know how to be sexy," she hissed out of the corner of her mouth.

"Just do it!" His words were a little slurred, but he was giving surprisingly coherent advice for a drunk guy.

She gently tugged her lower lip into her mouth and ran the tip of her tongue across it. Thank God for everlasting lipstick.

Seconds later she sensed the bartender's presence in front of her.

She lifted her head.

"Hey." His eyes were glued to her face.

"Hey." Her stomach began a series of acrobatics. She'd forgotten how terrifying and exhilarating this could be.

In spite of her nervousness, she managed to strike up a conversation, and twenty minutes later they were still discussing the year the bartender had spent living in Barbados. Until Ryan tapped her on the shoulder, interrupting them.

"Ainsley." Ryan's voice was still too loud for the cramped bar. "Did you know my fly has been down this whole time? Since I went to the bathroom? I really should work on that."

She swallowed a giggle as the bartender shifted his gaze to Ryan and narrowed his eyes.

Ryan was hopeless. First he told her to pick up the bartender, and now he was drunkenly cock-blocking her.

"I'm sure you can find someone to help you with your pants, Ryan."

There had to be some willing woman around here.

"Yup. I definitely could." Then, with a *thunk*, his head dropped onto the bar.

Irritation grew inside of her as she poked him with one finger. Exactly how much had he drunk?

"Is your friend OK?" the bartender asked.

"Snkjbjhreb." Ryan didn't lift his head.

She sighed. Only Ryan could go from coherent drunk one second to passed out cold the next.

The bartender arched an eyebrow at her. "You want help getting your friend into the car?"

She hesitated for a second, then pulled her credit card from her purse and slapped it down on the counter, right next to Ryan's head. He still didn't move.

"That would be just great."

Ryan owed her for this one.

CHAPTER TEN

The bartender slung Ryan's right arm over his shoulder and hoisted him by the waist. She hesitated for a moment, then wedged herself under Ryan's other arm. She planted one hand on his chest.

Her fingers met with hard planes of muscle, sending an unexpected wave of desire washing over her. She sucked in a shaky breath and planted her other hand on his back. Again, firm muscles met her skin from underneath the cotton of his T-shirt. Her knees trembled slightly and her heartbeat sped.

"You OK over there?" the bartender called.

"Um, yeah. Yup. Great. My car's parked just out front."

She swallowed hard. It was only Ryan. Nothing worth getting worked up over. She knew he was good-looking, she'd just never paid much attention. And right now she should concentrate on the bartender.

"What's your name?" she asked as the three of them staggered slowly toward the door.

"Mike."

She frowned. Mike. She'd never really pictured herself dating a Mike. Then again, she'd never pictured herself carrying a drunk Ryan Lawhill out of a bar. She'd never been the "carry you out of a bar" kind of friend. She was more the "plan your wedding" or "help you choose an outfit for your hot date" kind of friend. At least he was keeping his promise and pushing her outside her comfort zone.

She fished through her purse until she found her keys, then clicked the unlock button. A beep rang through the air. It was a good thing she'd found a parking spot right by the door.

When they reached the car, she eased from under Ryan's arm and pulled the handle of the passenger door. She was breathing heavily and beads of sweat were beginning to trickle down the back of her neck. She didn't even want to know what her hair looked like.

"On three, we'll set him on the seat. Then we can swing his feet around." Now that they were outside in the night air, she could hear Mike's voice more clearly. Its timbre was warm but light. She usually liked men whose voice had a little more gruffness.

She bit her lip.

Oh well. After this he probably wouldn't want to see her again anyway. And she was supposed to be trying new dating strategies.

Mike counted to three, then they shoved Ryan forward and into the passenger seat. The crushing weight around her shoulders lifted. He was a lean, lanky guy. How had she never guessed at the muscles that hid under his T-shirts and jeans?

There was a slight pressure against the small of her back.

"You got him from here?" Mike's warm breath brushed across her ear as his hand on her back inched lower.

Her spine stiffened. What was he doing?

"Um, thanks for everything." She abruptly stepped away and reached into her purse. She pulled out a five-dollar bill.

Mike let out a quick laugh and shook his head. "I'm not taking your money. But I would take your phone number."

His tone was teasing and he cocked an eyebrow, waiting.

Her face heated. This was what she wanted, right? This was what she was supposed to be aiming for?

"Oh yeah. Sure. Here, let me just put you into my phone."

She whipped her phone out of her purse and handed it to him. He turned it over, looking at her bejeweled Kate Spade case. "Fancy."

Her face flamed hotter and she bent to buckle the seat belt over his chest.

She paused for a moment, allowing herself to get a full look at his broad chest and the sinewy muscles of his forearms.

Her pulse raced.

"All done!" Mike called.

She jerked her head up, slamming it into the roof. "Ouch!"

That's what she got for checking Ryan out when he was asleep. Served her right.

Carefully this time, she eased her head out of the car and quietly nudged the passenger door shut. She might as well let him sleep.

Mike held the phone out to her and their fingers brushed as she took it. Nothing. Nada. No spark. No zing.

Frustration surged inside of her. He was hot enough. And he was interested. So what was she doing making eyes at an unconscious Ryan Lawhill?

Gross. Weird. Gross and weird.

"I'll call you later." She waved a quick good-bye, then rounded the car and climbed into the driver's seat.

After debating a few seconds, she decided to take Ryan back to her apartment. The last thing she needed was to try to fish through his pockets for his keys. With her luck tonight, she'd wind up grabbing hold of way more than she bargained for. She brushed aside her annoyance. After all, it wasn't as though she had anything better to do with her night. Babysitting Ryan may not have been part of her plan, but she'd live. And at least she'd left the bar with a phone number, although somehow she couldn't muster the excitement she knew she should be feeling. Which only made her more nervous. Why was she suddenly attracted to all the wrong guys? Like Ryan?

It was a five-minute drive to her apartment. Only when they reached the parking lot did it occur to her that she had no way to get Ryan out of the car and onto her sofa.

Shit. She couldn't exactly leave him there. She nearly threw her hands up in exasperation. Ryan had needed an outlet tonight, but wasn't he the one who was supposed to be helping her?

With a sigh, she unbuckled her seat belt and went around to the passenger-side door. She leaned across him to press the button to release the seat belt. He'd had a tough night, and the least she could do was look out for him. If the situation were in reverse, she knew he'd do the same for her.

"Ainsley?" She jumped, but a strong hand grabbed her wrist, pulling her closer so her long hair formed a curtain around them.

Ryan's eyes were a little blurry, but he managed to hold her gaze. "Did you go home with that guy?"

His voice was quiet, almost a whisper. It made the moment oddly intimate.

She swallowed, her body flush with anticipation. "Nope. I brought you home with me instead."

It was exactly the kind of joke he'd appreciate. And she really was joking, she told herself. Under more sober circumstances, with another, more sober man, this moment would have been full of promise. But Ryan didn't know what he was about. The sensation of closeness, emotional as well as physical, was a trick. It was the alcohol and Ryan's inhibition and her own loneliness. Nothing about it was real.

He lifted his thumb and ran it over her lower lip. Her breath caught and a surge of heat washed over her. Involuntarily, she parted her lips, even as she tried to bring herself back to sanity. Ryan was drunk, he had no idea what he was doing, but she knew better. He'd regret this in the morning. If he remembered it. Still, she couldn't force herself to pull away. It felt good to be looked at like that.

He watched her a moment longer, his gaze burning into her. "I forgot to tell you how beautiful you look tonight. Glad you didn't waste it on the bartender."

Wow. Drunk Ryan was even smoother than sober Ryan, a fact she hadn't imagined possible. She knew it wasn't real, knew it was just the alcohol speaking, but couldn't help soaking in the seeming genuineness of his words.

Before she could respond, he leaned forward and pressed his mouth to hers. His lips were warm and supple. A strong hand snaked around her waist, pulling her into him, as his tongue darted into her mouth, caressing.

For a second she was lost in the taste and feel of him. Then her senses returned and she yanked back.

"Wow. That was good," he said, before his eyelids flickered shut again.

* * *

Ryan woke in a haze, his head pounding and his mouth dry. With a groan, he turned to bury his head into the pillow.

A sweet, flowery scent met his nostrils. He jolted to a sitting position. Ainsley. The pillow smelled like Ainsley.

The room spun and it took him a moment to get his bearings. He lay in the middle of a white four-poster bed, wrapped in a soft, pink blanket. Next to him was a wall of pink and yellow throw pillows, from the headboard all the way down to the foot of the bed. The Great Wall of Pillows.

Anxiety pricked the back of his neck as he jerked back the covers. He was still wearing his jeans. Which meant they hadn't…

He shook his head. Of course they hadn't. This was him and Ainsley, for heaven's sake. She'd never sleep with a guy like him, even as part of the Lawhill challenge. She'd made that more than clear at dinner last night when laying out her dating strategies.

So how the hell had he gotten into her bed?

He squinted against the pain as he racked his mind for his last memory from the night before. Auto-tuned pop playing over the car radio. The bite of the seat belt against his waist. Soft, sweet lips. Cool stone against his forehead, followed by a throbbing pain. The burn of alcohol searing his throat.

With a grunt, he swung his legs out from under the covers and placed his bare feet on the soft carpet.

He glanced around, searching. There was his folded T-shirt, resting on top of his shoes and socks. He smiled to himself. Ainsley. She'd put him to bed like a damn kid.

A lump formed in his throat. Had he kissed her last night? There was the memory of lips against his, but details eluded him. Surely she would have kicked him out of the car and left him by the side of the road if he had. More likely he'd kissed some random woman on his way back from the bathroom. He felt a pang of regret at the thought. Part of him would much rather have kissed Ainsley. Then again, that could just be his ego talking.

He ran his hand through his hair and wandered into the living room. What he really needed was a cup of coffee.

"Morning, sleepyhead!" Ainsley stopped tapping at the keyboard of her laptop long enough to look up at him from her spot on the sofa. "How are you feeling?"

He trudged a few steps farther, then threw himself into an armchair. "I feel like hell. And I'd really love some coffee. Also, please tell me I didn't do anything stupid or humiliating last night. I'm fine with embarrassing myself, I just prefer to remember it so I can make fun of myself before anyone else does."

She stared at him for a second, then gave a little half smile. His heart punched against his rib cage. What did that look mean?

"Nope." She pushed up from the sofa and headed into the kitchen. "Nothing unusual in the life of Ryan. You want food too? I have strawberries, steel-cut oats, turkey bacon?"

At the mention of food, his stomach grumbled loudly. "Yes to food. You have anything that isn't hippie organic healthy from Whole Paycheck?"

She closed the refrigerator and rolled her eyes at him. "Since I carted your drunk ass home last night and tipped the doorman to help carry you into my apartment, I think you'll eat what I tell you and be grateful for the food."

"Well, aren't you bossy," he grumbled, mostly joking.

She shot him another icy look and he snapped his mouth closed again. She was right, he owed her. And he really, really wanted some food.

As if to punctuate the point, his stomach growled even more loudly.

She laughed, and opened the refrigerator again. "Eggs and turkey bacon and toast and fruit it is."

His mouth watered. "And coffee," he reminded.

From inside his pocket, his cell phone chirped. Had it been in there all night? No wonder he felt like he'd slept on a small boulder.

He fished it out. "Mom" was displayed across the screen.

"Hey, Mom."

"Hi, sweetie! I just wanted to call and let you know that a package arrived for you yesterday. It's from one of those online music stores, and I know how anxious you normally are to get your equipment."

His pulse sped. His new studio monitor stands. He'd been wanting to upgrade his for a while and had finally splurged last week. But he wasn't always at the studio, so he'd had it shipped to his parents' instead, where there was less risk the package might be stolen.

"Sweet. I'll be over in a little bit. Love you, Mom."

When he hung up, he caught Ainsley staring at him, tapping her foot impatiently. "For someone who just demanded coffee you aren't in a big hurry to tell me whether you prefer drip or espresso."

"Hell, yeah, espresso!" He blurted the words.

"I mean," he leaned back into the armchair and massaged his throbbing head, "espresso would be fine, thanks."

Normally there was no sleeping when he stayed over at a woman's house and he bailed when the fun part was over. He could get used to being served breakfast though.

He propped his feet on the coffee table. As long as he was hanging out, he might as well get comfortable.

There was a hiss and a whirr from the kitchen. A minute later Ainsley glided into the living room, cup and saucer in hand. She set it in front of him on the coffee table and pointedly eyed his feet.

"Well, look at you with your fancy espresso machine, your special cups and your matching saucers." He couldn't help but give her a once-over. Her long blonde hair was damp and combed, her face pink and without a trace of makeup. She wore a simple blue tank top that accented the curve of her breasts, and a pair of yoga pants.

He breathed faster.

She looked gorgeous. Real. Eminently touchable. He flexed his fingers. *Not touchable. Not for you.*

"If you spill espresso on my carpet or my chair, I will murder you myself. I hope you know that." She pointed to the cup.

He grimaced and lowered his feet back to the floor. Not so touchable after all. "I will not spill. I'm a big boy."

Ainsley's impeccable clothing and makeup were only part of the package. She also used her sharp tongue to keep people at a distance.

He lifted the espresso cup to his lips and grinned. Good thing he always knew how to get under her skin.

"Griffin always serves my espresso with a lemon twist on the side."

Her eyes widened and her cheeks turned pink. "I should have left you passed out on that bar last night."

He chuckled, his pulse pounding harder. What was it about her? He just couldn't help himself.

With a huff, she turned and headed back into the kitchen. Giving him a great view of her perfectly sculpted backside.

He didn't have any complaints about the view or the breakfast.

* * *

Ainsley slid behind the wheel of her car and waited for Ryan to climb into the passenger seat. She bit her lip while her stomach did another somersault.

She was not going to tell him about last night. He'd kissed her by accident. It had been a dumb, drunken mistake. And while she normally would have relished the chance to hold it over his head, it seemed safest to keep it to herself.

He settled into the seat and strapped on his seat belt. Then his eyebrows furrowed. "Were you listening to the Anaconda remix last night?"

Her throat grew dry. If he remembered that, what else would he remember? He'd kissed her not even five minutes later.

"Ummm, maybe?"

He shook his head and made a face. "That song is terrible. You have terrible taste in music. Step three of the Ryan Lawhill Life Plan is to make you some halfway decent playlists. Oh, and get you out to some great live shows. That's how you really fall in love with good bands is to see them perform in person."

She made a noncommittal noise in the back of her throat and kept her eyes on the road. One minute he was holding her hand, guiding her carefully through Kate and James's engagement party, and the next he was making fun of her. He could try to distract her all he wanted, but she was starting to see him for who he really was, and he wasn't as simple as he liked to think. His verbal barbs and constant joking were just a way of keeping other people at a distance. Deep down she had a feeling he was a big old softie, as evidenced by the fact that they were on the way to his mom's house.

"What are we doing at your mom's again?" He'd asked for a ride and she'd agreed. After all, he didn't have a car.

He shook his head. "I'm just going to run in and grab the package and run back out. No need for you to bother coming in for that."

This was it. The perfect opportunity to screw with him. She had to admit that she enjoyed the verbal back-and-forth. Ryan used it as a way to create distance with people, but she actually got the feeling that it was bringing them closer together. Kind of like their own secret language. Because after last night, she was positive the attraction wasn't one-sided, and while they both knew they shouldn't act on it, surely it wouldn't hurt to keep flirting.

"Oh, that's OK. I'd love to meet your mom. After all, we did sleep together." She had to work to keep her tone breezy.

His jaw fell open and stayed that way for a full second. Then he gave a bark of laughter. "Very funny. But seriously, my mom and my sister are nosy, so feel free to hide from them in the car."

"Sister?" Now he'd really picqued her interest.

He heaved a sigh. "Shit. I walked right into that, didn't I? Now you're dying to meet her."

Her face heated. After the toe-curling kiss last night, meeting his family seemed like a bad idea.

"On second thought, I will wait in the car."

Play with fire and you might get burned. Ryan was definitely fire. The flirting was fun, but she had to be careful not to let it go too far.

He glanced at her, a half smile on his lips. "Actually, I'm sure you have better things to do than drive me around. I'll get my mom to drive me to the rental-car place. She's always on my case about spending more quality time together."

She snickered and gave a small shake of her head. Somehow she didn't think that's what his mother meant by quality time.

"The house is right over there." He pointed and she pulled into the driveway he'd indicated and slowed to a stop.

He fingered the door handle. "I don't think last night really counted in the Ryan's life lessons department. What are you doing tomorrow?"

She slanted him a glance. "What do you mean, it doesn't count? You taught me how to pick up a hot bartender. Who then helped me carry your ass to the car and gave me his number."

His eyes widened. "You, Ainsley Slone, successfully picked up a random guy at a crappy bar? How do I not remember that?"

"You were sloshed. Blotto. Plastered. Shitfaced. Wrecked. FUBARed."

He cut her off with a wave of his hand. "OK, thanks, I get the picture. I guess that means tomorrow night would be lesson four. You in?"

Her heart rate sped. Of course she was. This plan was turning out to be more fun than she'd expected. "Yup, I'm in."

"Great." He opened the door and climbed out of the car. "Wear something comfortable. Like those yoga pants. They make your ass look good, by the way."

Then he slammed the door and turned to the house, leaving her staring after him openmouthed. *They make your ass look good.* Her palms began to sweat.

Damn Ryan and his smooth talk. She had to admit she was falling for it, but just a little bit.

CHAPTER ELEVEN

Ryan sat at the breakfast bar in his mom's kitchen, sipping coffee.

"Are you sure you don't want pancakes? I can whip them up in no time," she offered for the fifth time.

"Nope, I'm good."

Claire narrowed her eyes at him. "Are you sure you're OK? You never say no to pancakes."

"Yup. I already ate breakfast." After Ainsley's eggs, turkey bacon, whole wheat toast, and strawberries, he couldn't eat anything else. Although if he hung out at his mom's for long enough, he'd work up an appetite again. Another thing his loft lacked: someone willing to feed him.

"Does this have anything to do with the girl who dropped you off in the driveway?" Claire kept her eyes on her own coffee mug, but her cheeks flushed pink.

"A girl dropped you off?" His mother dropped the spatula

she was holding and spun to face him. Her eyes danced with excitement. "Who is she?"

He groaned and fought the urge to bury his head in his hands. He knew better than to bring a woman within five hundred feet of his mom's, but it had been an emergency. And it was just Ainsley.

"Don't get all excited. It was Ainsley. I've told you about her before, I met her through Kate. They're good friends, she's a bridesmaid in Kate's wedding. She grew up with Kate's fiancé, James."

"Oh." The smile dropped from his mom's face.

He almost felt guilty but then reminded himself. He wasn't a relationship person and his mother knew exactly why. They never talked about his dad, but he was sure that deep down she understood his reluctance.

"Don't worry, Mom." He stood and approached her, then placed a hand on her shoulder. "Next time I'll invite her in so you can tell embarrassing stories about me. I know she'd love to meet you."

Ainsley wouldn't mind or read anything into it, especially since he'd already met the human ice sculpture she called Dad.

Gremlin trotted up to him and dropped a tennis ball at his feet, whining loudly.

His mother smiled. "I'm going to hold you to that, you know."

He reached to rub the back of his neck. "Yeah, I know. I'm going to throw the ball for G here and when you're done can you drop me by the car rental place?"

It was like he was back in high school, asking his mom for

rides and inventing excuses to avoid her inquiries about his personal life.

"Of course, honey. You and G have a nice time. Try and take Hippo too, won't you?"

He glanced at the gray pit bull, who was laying on her back, feet up in the air. She had to be the world's laziest pit bull, which was really saying something.

Claire jumped from her stool at the counter. "I'm coming too!"

Claire followed behind him as he opened the door to the yard and let Gremlin out. The porch was littered with tennis balls that had all been chewed into various states of destruction. He chose one at random and chucked it. Gremlin went streaking after the ball.

"So." Claire sidled up beside him. "Ainsley, huh? What's the deal with that? Did you, you know, stay together, last night?"

He fixed her with a look. No way he was talking about that kind of thing with his little sister.

She tilted her chin defiantly and her cheeks grew redder. "You know. Did you have sex with her? You can tell me, I won't tell Mom."

He snorted in amusement. "No, I did not have sex with her, and I wouldn't tell you even if I had."

The corners of her mouth fell. "Why not? I'm almost eighteen. You can tell me those kinds of things."

His hands balled into fists and his spine prickled. How was Claire almost eighteen? Regardless, he most certainly could not tell her those kinds of things.

"Ainsley knows better than to get mixed up with a guy like me. You should too."

She sighed loudly. "Don't be ridiculous. I know you act like an ass, but that's all for show. She probably knows it too."

That warmed his heart for a second, before he came to his senses. That wasn't a healthy attitude for his sister to have.

He turned to her and gripped her by the shoulders. "Claire, this is something very important for you to understand. When a man shows you who he is, through his actions, you trust him. Don't imagine you can change him. You can't."

She cocked her head and stared at him. "What's your deal anyways? You never have a girlfriend. I can't think of one woman you've ever brought home, well, other than Kate. Don't you want to find someone? I know it's scary to put yourself out there."

"You don't know what you're talking about." A muscle in his jaw twitched. He wasn't single because he was scared. He was single because it worked for him. It was the right thing for everyone: him and the women he hooked up with. All of which was entirely too complicated to explain to a seventeen-year-old.

Her eyebrows furrowed and she shrugged his hands from her shoulder. "Fine. I won't help you. But someday, after a lot of therapy, you might find that you want something more from someone."

Exasperated, he exhaled loudly. She was only trying to help. She just didn't get it. It wasn't as simple finding a woman he liked, spending time with her, and having sex. There were all kinds of bullshit adult responsibilities and repercussions to think about. How could he promise to love another human being forever? The very idea was too daunting, too overwhelming. It had been too much for his dad and it was probably too much for him too. He was happy having his mom and Claire and Hank and his friends. How was he supposed to have enough love left over to satisfy yet another person? He worried he might run out one day without warning.

It was better to value the love he already had in his life and make sure the people around him knew he valued them. People like Claire.

"Thank you for trying to fix me, Claire."

She turned and glanced at him over her shoulder, wrinkling her nose. "Let me guess. You're about to say you're beyond fixing."

He called Gremlin, then strode toward his sister and looped an arm around her shoulder. "Exactly. I'm glad to see that you got the message. Now just remember, don't date guys like me."

Wouldn't that be a great karmic kick in the ass? His temple throbbed. No matter what, he had to make sure Claire didn't fall for someone like him. She deserved better.

From inside his pocket his phone chirped. He cracked the door open and held it as Claire, then Gremlin, passed through. Hippo was walking at a speed of one mile per year and he waited impatiently as she ambled her way inside.

On screen was a text message from Beth.

Beth: Hey, what are you up to this week?

His fingers flew across the screen and he barely glanced at what he entered before he clicked send. He could text in his sleep.

A second later the phone chirped again and he glanced down.

Beth: Um...what on earth does that mean?

He scanned up to his reply.

Ryan: DEEZ NUTZ have a show on Tuesday and Thursday, any other time DEEZ NUTZ'm free. What did you have in mind?

He frowned as he stared at the phone. What the hell was going on?

He tried again, slowly and deliberately picking out his response on the keyboard. I said I, he typed.

The minute he clicked send it popped up on the screen.

Ryan: DEEZ NUTZ said DEEZ NUTZ.

Understanding dawned on him. Someone had hacked his phone. Which was his trick, damn it. Someone had stolen his prank.

"What are you doing?" Claire asked.

He jerked his head up to look at her. Her forehead was creased in confusion and there was no trace of a smile on her face.

Not Claire. And it wasn't like his mom. So who could've done it?

The lightbulb turned on. *Ainsley.* He had, after all, been passed out for most of last night. If the roles were reversed he would have messed with her phone.

He chuckled. He had to admit, it was damn funny.

He quickly typed a response to Beth, "Let me guess. Ainsley told you to text."

She would have been itching for him to discover her prank. But when he hit send, that wasn't what showed up on the screen.

Ryan: Let me guess. AINSLEY IS PERFECT IN EVERY SINGLE WAY told you to text.

He chuckled. Who would have thought Ainsley would be the one to provide a much needed laugh?

He shoved the phone back in his pocket. He wasn't changing anything back. But he was going to text Ainsley just the words "I" and "Ainsley" until she got sick of her own joke. That would show her.

* * *

Ainsley fought the urge to throw her phone across the room and stuffed it under a pillow instead. She couldn't take any more of Ryan's text messages. All day he'd alternated between sending her texts that read simply Deez Nutz and Ainsley is perfect in every single way.

She turned her attention back to the laptop that was propped on her lap.

Leave it to Ryan to turn her brilliant prank around on her. It was, after all, one she'd learned from him.

She clicked on the Matters of the Heart link, which she'd added to her bookmarks, and navigated her way to Breaking Up Is Hard to Do, where she only had to scan a few posts before she found one from Glowbugdoodle, labeled Update. She clicked.

WHAT A HUGE DISAPPOINTMENT.

The words, in all capitals, jumped off the screen at her. She blinked before she read further, her stomach dropping for this internet stranger.

Well, I did it. Just like MsRelationship and ASplanner suggested, I slept with him. My thought being it would definitely count as a fling, and whether he was the one before the One, or a potential soul mate, or just the person to help me get back out there, it would be worth it. I was wrong. I was so, so wrong.

You guys, his dick is the size of a pencil eraser. It was so small and stumpy it literally defied imagination. I almost laughed when he took his pants off, but I almost cried when he climbed on top of me. I couldn't feel anything. A N Y T H I N G. I've had sex with the same man for the last three years and now that he's dumped me and I'm back on the market? Worst sex of my life. It's so depressing.

I'm glad I came here for advice because at least it wasn't as much of a letdown as it would have been if I'd gone in still thinking he could be the One. He's definitely not. I basically want to forget I ever slept with him.

There were a few sympathetic replies before Ainsley reached the one from Ms.Relationship728.

At least now you know why none of his flings come back for more. And why he's so good at playing the game, flirting, and building his reputation as a player.

An uneasy feeling crept up on her. That couldn't be true of Ryan, could it?

She recalled his firm stomach and chiseled abs, which she'd glimpsed while helping him out of his shirt the night before. A wave of heat swept over her. Nope. There was no way Ryan had eraser dick. There were some things a person just knew, and this was one of them.

Good news is, you got back out there. And hopefully he is the one before the One. You need to start internet dating immediately. Before your vagina starts to feel neglected and unloved and develops a complex and you have to take it to therapy.

Ainsley snorted with laughter.

She finished the rest of the responses and opened a text box to reply but then sat there staring. What could she say? She'd never been where Ms. Glowbugdoodle was before. She was able to identify with the poster's original problem, but now what? Ms.Glowbugdoodle had already surpassed her when it came to getting on with life. And she refused to be left behind by anyone, even an internet stranger.

Before she could think twice, she opened a browser window and typed in online dating. She scanned the results and clicked on something about Just Coffee. She liked coffee. Meeting for a cup of coffee was harmless, right? Quick and painless, with the added benefit of a caffeine jolt. Ryan had said she needed to start dating more casually and without expectations. Online dating fit in that category.

Her mind whirred as she typed into the blank boxes to create her profile. When she was younger she'd always imagined herself going off to college, finding the right guy, moving in together when they graduated, and marrying around the time they were twenty-five. Which would give them enough time for him to get established in his career before marriage and enough time to enjoy being married and do some traveling before they had their first child at thirty. Instead she was approaching thirty, single, unmarried, not very well traveled, and childless. Which wouldn't be so bad if she didn't find the prospect of dating daunting and the pool of available men dismal.

She didn't want to settle. She still wanted it all. Was that so much to ask for?

She stood up from the sofa and placed her laptop, still open, on the coffee table. If she was going to try this online dating thing, she needed a big glass of wine. It was four o'clock on a Sunday, which was as good a time as any to start drinking.

She was still in her kitchen, struggling to extract the cork of a French chardonnay, when she heard her computer *bing*. With one last yank, she jerked the cork free, poured a healthy slug of white wine into a wineglass, and carried it into the living room. As she sat she whispered a silent prayer to herself.

Please let this go well.

This was exactly what she was supposed to be doing, right? Putting herself out there, breaking out of her normal pattern, and trying to meet new people? Ryan was going to take all the credit, even though they were only a week and a half into his plan, but she didn't care. Mike hadn't inspired any real butterflies in her belly, but that guy was out there. Maybe he was online right now, waiting for her.

She took a large gulp of wine and lifted her laptop back onto her lap, then clicked on the text box. There was a series of *bing*s as a number of other messages quickly popped up on the screen.

Her heart raced. *This was good.* She was getting responses.

Now she just had to go through them one at a time. She clicked the mute button. Each message deserved her undivided attention and she had to focus, without the distraction of alerts, if she was going to get to know these guys well enough to decide whether they warranted an actual face-to-face meeting.

Markymarkmark: Do you like cheese?

She wrinkled her nose at the name. Talk about a dated reference. Plus, Mark Wahlberg wasn't entirely her type. She liked taller. Blonder. And single.

She sighed. So what if it was a weird question and a shitty screen name? What was the harm in playing along for a few seconds? Maybe he was just trying to grab her attention and stand out.

ASplanner: I love cheese. Doesn't everyone?

Markymarkmark: Does that mean we're in love?

Her eyes widened. What the hell? Was he kidding? She seriously hoped he was kidding.

It only took her a few seconds of searching before she found the "block" button. She clicked without hesitation.

All right, so that was a bust. Still, it wasn't as if she'd expected to find Mr. Right on her first try. She clicked to the blinking box beside it. By now five had appeared. Surely at least one of them was decent?

Hornybigman: What's up Princess?

She clicked block again.

Next.

Jrbeachlovr: Can I play some important role in your wedding?

She was about to close the box, without blocking, when another line of text appeared.

Jrbeachlovr: Like the groom?

Once again, her finger found the block button.

As quickly as she closed text boxes, new ones opened.

Raulhottie: Show me bagina.

She gagged. What the hell was wrong with men? Did women actually fall for this kind of shit?

This time she moved the cursor until she found the "cancel service" button. With her index finger, she punched the trackpad once, then three more times just to be sure.

She heaved a long sigh and reached to rub her throbbing temple. Online dating wasn't going to work, she could tell already. It was a freak show out there.

At least now she knew what to tell Glowbugdoodle.

She navigated back to the post on Matters of the Heart and opened a reply to the thread.

Online dating is terrifying. I don't have any better suggestions, but proceed with caution!

She clicked post, then closed the lid to her laptop.

Wherever she was going to meet someone, it sure as hell wasn't online.

CHAPTER TWELVE

A few days later, Ainsley was holed up in her office at the Meridien sneaking a peek at her phone in between high-strung clients. At lunch, a mother of the bride had yelled at her regarding the unavailability of oysters for a wedding in May. She'd had to swallow the urge to yell, "It's not like I can raise them myself in my freaking bathtub!" No, that was the kind of thing Brett would fire her for. Instead, she'd smiled brightly and suggested crab legs.

That meeting was followed by a walk-through with a bride who panicked when she realized the bride's suite was located on the same hallway as the groom's. Which, in her mind, meant a possibility that the groom or one of his groomsmen might see her in her dress before the ceremony. Luckily, Ainsley's promise to personally stand guard in the hall had reassured her.

She only had ten minutes before the next bride and her mother arrived. They'd spend an hour going over china, linens, and flatware. Then she was free and due for her next Ryan-or-chestrated adventure.

Her phone chirped.

Ryan: You all set for tonight?

Ainsley: Yes. When are you going to tell me where we're going? I don't like surprises. I need to plan my outfit.

He sent an emoticon rolling its eyes.

She fought the urge to roll her eyes back at him. What was wrong with wanting to dress appropriately? This was Ryan they were talking about. It wouldn't be totally out of left field for him to take her to play paintball or something.

She shook her head. Better not mention paintball to him, ever. He'd get entirely too much pleasure from shooting her with paint pellets.

Although she did have an idea for how to get the details from him.

Ainsley: Let me guess: You're taking me to that new French restaurant down by the water. The one with views of the sunset and a top-level sommelier. I knew you were a romantic. Should I get my nails done beforehand? And do you think diamonds or pearls for jewelry?

Ryan: Oh hell no. No. This is Ryan time. I'm planning, not you. No French anything. No sommelier. No romance and no beach views. Just no.

She chuckled, a ripple of satisfaction spreading through her. It was entirely too easy, and too much fun, to get under his skin.

Ainsley: Tell me this much: should I wear a dress or not?

Even Ryan should be capable of answering that question.

Ryan: Wear whatever you want. A poncho or a muumuu or overalls. I'm still not telling you where we're going.

She frowned. No luck. For a second she'd thought she had a chance of egging him into spilling.

Ryan: I can tell you to clear your schedule for next weekend, though. We're going camping.

Her stomach dropped. Camping? The very thought made her skin crawl, as if it were already covered by a thousand bugs. She shuddered.

She was in the midst of drafting a long, strongly worded diatribe about her unwillingness to participate in this particular aspect of the Ryan program when there was a rap on her office door.

She immediately dropped the phone into her handbag, which sat open on her desk.

Without waiting for a response, Brett entered. His eyebrows were knitted together and his lips formed a deep frown. "What are you doing in here?"

Her cheeks heated, and she took a deep breath before she replied.

"Just checking a few emails! I'm waiting for a new bride to send over her contract tonight or tomorrow and I thought I'd get a jump on it before the Sylvester bride arrives." It took effort to keep her voice bright and cheerful.

His eyes narrowed. "This isn't like you."

She swallowed hard. What did he mean by that?

He tapped his foot on the ground. "Usually you're out chatting and schmoozing with the customers. That's part of the reason we hired you, Ainsley. It's all about image. You're the face of events for the Meridien. You need to be charming every person who is currently seated at the bar, so when they get engaged or their kids or cousins get engaged, we're the first place they think of."

She had to work to hold in her sigh. Brett had always been good about deferring to her judgment and listening to her opinions. She knew she wasn't her usual enthusiastic self, but so what if bubbly Ainsley was on temporary hiatus? She was tired, damn it. Didn't she deserve a tiny break?

Her insomnia had returned in full force and she felt like a zombie, dragging herself through the day. A well-dressed zombie with blown-out hair and carefully applied makeup, but still, a zombie.

Brett slumped into a chair next to her. "Look, I know you're down in the dumps. I do. And I get that this job is really hard under the circumstances, but the company hired a new regional manager, and everything we do is going to be under the microscope for a few months. You've always been one of our top-performing event planners, and I'm counting on you to make us all look good."

She immediately regretted her impatience with him. Brett wasn't a bad guy, he'd just had to ride her more than usual lately. Once she got past this bout of insomnia, she'd be back to performing her job flawlessly.

She forced a small nod.

"How about this? I'll give you next weekend off if you promise to go out there for one more hour and pretend to be happy," he offered.

Normally she would have jumped at the offer, but of course

Brett had no way of knowing she was supposed to go camping next weekend. Maybe it was a sign. Maybe she was supposed to spend her weekend slogging through the woods smelling like bug spray.

"Thanks, Brett."

She could do this. She would fake feeling chipper for one hour, then she'd go home, get dressed, and get drunk. There was one thing she knew for sure: Wherever Ryan was taking her, there would be alcohol.

* * *

Ryan perched at the bar of Diver's, sipping on a craft beer. He didn't need a repeat of his last time here with Ainsley. At least he didn't think he needed a repeat. The exact details remained fuzzy. Still, it was one of his favorite places. He never had to worry about crowds or schmoozing, he could just kick back and relax.

The bartender with the thick-rimmed glasses and goofy-looking hair approached and leaned with both elbows onto the bar in front of him. "How's your friend from the other night? Ainsley?"

The nape of his neck prickled in irritation. Why did this guy care?

"Fine."

"Is she joining you later? For a drink?" The bartender arched an eyebrow.

A pang of jealousy hit him as he realized the bartender had a thing for Ainsley.

His jaw tensed in annoyance. Of course the guy had a crush on Ainsley. She was beautiful, funny, charming. The bigger question was why he cared.

Because as much as he wanted to deny it, he did care. He liked the time they spent together, ribbing each other. And he was one hundred percent sure the bartender wasn't the right guy to make her happy.

"Sorry, man. I don't think so." He took another swig of beer.

There was only a week and half left to his plan. As much as Ainsley had learned to loosen up in the past ten days, part of him worried she'd go right back to dating stockbrokers from the Point when this was all over.

The corners of the bartender's mouth fell. "OK, well, tell her Mike said to give him a call."

He almost felt bad for the guy.

As if on cue, his phone chimed.

"Excuse me." He glanced at the phone, hoping Mike would take the hint to scram.

Ainsley: I'm so sorry but I can't go on this mystery Ryan-prescribed adventure tonight. I'm stuck at work.

Disappointment filled him. She was bailing?

He swallowed. It would be better not to let her know he felt let down.

He typed his response quickly.

Ryan: Hmmm this sounds made up to me. Are you trying to get out of tonight? Because I won't tell you where we're going?

He'd been half hoping she'd show up in a dress. A shorter one, so that every time she took her turn to bowl and bent over...

Blood rushed below the belt, and he had to shake his head to clear the image. He'd given up trying to convince himself not to be attracted to her and was clinging to his last remnants of self-restraint. Ainsley had come a long way, but he didn't think she was capable of having a casual fling, especially not with a good friend. Because they were good friends now. The past few weeks had brought them closer, and he didn't want to mess that up.

Ainsley: Trust me I'd rather wear a poncho and a muumuu and overalls and go camping with you than be here tonight.

Ryan: You're going to be missing out on a sweet ride in my rental minivan...

His options had come down to that or some smart car he couldn't shove his legs into. He missed his Mustang so much it made his chest ache. Meanwhile, he was no closer to finding out who'd smashed out his window.

Ainsley: You? Have a man van? I never thought I'd see the day.

His nose wrinkled. *Man van?* He just hoped the rest of their friends didn't pick up the term. Good thing he only had to drive it for a few more days.

Ryan: And I was going to take you bowling.

He'd put some thought into choosing tonight's activity, figuring Ainsley had never rented shoes and chucked heavy balls at a dozen pins. He was fairly confident she'd enjoy it, once she got past the footwear issue. And if not? Watching her try would be amusement enough for him.

Ainsley: Bowling and a van? You really know how to charm a girl, Ryan Lawhill. Let me guess, you have a mattress and a six-pack in the back?

He scoffed. Even in high school, he'd had more game than that. But hey, what was the harm in playing along?

Ryan: I bet you're dying to find out.

Barely a second passed before she sent an emoji of a hand holding up the middle finger.

He snorted in laughter, then glanced up to make sure no one at the bar had noticed. Luckily, it was early and the bar was pretty empty.

His phone pinged again and he found himself grinning before he even opened the message. He liked this, the way they teased each other. It felt good.

Ainsley: Gotta go. At least boss man agreed to give me next weekend off.

At least he'd gotten her to agree to camping, a task he'd expected to be a lot more difficult.

Ryan: Trust me, you'll love camping.

He was pretty sure she'd rather gnaw off her right arm than spend a day hiking and a night sleeping on the ground. Which was exactly why he was making her go. Their three weeks were almost over and he was determined to make them count. Plus, he had to admit he enjoyed pushing her buttons and getting her to do things she'd never normally agree to.

Ainsley: I'm not going camping. You and I both know it.

He grinned. That was more like it. With Ainsley it was partially the challenge he enjoyed. She'd protest or complain and he'd have to think of ways to convince her.

Ryan: I knew you'd be too chicken. And I knew you'd invent any kind of excuse you could to get out of it.

He'd even briefly contemplated fake-kidnapping her but

then figured she was the type of woman who would kick him in the balls. So he'd scrapped that plan and steeled himself to dare her, challenge her, and goad her until she gave in.

Ainsley: I can camp. I just refuse to.

The anticipation built as he planned his next words.

Ryan: Figures. I thought you might balk, but I was hoping you'd decide you were tough enough to handle it.

There was a moment's silence as he stared at the phone, his pulse pounding as he awaited her response. This back-and-forth with them? It was addictive.

Ainsley: I know exactly what you're doing. And that's not why I'm going to agree to go camping. I'm going to go for me, to prove to myself that I can do it.

He grinned. Atta girl. He'd figured she would rise to the occasion eventually.

Ainsley: Also, screw you. I know you're patting yourself on the back right now for getting me to do this. Let's be clear, it's my decision. You have nothing to do with it.

Blood thrummed in his veins. *Sure.* She could tell herself that, but they both knew she was having fun following his life plan. The question was whether the changes would stick, or whether Ainsley would go back to the way things had been.

Worry threaded through his brain. He hoped she wouldn't. They'd been having too much fun together lately. Not that he could tell her that.

So he let the comment go.

Ryan: Camping it is. Next weekend. Oh, and one of my bands is playing a show next Thursday. I got you a ticket.

Ainsley: I'll be there. But I have to run now before boss

catches me texting. Don't do anything I wouldn't do tonight.

He frowned. That ruled out practically everything fun.

He caught the bartender's eye and lifted one finger. As long as he was here, he might as well have another beer.

Someone slid into the seat next to him, and he glimpsed a flash of dark hair as the strong scent of flowers assaulted his nose. His nostrils tickled, then burned, and he held his breath in an attempt to keep from sneezing.

"Are you buying me a drink or not?" The honeyed voice purred into his ear. He didn't even have to turn. He already knew it was Melanie.

He tried to muster his most charming smile as he turned to face her. "Hey, Melanie. Of course I'll buy you a drink. How are things?"

His voice was flat, even to his own ears. Suddenly the prospect of spending the night with Melanie felt like…work. Even if the sex was usually good.

She rested a hand on his arm, her long fingernails pricking against his skin. "I'm better now that I've seen you."

He watched mutely as she pulled a tube of lipstick from her purse, applied the dark red, and puckered her lips. Normally the gesture would have had him sweating, ready to chug his beer and make a beeline for the door with her in tow. But tonight? A vague sense of dissatisfaction had settled over him.

Melanie shifted her leg to rest against his. Carefully, slowly, he angled himself in the other direction, creating a few more inches of space between them. He really wasn't up for her games tonight.

She grimaced then, small lines creasing her forehead, her

lips twisting downward. "So who are you supposed to be meeting? The blond in the sparkly dress?"

His skin tingled in warning. How the hell did she know about Ainsley?

The muscles in his back and neck bunched. This felt weird, wrong. He made up his mind to get out of there.

He pulled his wallet out of his pocket, extricated his credit card, and slapped it down onto the bar. "Actually, I'm not meeting anyone here, but I lost track of the time, and I do need to go by the studio."

She let out a dramatic sigh, which irritated him. "Well, are you going to call me later? After? It's been a few weeks since you *really* called me."

Her words hung in the air, their meaning clear. And yet he still didn't feel any real desire. No pounding heart or restless fingers or tingling spine. Instead, he was annoyed.

What the hell was wrong with him?

He swallowed hard. "Thanks for the offer, but tonight isn't good. I'll call you soon."

Maybe he was coming down with something, but right now he needed to get home, watch some ESPN, and drink a few beers. If he gave himself a night off, his mojo would return. Right? It had to.

CHAPTER THIRTEEN

Ainsley sat outside Club 812, her car running as she drummed her fingers on the steering wheel impatiently.

"...then you need to check on the Colishaw contract. This wedding is a big get for the hotel, but she's already changed the venue twice, so we need to keep her on board. Apparently, ethically sourced flowers are a major sticking point for her," Brett droned.

Ethically sourced flowers. Check. They'd been the latest wedding trend for at least six months, and she already knew the right florist.

"I'm on it, I promise." After their talk she was trying to bring a renewed enthusiasm to work. Still, it was proving to be harder than she'd expected.

After a quick good-bye, she punched the off button and flipped down her driver's side visor to examine her reflection in the mirror.

With deft hands, she gave the corner of her eyeliner one last smudge, then flipped the mirror up again.

She turned off the car and climbed out. Then she squared her shoulders and smoothed a hand over the skirt of her pink sundress. In spite of herself, she was a little nervous. Tonight they'd be hearing one of Ryan's bands, and it wasn't her normal crowd. She wasn't entirely sure what to expect.

"Hey, Ainsley!" Ryan's voice boomed from the alley behind the club. She spun to face him and found him grinning at her, waving one hand in the air.

His enthusiasm had her heart skipping a beat. Then again, he'd invited her tonight, so of course he was happy to see her. Probably it meant nothing. It was just that there'd been this…tension between them ever since the kiss in the car. Ryan might not remember the kiss, at least not that he'd acknowledged, but things were definitely different.

In her eagerness, she crossed the distance to him quickly, her pink high-heeled sandals clicking against the pavement. When she reached him, he pulled her into a boisterous bear hug, which filled her with happiness. He was warm and the tiniest bit sweaty, which accentuated the spicy scent of his cologne.

"Hey, guys, this is my friend Ainsley!" He released her from the hug but kept one hand draped across her shoulders. Her pulse did a joyful tap dance. Then he motioned at three men who were unloading equipment from the trunk.

The first guy, who had a long beard and wore an outfit made entirely of leather, gave her a quick grunt in greeting. She glanced at the other two, one of whom had a skull tattoo on his cheek. None of them spoke, choosing instead to nod in her general direction.

Her face heated, her previous nervousness returning. Bearded leather-clad men with face tattoos? This wasn't exactly her scene. Was that why Ryan had brought her?

He lowered his head until his mouth was inches from her ear. "They're not big talkers. Good thing they make kick-ass music."

Her mouth relaxed into a smile. At least Ryan was here to look out for her. Then he cupped her elbow with his palm and led her through the door, into the darkness of the club.

"They don't go on for an hour, but I wanted you to come by early so you'd have a chance to get a feel for the place. There's something really great about the silence before a big show, followed by the craziness, and then the adrenaline high that lasts all night. You'll see. It's a feeling I can't entirely describe."

The excitement in his voice made her grin as she allowed him to guide her through the dimly lit club. His enthusiasm was contagious.

The space was strange in its emptiness. Without the flashing neon lights, the pulsing music, and the crowd of dancing bodies she could see the scuff marks on the black walls, the metal light rigging that crisscrossed the ceiling, and the stains on the cement floor. When they'd been here the other night it had felt alive and electric with energy. Now it was quiet and bare.

She suppressed a shiver of unease. Still, she could see why Ryan loved the contrast between this and the craziness that would follow. After all, that was what she'd always loved most about planning events: taking a blank canvas and turning it into a full-fledged experience. In that way, they weren't so different after all.

They climbed the stairs from the dance floor into the bar area, where a few people clad in all black were setting up chairs and arranging liquor bottles.

Ryan stopped in the middle of the room and shoved his hands in his pockets. His brow creased slightly. "Huh. I was so focused on wanting you to see what the place looked like before it was set up and people poured in that I kind of forgot how boring this part would be for you."

A bemused smile crossed her lips. It was obvious that Ryan loved what he did. And for some reason he'd wanted to share it with her, the whole experience.

Warmth flooded her. What did that mean?

A crash sounded from onstage and Ryan jerked his head in that direction.

"Don't worry about me. I can entertain myself. You go do your thing. Besides, Griffin and Beth should be here before the show starts, right?" She'd be fine on her own.

The furrow in his brow eased and he stepped toward her to rest a hand on her arm. "Thanks for understanding. Things are always crazy for me before the show. There are going to be a few representatives from larger venues and labels here, so I need to touch base with them. And I have to make sure the guys have everything set up correctly."

His eyes darted anxiously back to the stage.

She gave him a small push. "Seriously. Go. Before they break something important."

He grinned at her, then trotted in the direction of the stage.

With nothing else to do, she perched on a bar stool and watched him work.

The minute he reached the stage he began to motion and bark orders.

"Amps go over here. Hugo, I already told you once today, don't wear that color green onstage. It looks like puke. It makes you look like you're going to puke, it makes other people want to puke, I swear to God if I see you wear that shirt in a venue ever again I'm going to burn it."

She chuckled softly. He was right. That color was puke personified.

Then he strode to a booth slightly offstage, pulled a folded piece of paper from his back pocket, and began to reel off directions to a man clad in all black and wearing a pair of headphones.

She cocked her head to the side and studied him, a small thrill running through her as she watched him work. She'd only gone to a few of Ryan's shows. Generally their tastes in music didn't align, and the bars and clubs his bands played weren't her scene. Before now she'd never really had a chance to examine him in his element. And he was, one hundred percent, in his element. Confident, in control, and self-assured.

Her heart thumped faster in her chest.

No. She'd call Mike the bartender, she'd try online dating again, but she would not let herself develop real feelings for Ryan. That could only end in disaster. Not the same kind of disaster as Glowbugdoodle, but definitely some kind of disaster.

"Are you here with Ryan?" A purple-haired woman dressed in all black approached from behind the bar.

"Mhmm." She flicked a glance at the woman before her gaze automatically strayed back to Ryan.

There was a series of clanks, glass against glass, as the bartender began to stack glasses on the shelf behind the bar. With effort, Ainsley pulled her attention from Ryan and smiled at the woman standing behind the bar.

"I'm Ainsley." She extended a hand.

The bartender grinned knowingly as she took Ainsley's hand. "Sarah."

There was a brief silence and she had to fight the urge to let her attention stray back to Ryan, onstage.

"So how long have you known Ryan?" Sarah asked.

Her face burned and she swallowed hard. "A while. We have a good friend in common, Kate Massie?"

No doubt Sarah thought she was one of Ryan's many adoring flings, which she wasn't. Her throat turned scratchy. How was she supposed to communicate that without sounding suspiciously defensive?

For starters, stop staring at him. It hadn't been that long since she'd had sex. So why did Ryan make her feel like this?

To her relief, Sarah's smile broadened. "You're friends with Beth and Griffin too, right? You're an event planner?"

She nodded quickly. Yes, Ainsley the event planner. Not Ainsley with the unrequited crush on Ryan.

She nearly pinched herself for thinking the words. *It's not a crush. There is nothing going on.* She was just recalibrating and adjusting to the single life. Or maybe the tiny tingle of attraction was her body's way of telling her mind…something. That she needed to get laid?

She squeezed her hand closed and let the half-moons of her fingernails prick into her palms. "Yes, I work at the Meridien as a wedding planner."

Sarah let out a breath and leaned toward her, a look of relief crossing her face. "Talk about lucky run ins! I work for Griffin at Little Ray's. Beth said you might be here tonight, and I was hoping I'd have a chance to talk to you."

Automatically, her eyes went to Sarah's left ring finger. No engagement ring. So why did Sarah want her help?

"Griffin scheduled a charity event at Little Ray's. It's for the Mid-Atlantic Bully Breed rescue, and it's supposed to be in three weeks. Since I'm the assistant manager, a lot of the planning falls to me, and I have no idea what I'm doing."

She gestured to the bar. "I mean, I can make drinks and talk to customers, obviously, but I'm in way over my head when it comes to decorations and arrangements and silent auction items and all that stuff."

Sarah bit her lip for a second. "I really want it to go well. If you don't mind, I'd love your help. I know you're busy, but I would be so grateful. And I don't need you to do everything, I just need to pick your brain and get some ideas and make sure everything I'm doing makes sense."

Ainsley found herself nodding, slowly at first, then more enthusiastically. Already her brain began to hum with ideas. They could do an art auction, with portraits of people's dogs, Beth could make special dog biscuits for guests to take home in doggie bags, and she'd convince a few restaurants to donate gift certificates to be auctioned to the humans. She flushed with pleasure as her excitement built. This would be fun.

She leaned forward and placed her hand on Sarah's arm. "I'd love to do it. And I'd love to be there to oversee everything and help you at the event as well."

Sarah let out a nervous laugh. "Thank God. I was hoping you'd say that."

The low strum of a guitar resonated from onstage. She swiveled on her stool and caught a glimpse of Ryan, legs planted wide and hips jutting forward, as he strummed the guitar slung over his chest. His face was intent as he watched his fingers on the instrument.

The sight of him up there sucked all the air out of her chest.

With a slight shake of her head, she turned back to Sarah. In less than a week the Ryan experiment would be over and it would be back to her regularly scheduled life. In spite of herself, she'd been almost dreading it. What would she do with her time? Would things go back to normal between them? She'd miss him, miss all the time they'd been spending together. Planning this event would give her something to focus on, and it would help her tap into the essence of herself. After all, she wasn't meant to be like Ryan. She was good at planning and organizing, it was what she loved most in life.

Then again, maybe things didn't have to go back to the way they were. Maybe she could find some happy middle ground between her previous life and Ryan's life. She could be the new Ainsley, still herself, but better. First, she had to survive the camping trip though.

CHAPTER FOURTEEN

They were backstage, caught in the crush of people darting around to complete last-minute tasks. Ryan's gaze roamed over the onstage setup as he ticked through his mental checklist one last time. The band members' spots were marked onstage with gaffer tape, the spare guitar was cradled in its stand, and an extra mike rested next to the mike stand. It was already loaded with spare batteries, just in case. Over the years he'd learned to plan for every contingency.

Someone pushed past them, thrusting Ainsley closer. Her palms came to rest firmly on his chest and she left them there for one long, lingering second before she blushed and stepped back.

"Sorry. It's crowded back here."

Another stagehand, clad all in black, pushed past her, forcing her closer to Ryan again.

Pleasure and pride swelled inside him and he looped an arm around her waist. "Don't worry. I won't let anyone squash you."

Her breath was warm against his shoulder as she gave a little laugh.

His heart hammered in his chest. He sucked in a breath and held it, willing his body to come back under control. This was wrong. For a million reasons, this was wrong. One of his bands had a show, which meant he had to be on point the entire night. His focus, all of his focus, needed to be on the band and the crowd. Not to mention, this was Ainsley. The more time he spent with her the more he liked her, and he didn't want to screw up their friendship.

He reluctantly gripped her upper arm with one hand and took a step back. There. They needed more distance between the two of them. Not that he wanted it.

"Are you excited about camping?" He smirked in self-satisfaction, another attempt to goad her. The topic should get them back on safer ground.

She sighed with overemphasized reluctance. "Absolutely. I dug out my old hiking boots, and I bought five different kinds of bug spray. I'm prepared, so do your worst."

He chuckled. "Five kinds of bug spray?"

She slanted him a look. "I don't know what kind of bugs I'm dealing with. I need to be prepared for all possibilities."

He couldn't help but grin. She was the same old Ainsley. He could take her bowling and tromping through the wilderness, force her to drink cheap beer in dive bars, but she'd always do things her way.

Satisfaction filled him. It was one of her best qualities.

She raised an eyebrow. "You're not going to make some snide comment about the fact that I own hiking boots?"

A spike of adrenaline shot through him. This was their banter, which he loved. "Of course I am. Give me a second, I was just working up to it."

He paused and frowned, feigning deep thought. "There are so many angles I could take here and I'm really not sure which one to go for. Are they high-heeled? Pink? Sequined? Did you buy them because *Cosmopolitan* said they were the latest trend? Or maybe you saw one of those Kardashians wearing them on the red carpet?"

"No to all." She planted her hands on her hips and narrowed her eyes, giving him exactly what he'd craved. "If you must know, I have gone hiking before."

His eye widened in real surprise. "No shit! And you lived to tell the story. Who would have thought?"

She grinned at him and his heart jumped in his chest.

"I'm a lot tougher than you think I am." She tilted her chin upward and held his gaze, her demeanor suddenly serious.

His throat squeezed, forcing him to swallow hard. This wasn't a moment for joking. She was being genuine. And she deserved to hear what he really thought of her. "I know you're tough, Ainsley."

They were silent for a second, oblivious to the people rushing around them. He couldn't help but really look at her, admiring the arch of her eyebrows, the sparkle of her eyes, the sensuous bow of her top lip. She was obviously doing the same, drinking him in with her eyes. For once neither of them tried to back away or change the mood or make a wisecrack. They were content with being their authentic selves, in the same space, together. The air between them crackled with possibility.

Fuck it. Without thinking, he wrapped his hand around the back of her neck and tilted her chin toward him. He stepped forward until their faces were nearly touching. Ainsley sucked in a breath, causing her chest to jump. She gave a small shiver but didn't pull away and didn't break eye contact.

He waited. One second. Then another. He closed his eyes and inhaled her flowery scent. The same scent that had wrapped around him when he'd slept in her bed.

Blood pounded in his veins. With aching slowness he closed the distance between them, brushing his lips softly against hers, allowing himself to be guided by instinct. He kept his eyes closed and lost himself in the feeling of her body pressed against his, the warm pressure of her lips on his lips.

Need crashed into him, pulling him under. He wrapped his arms around her, crushing her into him. His mouth opened, and he tugged her lower lip into his mouth, his tongue caressing. A moan built inside of him as he pushed farther. She angled her head back, opening to him. His tongue twined with hers, tasting and exploring.

Next to them, someone loudly cleared his throat.

Frustration flared inside of him. What the hell? Didn't people know when to leave a person alone? Then again, he was technically working.

He eased his mouth away from Ainsley's and opened his eyes. A smile crossed his lips as Ainsley's eyelids fluttered, a dreamy expression on her face.

It had been one hell of a kiss.

The throat clearing came again and he jerked his head in the person's direction.

Griffin. His body went cold and he jumped, abruptly creating a respectable space between himself and Ainsley.

Griffin's eyes were narrowed in concern.

His jaw tensed, the regret instantaneous. What the hell had he been thinking? He had no business kissing Ainsley. None.

His face was on fire and all the muscles in his back went rigid.

Shit.

"Hey, man, where's Beth?" He glanced around quickly. *Please don't let her have seen us too.*

Shame engulfed him. He knew better. He should have shown some damn self-control.

In front of him, Ainsley kept her eyes on Griffin. He watched her out of the corner of his vision, but she held herself stiffly and stared forward.

An uneasy feeling built in Ryan's stomach. What was she thinking? Did she know it was a stupid momentary mistake? Did she regret it? Or did she want to kiss him again?

He gritted his teeth. No. No more kissing. As much as he wanted to, he simply wouldn't let himself. Their lives were too intertwined to keep things casual, and if he continued he'd hurt her the same way his father had hurt his mother. And him.

Griffin narrowed his eyes, his stare burning into Ryan. "Beth's just grabbing a beer. I told her I'd come back here and find you guys before the show started."

Ryan ducked his head, looking at his shoes instead. Griffin was one of his closest friends, but he cared about Ainsley too. They all did. Which was why he needed to get things under control now.

He glanced back up and placed a hand on Griffin's shoulder. "Sounds good. I have a few things to finish up back here. You wanna help me for a second? Ainsley, maybe you should meet Beth over by the bar and get a beer too?"

It was a good enough cover. Griffin was a musician and could technically help him, not that there was anything left to set up. But it would give them a moment to talk. He needed to make it clear to Griffin that he understood. That he wouldn't screw up like that again.

"Yeah, sure. We'll see you guys out there." Ainsley's voice was soft and he could barely make it out over the backstage bustle.

He listened for the sound of her heels clicking on the floor and as soon as it receded he gripped Griffin by both shoulders.

"It was a momentary fuckup. It won't happen again."

Griffin's shoulders sagged beneath Ryan's grip. "Dude." He shook his head. "This is bad, man. Really, really bad. I know that you're trying to teach Ainsley not to invest all of her emotions in every relationship, but this isn't the right way to do it. You're better than this."

His words hit Ryan like a punch in the gut. Is that really what Griffin thought he was trying to do?

"No." His voice was a growl. "No. I wouldn't do that to her, I swear. I just got caught up in the moment or something. I don't know. I'll stay away from her, I promise."

Anxiety coursed through him. Griffin would tell Beth who would tell Kate who would tell James. And they'd all be furious at him, with good reason. He cared too much about Ainsley to be this careless with her feelings.

Griffin's brow furrowed. "I thought you were going camping for the weekend. Together."

"I'll cancel." His stomach twisted. He didn't want to, but it was for the best now that he'd gone and screwed everything up. "She doesn't want to go anyway. This whole thing was just to get her mind off of Scott and the breakup."

"Well, I think it's fair to say you've done that."

He scowled. "I'm not an asshole. It was just—something happened…" He trailed off. The words were lame, even to his own ears.

Griffin caught his gaze and held it, his eyes filled with sympathy. "I know you're not an asshole. We can all tell there's something going on with you two. Chemistry, flirtation, I don't know. But do you really think Ainsley's ready for a relationship?"

Relationship. His throat constricted in panic.

"Are you ready for a relationship?" Griffin's tone was low and probing.

Because that's how it would have to be between them. Ainsley wasn't the kind of person who dated casually. Sure, she'd lived up to the three-week Ryan challenge, but deep down she was a relationship kind of person. And he wasn't. For a second he'd thought maybe it could be like it was with the other women he saw. They'd have an understanding, just fun, and then when it had run its course they'd go their separate ways.

His mind flashed back to his beloved Mustang, its windshield shattered. Not everyone wanted that kind of arrangement, though. Sometimes people got hurt, even if they'd gone into it with their eyes wide open.

His gut twisted. Ainsley was one of those people. She might fool herself into thinking she could date casually, but he knew her better than that. He'd wind up hurting her and then he'd hate himself. He looked at Griffin. He'd lose his friends too.

He gave a small shake of his head, then forced a chuckle. "Of course I'm not. You know me."

Griffin's eyes were full of concern, but Ryan dropped his hands from Griffin's shoulders and turned so his friend couldn't see his face anymore. He felt like absolute, utter shit.

"I just have a few things to finish up back here. Go find the ladies, I'll meet up with you all in a little bit."

He'd cancel the camping trip. He'd limit contact with Ainsley, and he'd let them both get back to their regular lives. The Ryan-Ainsley experiment was officially over, but damn was he going to miss her.

CHAPTER FIFTEEN

Ryan: I'm canceling the camping trip. I don't think it's a good idea. And I hereby announce that you're a graduate of the Lawhill Life Plan.

She stared at the text, anger and sadness warring inside of her. She couldn't help it. Tears spilled over.

So, what, he was just done with her now? He'd kissed her and dropped her? All last night he'd avoided her, but she'd hoped they'd have a chance to talk it through. After all, they had planned a two-day excursion in the woods. There'd been lots of time to talk.

Under any other circumstances she would have drafted a witty, cutting reply. Something to keep the banter going between them. But she couldn't think of a valid response. She was simply angry, and more than a little bit hurt.

She tapped into the anger and decided to channel it. So Ryan didn't want to go? Fine. She didn't need him. She was becoming a new woman, and she could do this on her own.

No more pining after unavailable men. If anything, Ryan had probably done her a favor and saved her from another mistake.

Ainsley shoved the socks into a corner of her hiking pack. She lifted it and slung it onto her back, testing the weight.

Heavy, but not too heavy. She could walk thirteen miles with this, couldn't she? It would be like one long drawn-out arms and back workout, which would be almost as satisfying as attacking a punching bag with Ryan's face painted on it.

She glanced through her apartment one last time. Everything she'd piled on the coffee table was packed and on her back. All appliances were unplugged and she'd made sure to charge her cell phone.

She straightened her shoulders, shifting the weight on her back. Her stomach did a little flip of remorse.

She'd known immediately that he'd regretted kissing her last night. The second he pulled away, his eyes went round and his mouth fell open, as if he'd forgotten that she was the person attached to her mouth.

The memory of that kiss sent a flush through her body. It had been fantastic. Tantalizingly slow and sensual. The kind of kiss that made her toes tingle when she saw one in movies. The kind of kiss that wasn't supposed to happen to people in real life.

She bit the inside of her cheek, willing herself not to think about it. Surely there were plenty of men in the world who could kiss like that. Wasn't that what Ryan had set out to teach her? She just needed to get out there and find one of them, one who was relationship material.

Damn it, she was still going to miss him. Because they both

knew what had to happen now. They had to pretend like there'd been no kiss, that it had just been a silly spur-of-the-moment mistake and that they both knew they were better off as friends.

We are better off. They could never be what the other one needed. At least now there was a chance they could salvage the friendship. After she licked her wounds, of course.

With a renewed sense of determination, she grabbed her keys off the counter and headed for her car in the parking lot. She'd gone camping before, one time in college. She still had the boots and the pack and she had a phone with GPS. All she'd had to do was look up Craggy Peak, the location Ryan had mentioned, and get directions. In two hours she'd be climbing the side of a mountain without him. This was a chance to prove something, to herself and to him. She was strong, she knew it.

She picked up her phone and typed a message to Kate and Beth.

Ainsley: Leaving now! I'll be at the campsite by seven p.m. and back down the mountain, in the car, and on my way home by seven p.m. tomorrow. Wish me luck!

Kate: Have a blast. You have extra batteries and enough food?

She rolled her eyes. Of course she had all those things. She'd even Googled how to start a campfire.

Beth: Be careful. We're proud of you. Kick ass!

She smiled to herself. That was more like it. For now she wasn't going to mention the fact that Ryan had bailed. It would be too humiliating. She'd have to explain the kiss and then she'd have to pretend she wasn't hurt. It was better to go into the woods, clear her head, and come back with a triumphant story to share. That way she wouldn't have to suffer through everyone's pity and she'd have tangible proof of her perseverance.

Four hours later, Ainsley was plodding up the side of the mountain when the first drops of rain fell. She paused and tilted her head back, examining the sky. A tingle of trepidation climbed her spine. The parking lot had been nearly empty when she'd arrived and she'd passed only one other hiker on the way up the mountain. But she'd figured that was because she'd gotten a late start or it was still early in the season or something.

Another fat drop landed on her cheek, then another and another, until her wet clothes stuck to her body.

Her eyes burned as tears threatened, but she gritted her teeth. No. She was stronger than that.

She heaved the pack off of her shoulders and unzipped the small pocket in front, pulling out her cell phone.

No signal. Shit.

She had two choices, go back down the mountain and drive home in defeat or suck it up and keep climbing. After all, she was maybe a quarter or a third of the way to the top. She was already soaking and the rain had to stop eventually. Plus her pack was waterproof, wasn't it? Once she got to the top of the mountain, she'd find a campsite and start a fire. She'd have food and dry clothes.

She bit her lip. Then again, if she retreated and went home she could have a hot shower and a nice glass of chilled sauvignon blanc. Beth and Kate were the only ones who knew she was up here and they wouldn't judge her for quitting, not in the middle of a rainstorm.

She stood for a moment, raindrops falling from her body in rivulets. *There's no shame in quitting.* Her throat began to burn. Except there was. She'd done plenty of things harder than this. Like Kate and James's engagement party, where she'd mingled in a room full of people who pitied her.

Only Ryan had been there to help.

Determination swelled inside of her. Screw Ryan. She could do this without him.

She set off again, at a fast clip. The sooner she got to the top the sooner she'd be able to get dry.

* * *

Ryan fingered the phone in his hand, debating.

Should he text Ainsley? Or should he leave her alone? What was she doing right now? Was she angry? Relieved?

He squeezed the bridge of his nose between his thumb and his forefinger. No doubt she was glad to be back to her normal life without him challenging her and goading her into things she never wanted to do in the first place.

He clenched his hands into fists and forced himself to focus on the computer screen in front of him. It displayed his calendar for the month, with all the shows his bands would be playing.

Hmmm. He frowned. His mom's fund-raiser for MABB, Mid-Atlantic Bully Breeds, was set for two weekends from now at Little Ray's. Griffin's band, which he managed, would provide the entertainment, but he'd also agreed to provide concert tickets, CDs, T-shirts, and other swag to be raffled off.

He reached for his phone just as it chimed. A text message from Kate. He opened it.

Kate: It just started raining here. You guys ok out there on the mountain?

His heartbeat sped as he reread the message. What the hell was she talking about?

Ryan: I'm confused. We canceled the hiking trip.

Kate: What? She texted me this morning at 7 that she was leaving and would reach the top by 7 pm! When did you cancel?

Something cold and hard formed in the pit of his stomach. Panic flooded his body. He'd texted her a little bit before seven a.m. Had Ainsley really gone up there? By herself? Was she nuts?

He stood and strode to the window, then glanced outside. The rain had begun to fall harder now, in unrelenting sheets.

Panic threaded his lungs, then shifted to cold, hard resolve.

Ryan: I canceled before that. Don't worry. I'm going to get her now.

Without another glance at his computer, he hurried from his music studio, slamming the door behind him. He climbed into the driver's seat of the man van, whipped out of the parking lot, and pressed his foot to the gas pedal. Self-loathing filled him. This was all his fault. He'd done exactly what he swore he'd never do, and Ainsley was in danger because of his selfish, impulsive choices.

Anything could happen to her up there. She could lose her

footing in the rain and fall down the mountain. Nobody else would be there today—it would take days to find her. If she wasn't dressed properly she'd get cold and wet and develop hypothermia. Or a wild animal might smell her food and decide it was worth encountering a lone hiker.

Shit. He stepped harder on the gas pedal, wishing desperately for his Mustang. He glanced at the clock. Four twenty-three p.m. If he drove fast enough, he could be there in an hour and a half. The sun wouldn't start to go down until around seven. That left him an hour and a half to make it to the top. Or maybe he should contact the rangers and see if they could look for her? Surely they had an ATV that could handle the access roads to the top?

His gut clenched in fear. He should have been there with her. He should never have kissed her or canceled. Then she wouldn't have wanted to go up on the mountain alone. He was supposed to be there with her, to protect her.

If something happened to her he would never forgive himself.

CHAPTER SIXTEEN

She stepped into another puddle, icy wetness soaking through her boot and chilling her toes further, but she barely noticed. It was no use trying to avoid the puddles or keep dry anymore. She was soaked through and through, and there was no way around it and no end in sight. At least not until she got to the top.

The wet straps of her backpack hung heavier, dragging her down into the muck and goo. She bowed her head and struggled forward. The last trail marker had said there was less than a mile to go. Maybe there were already some hikers at the campsite, hopefully with a fire and shelter and food. Or at least shelter. They had to have a lean-to up there or something, didn't they? She'd heard those were common on trails.

Please let there be something. She was wet, miserable, shivering. What the hell had she been thinking?

She hunched her shoulders and pushed forward, willing herself to lift her sodden feet and place one in front of the other. It was almost over, and going up had to be the hardest part, didn't it? She'd shiver her way through the night, then scoot her ass back down the mountain. And call in sick for the next two days while she recuperated in a spa.

Finally she reached the clearing. She lifted her head, her heart dropping as she took in the campsite. It was abandoned. Just her, a tiny four-foot by six-foot wooden awning with water dripping through the cracks, and a soaked ring of stones where a campfire would go.

She trudged to the pathetic shelter, dropped her pack onto the wet ground, and stared at it woefully. Was there any point in changing her clothes? A droplet of water trickled its way down the center of her forehead and onto the bridge of her nose. She couldn't even muster the energy to wipe it away. Instead she wrapped her arms around herself.

Stupid rain. From now on all of her weekends off would be spent indoors. Or on a porch with an airtight roof, a glass of sparkling wine in her hand.

Beth had compared Ryan's three-week challenge to a reality TV show, but right now she felt as if she'd been cast in a wetter version of *Naked and Afraid*. Only she wasn't afraid. She was a little pissed and incredibly weary. In fact, all she wanted was to curl up on the ground and drift off to sleep. But even she knew that would lead to hypothermia or gangrene or whatever it was a person could get from traipsing around in the wet forest.

With a sigh, she unzipped her pack and felt around inside. A bubble of relief swelled inside of her. Dry. Thank God. Dry clothes, dry food, all things dry. She lifted her eyes from the pack and glanced around the abandoned campsite one more time, as if someone might have mysteriously disappeared.

Just me and the rain and the wildlife. What did it matter if a squirrel saw her naked? Or a bear? She shuddered. Nope. No bears. Nature couldn't hate her that much, could it?

She peeled her shirt off and over her head, then shimmied out of her wet jeans. They weighed a million pounds and stuck to her legs.

From somewhere out in the darkness there was a cracking sound, followed by a squish and a shuffle. She tilted her head, trying to focus on the sounds, while the *whoosh* of her heartbeat thundered in her ears.

Shit shit shit. She was going to be eaten out here while she stood in just her underwear. She'd never been one to believe in Sasquatch and all that crap, but what did she know? These were the woods, for heaven's sake, she didn't belong here!

Her legs shook harder, her entire body quaking from cold and fear and confusion. Her heart lodged in her throat.

Please don't let this be how I die.

* * *

Ryan skirted a fallen tree, only to tromp directly into a deep puddle.

Shit. What had Ainsley been thinking, coming up here in the rain by herself? It had taken longer than he'd expected to reach the base of Craggy Peak. Then he'd had to convince a ranger to let him use one of the ATVs, which added another hour and cost him a hundred dollars. Even with the ATV, climbing the mountain had been slow going, and the sun had disappeared below the skyline a while ago.

He tried to pick up his pace, bowing his head against the pelting rain and the whipping wind. Almost there. The access roads didn't reach all the way to the peak, and he'd had to leave the ATV behind around a mile ago. Once he reached the top he'd do a quick search for Ainsley, then begin to descend the mountain.

His throat was raw with fear. He'd seen her car in the parking lot, but how far had she gotten in the rain?

He cursed himself, his hands clenching at his sides in frustration. This was all his fault. He'd convinced Ainsley to agree to the camping trip by challenging her, daring her, and playing on her pride. He should have known she'd try to do it on her own when he bailed. She cared too much about what other people thought. Even him.

He squeezed his fists tighter. *Idiot.* He liked to think he had a gift with women, but what he really had was a gift for fucking things up.

He stepped on a branch, heard the long, loud crack beneath his boot, but kept climbing. Just a few more steps and he'd be at the top, where he'd start his hunt for Ainsley. The ranger had tried to scare him to not go into the woods to search in the rain in the dark, but screw that guy. Who knew what could happen to Ainsley out here overnight?

Anxiety and determination coursed through his body as he took the final step into the clearing.

His eyes swept across the space and came to rest on Ainsley, wearing only her underwear, huddled beneath a flimsy wooden roof propped on four rickety poles. Relief crashed over him.

"Ainsley?" He broke into a run, his pulse pounding in his ears.

He snatched her up, joyfully crushing her against him. Through his layers of waterproof clothing, he could feel her shiver and quake against him.

"Ryan?" Her voice was a small squeak against his chest.

"Yes." His breathing was ragged with emotion. Thank God. She was here. She was safe. She was…naked?

His hands skimmed over her cold, wet skin, down to her sodden underwear.

Then his fingers brushed the tiny triangle of lace just below the small of her back. A thong? Blood rushed below the belt, but he clenched his jaw and forced himself to focus. *This is not the time to think with your dick.* That's how they'd gotten into this mess in the first place.

Instead, he set her down gently, only releasing her when her feet rested firmly on the ground. He unzipped his waterproof jacket and whipped it off his shoulders, tenderly placing it on hers instead.

"You're freezing, Ainsley. We have to get you warm before you get hypothermia. How long have you been this wet? How long have you been up here?"

And why are you naked? He choked back the last question and forced himself to keep his eyes on her face.

People forgot that the mountains got cold at night, even in May, and especially when it rained.

She stood, staring at him, her mouth agape. "What are you doing here?"

Her wet hair was plastered to her face, hanging in tangles. Instinctively he reached to push it away from her eyes.

"I came to get you, of course. It's not safe to be out here." He bit back the rest of his words. *What were you thinking? Why are you out here alone? Where did your clothes go?*

Instead, he riffled through her pack and jerked out the first two articles of clothing he found. "Lift your arms."

She handed him back the jacket, which he slung over one shoulder. Then she raised her arms above her head even as another spasm of shivers racked her body.

Shit. He clenched his jaw and tried to be gentle as he placed her hands into the sleeves and pulled the shirt down over her body. When he was done he wrapped his waterproof jacket back around her, lifting the hood over her head and zipping up the front. It nearly swallowed her frame, but she simply watched, pale-faced, and allowed him to dress her.

Next were the jeans.

"Put your hands on my shoulders and lean on me. One foot at a time." He tugged her left foot from the mud, creating a sucking sound. Why was she barefoot? Where had her boots gone?

He scanned the ground and found them several inches away. Next to a pile of discarded clothes.

He grabbed the boots and the wet clothes and pulled them toward him. He used her wet T-shirt to rub her foot until he'd managed to remove most of the mud, then he dried it with the bottom of his T-shirt. When he was done, he guided her dry foot through the jean leg, located a pair of clean socks in her pack, eased her foot into one, then guided it back into her boot.

"Time for the other foot."

Obediently, she lifted it out of the mud. He repeated the same actions, wiping the mud off with her shirt, drying her foot, then sliding her foot through. Then he slipped on a dry sock and guided her foot back into the boot.

"Done."

He stepped back and tried not to watch as she shimmied her jeans up over her hips, then buttoned and zipped them. Even though his jacket covered most of the good parts, some of her smooth, tan thighs were still exposed. Instead, he stared at the ground and measured his breathing.

You found her. Now to get her back to the ATV, down the mountain, and warm her up.

Warm her up. The words rang in his head, lighting a fire inside of him.

He was in the process of chiding himself when she wrapped her arms around his neck, pressing her body against him. Without thinking, he returned the gesture, squeezing her closer with one hand and rubbing her back with the other. Friction helped people heat up, didn't it?

Her breath was warm on his neck.

"Thank you for coming to get me."

He lowered his head, inhaling the rain and earth mixed with the floral scent that was pure Ainsley. "You scared the shit out of me."

She gave a little laugh then. "I scared the shit out of myself. I told you I'm not good at outdoor stuff. And I really do hate camping."

She pulled back slightly and frowned. "Since you rescued me does that mean I don't get credit for camping overnight?"

"Fuck camping." He fought the overwhelming urge to scoop her into his arms and carry her down the mountain, her body pressed against his chest, her breath coming in small puffs as she nestled into his neck.

Instead he reached for her pack.

"I don't need that stuff." She waved her hand in its direction. "I promise you, I'm never going in the woods and never using that crap ever again. Leave it for the bears or the next person who comes up here, or the mountain men or Sasquatch or whoever the hell is crazy enough to enjoy being this far from civilization. From now on, I am a resort and spa only kind of girl. No more tents and shacks and lean-tos and nature and shit."

He chuckled before he pulled her in for another hug, and he planted a kiss on her forehead. His throat grew thick with emotion, but he reminded himself he had to release her in a minute. They had to get back down the mountain. His anxiety wouldn't dissipate until she was indoors somewhere, warm and dry.

"I swear to you, Ainsley Slone, I will never even think of suggesting you go into the woods again. In fact, if anyone ever mentions it to you, refer them to me. I'll set them straight."

She sagged against him and he was slightly reassured by the feel of her.

"Let's get out of here. The nice ranger loaned me an ATV after I permanently loaned him a hundred dollars, and he said there's a nice B&B by the entrance to the park that usually isn't booked this time of year. It's not a spa, but we can have you in a hot bath in an hour."

It took effort to pull his arms back to his sides and step away from her. The physical distance reignited his concern. They weren't out of the woods, literally, just yet.

She glanced at him, worry in her eyes. "What about you? You need your jacket, and all you're wearing is a T-shirt." She grimaced. "With my foot mud on it."

He couldn't tell if the moisture on her face was rain or if she was starting to crack under the weight of the day. Regardless, he was so happy to have found her that he didn't give a damn about the rain or the cold, at least not for his own sake.

As usual, he chose to deflect the moment with humor.

"You know me. I'm a freak. Can't resist me a little foot mud." He waggled his eyebrows. "Besides, that's the closest thing to a spa treatment you'll get from me, so you might as well enjoy it."

She laughed and brushed at her cheek. The muscles in his forearms tensed with the desire to reach out to her, to feel the comfort of her presence, but he stopped himself. They really needed to get down the mountain and get her warm.

He grabbed her arm and stepped confidently into the downpour. It pained him to force her into the rain again, but he told himself they had to get this part over with. "Besides, I'm warmer than you. I haven't spent the day slogging through the rain, and we'll be back to the bottom in no time. I'll take a hot bath right after you and we'll both be good as new."

"OK." She fell into step behind him and they descended the distance to the ATV in silence, surrounded only by the sound of the rain. Finally, the panic and anxiety that had plagued him since Kate's texts began to ease. He couldn't fix what he'd done, but he was going to try his hardest to make things right. In spite of the situation, he even found there was a small spring in his step. He had Ainsley safe and sound. That, at least, felt right.

CHAPTER SEVENTEEN

For once in her life, Ainsley had done exactly what someone else told her to do. When they reached the ATV she'd climbed on the back, as Ryan instructed, without any complaints. So what if she had to press her body intimately close to his and hold on for dear life as he floored the thing? He was saving her. So she let her cheek rest against the damp of his T-shirt, the muscles of his back tightening and clenching as he steered the ATV. At one point her eyes even drifted shut, Ryan's warm presence soothing her nearly to sleep.

Before she knew it, the bouncing had stopped and they came to a halt in front of a wooden log cabin–like structure.

Ryan climbed off the ATV, then turned and extended a hand to help her off. She accepted, giving in to her weary muscles as she leaned against his strong body. He looped a hand around her waist and waved to the ranger who'd appeared in the doorway. With his free hand, Ryan tossed the man his keys.

"Thanks so much. Hope the rest of your day is a lot less eventful."

The ranger gave a curt nod but made no motion to step out into the downpour. "You all just be careful. And stop at that place I told you about. We've gotten at least five inches of rain today, some of the roads are going to flood, and we don't need to be out there saving you twice today."

Ryan chuckled, but she felt his muscles tense against her. "Will do," he called back.

He pulled a set of keys out of his pocket, and Ainsley turned in the direction of the chirping that indicated he'd unlocked the car.

Immediately, her mouth fell open in surprise. "You brought the man van?"

He shrugged, then strode in front of her and opened the passenger side door. "Yup."

"Did you remember the mattress and the six-pack?" The words died in her throat as her face flamed. She'd intended it as a joke, but out loud it had sounded like so much more.

He froze before he turned to face her, but his face was tender in its seriousness. "No."

No jokes, no wisecracks. The realization hit her in her chest, filling her with a hazy sense of longing. As much as she loved the banter between them, she loved this too. The way he looked at her as if she were the only person in the world.

She strode toward him and cupped his strong jaw between her two hands. "Thank you, Ryan. Thank you for coming to get me and not judging me and not making fun of me."

She'd given him the perfect fodder, of course, by trekking up a mountain in the rain just to prove to herself she didn't need him. It had been an attempt to convince herself she didn't care, that his regret for the kiss hadn't penetrated. All she'd done was prove how much she did need him after all.

"It was my fault." His voice was thick, his eyebrows knit in contrition. It was a look she'd never seen on him before: real, genuine remorse.

"No." It would be unfair to let him take the blame for this. "It was my decision, and it was a bad one. I don't want to think about it anymore though. You and I? We need to learn to let the past go."

There had to be a way forward for them. They couldn't go back and change things, but they could learn to make better decisions in the future. She was willing to try to change, for Ryan. Hell, she had changed for him, hadn't she? Old Ainsley would never have gone hiking in the rain. Much as she was loath to admit it, he'd gotten to her core.

She closed her eyes and inhaled the spicy scent of him, then closed the distance. This time she would be the one to kiss him. It would be an affirmation of the other night at the concert. She'd make him understand that it wasn't a mistake. Nothing that had happened between them so far had been a mistake, there had been a purpose behind all of it. To her relief, his lips met hers hungrily and her grip around his neck tightened. She kissed him hard, their tongues tangling together.

She nearly sagged with relief. As he kissed her back, she could almost feel his walls and his reserve, his sarcasm and his jokes, melting between them. He was opening up to her, showing her parts of himself he normally kept closed off.

He let out a low growl, then pulled back to stare at her. Her heart pounded in her ears as she met his gaze. There was a vulnerability there she'd never seen before. She almost smiled. Griffin was right, she'd had a thing or two to teach Ryan about relationships after all. It had just taken him a bit to catch on.

Keep kissing me.

As if he could read her mind, as if kicking down the last of the emotional walls that divided them, he lifted her, cupping her butt in his hands. She wrapped her legs around his waist as he tilted his head toward her and kissed her again. This time his tongue stroked hers, massaging and caressing.

A shiver ran through her and she moaned into his mouth. It was a shiver of desire, of expectation. The cold and the wet had melted completely away, as if kissing Ryan had cocooned her in a protective bubble. She didn't care about anything other than him and the fact that they were suspended in this moment together. It was real. He was real. And, for the first time, she was pretty sure they were real together.

He pressed her against the van and his mouth trailed down to her throat. Her head fell backward and sensation throbbed inside of her as he found the hollow of her throat. He sucked gently, sending a tsunami of need through her body. For the first time she was sure that he saw her, all of her. They'd let go of their pride and ego to be in this moment together.

She eased away from his mouth and held his gaze. He looked at her longingly and gave a small, crinkled smile. It was more boyish, more filled with hope than she'd ever seen him.

Suddenly she was filled with resolve. They should get out of here. Go somewhere more…private. Comfortable. Because she knew exactly what they both wanted to come next.

Impulsively, she reached out and placed her thumb on his bottom lip. "You have a great mouth."

He used his teeth to graze her thumb.

She gasped, her hips arching against him. He lowered his head, burying it in her neck. He nipped and licked at her neck, creating shocks of pleasure pain. After the past twenty-four hours, the certainty in his touch meant more than words could.

"You smell amazing. And you have the softest skin," he murmured.

Not that she minded those words. "I...um." She swallowed hard. "It's a special lotion."

He pulled his head back and grinned at her. "Oh yeah? Let me guess, from Paris. Or handmade by oompah-loompahs."

She slanted him a look. "I like you so much more when you're not talking. I can think of much better things you could be doing with your mouth."

His jokes were a defense mechanism and she wasn't about to let him retreat back into himself.

His grin faltered, then faded, but the sincerity in his eyes remained. "Agreed."

He lowered her to the ground slowly, her body flush against his as she slid to the ground. The hard muscles of his chest under her hands, his hard...a surge of dizziness snuck up on her.

His grip on her arms remained firm. When she'd regained her bearings he tilted his chin down and brushed his lips across hers again. The kiss was gentle and soulful but full of need, all at the same time.

And it reignited the throbbing need inside of her.

"We should go somewhere." Each ragged breath she took pushed her breasts into his chest, teasing the already hard peaks that lay beneath her bra.

He nodded, uncharacteristically mute, as if he was also loath to break the spell between them. Without a word he cracked open the passenger-side door. When she was safely inside and out of the continued rain, he jogged to the driver side and climbed in. He started the minivan and activated the heat, focusing all of the air vents in her direction.

She began to shiver violently, her teeth clacking together, as if suddenly reminded that she was freezing.

He frowned in self-reproach as he shifted the van into drive. "Sorry. I don't know what I was thinking. I should have gotten you into the warm faster. Don't worry, I'll find you a hot shower."

Hot shower. She forced her head back against the headrest and closed her eyes. The image of her and Ryan, naked in a shower, steam billowing around them, his hands on her body...she gasped and snapped her eyes open again.

"What about you?" Her voice was wobbly as she examined his T-shirt, damp and muddy from her feet.

He reached across the divide between the seats and brushed a hand over her damp hair. "I think I deserve one too."

Happiness bubbled inside of her. Ryan was the one before the One, or just a friend, or a friend with benefits, or something else entirely, she didn't care right now. All she wanted right now was him.

* * *

Ryan eagerly accepted the key from the elderly woman at the front desk of the B&B.

"Thanks. We're glad to get out of the rain."

The woman shook her head, her gray hair secure in its bun at the back of her head. "I can't imagine that you all were out there hiking today. Good thing you found us."

The muscles in his stomach unknotted, finally allowing himself to relax fully. It definitely was. Ainsley needed to get warm and dry. He'd done his best with the tools at his disposal, but the ranger was right, and all the roads off the base of the mountain had flooded.

He looped his thumb through the key ring and picked up his leather toiletry bag from the counter.

With his other hand, he protectively placed his palm on the small of Ainsley's back and guided her toward the stairs. The owner had said their room was on the third floor, a suite with its own bathroom. No other rooms on that floor and no other guests in the house. She'd winked when she'd said that.

He'd watched Ainsley carefully when he'd requested the one room. And he'd taken her small smile and silence as agreement.

Good. He didn't think he could keep his hands off of her anymore. More than that, he didn't want to. He sensed that they were on the threshold of something great, something they'd both been dancing around for weeks. The thrill of possibility hung in the air, and this time he wasn't about to let him pass it by. He'd hated himself this morning for kissing Ainsley, then canceling. He'd been a ball of self-recrimination. Now, though, he knew exactly what he was supposed to do. Ainsley was safe and he had another chance.

They reached the door and he stepped in front of her to unlock it. When they were inside he kicked his shoes off and handed her the toiletry bag. "There's shampoo and soap and some other things in there."

She stared down at the bag in his hand, her forehead furrowed. "Where did you get that?"

His mouth opened, but nothing came out. *Shit.* He swallowed hard. He always kept a bag of overnight essentials in his car. Shampoo, toothpaste, condoms.

Then the corners of her mouth lifted and her eyes turned playful. "Why don't you bring it into the shower yourself?"

She raised an eyebrow and shot him a look over her shoulder. Relief swelled in him. Good. This was good. He liked the mixture of playful banter and seriousness. Why hadn't he realized that sooner?

As she walked to the bathroom she unzipped his rain jacket, which was too large on her, and let it fall to the floor. It was followed by her T-shirt, then her jeans, which she had to shimmy out of. When she was done, she stood clad in only her thong and bra, her back to him.

He let his eyes travel over the curve of her shoulders, the exposed skin of her back, past the tuck of her waist, down to the flare of her hips. His mouth went dry. God, her body was perfect. And this was only from the back. There was something more to it, though, as if she were allowing him a clear, unobstructed look at the real Ainsley. Without makeup and high heels and coordinated outfits. She was one hundred percent Ainsley, and he found he liked her even more than before.

He stumbled as he kicked off his shoes, dropped his jeans, and yanked his legs out of them. Ainsley stepped into the bathroom and the sound of running water started.

He followed her, his penis already hard from that glimpse of her. When he entered the bathroom, he spotted her through the glass doors of the shower, rivulets of water trailing down her perfect body.

The air left his lungs in one hard whoosh. He really saw her now. All of her. Her round breasts, with the perky, dusky-pink nipples. Her flat belly and the manicured thatch of hair between her legs.

His tongue grew thick with nerves.

"Are you coming in? It's really nice and warm." Her voice was teasing.

He nodded seriously. She'd been right earlier. Talking was a waste of his mouth's abilities. He had so much he needed to communicate to her and he could think of the perfect way to do it.

The moment he stepped into the shower he grabbed the bar of soap and began to form suds with it between his palms. When he had a good lather worked up he reached for her. He closed his eyes and let his hands slip and slide over her soft skin and her curves. She let out a moan as her body relaxed into his hands, as she gave herself over to him. For several minutes he simply explored: over her firm ass, the indentation of her waist, across the hard peaks of her nipples.

His heart punched against his ribs.

"Kiss me," she whispered. Then her lips were warm and firm on his, her tongue silky and supple as it slipped into his mouth.

He wound one hand around her neck and cupped her butt cheek with the other as she lifted a leg to twine around his waist. He advanced, pressing forward slowly and carefully until her back was against the shower wall.

She arched, pushing her body into to him and he drew closer to the point of no return.

"Please tell me you have a condom in that bag of yours."

He let out a jagged sigh of relief. His sixth sense hadn't failed him. She wanted it too. As much as he did.

He leaned out of the shower, unzipped the bag, and groped for a condom. When his fingers skirted the smooth plastic he yanked it out. With deft hands he tore open the packaging.

Ainsley watched in rapt silence, her chest heaving with each breath, as he wrapped the condom over his length. Her eyes sparked with hunger, and satisfaction surged through him.

Ainsley. Completely unguarded, completely in the moment. With a body that was hot as hell. His chest squeezed as he glanced at her, naked in front of him in the shower.

"Where were we?" he growled.

She giggled as he resumed their prior position, her back against the shower stall and with one leg wrapped around him.

He eased himself closer to her opening, teasing her for a second by rubbing against her. When he brushed past the hard nub of her clitoris she gasped, tilting her head back.

He kissed her then, plunging his tongue into her mouth. Gently he entered her, stroking slowly.

She bucked hard, her hips tilting to plunge all of him inside of her, and his grip on control began to slip. Instead, he grasped her harder around the hips and willed himself to move slowly. He'd tease her, make sure she was good and ready.

Ainsley's head dropped to his shoulder, her breath coming in frantic puffs against his collarbone. She whimpered softly, her voice gradually rising in pitch.

"You OK?" He pulled back far enough to look her in the eye. Her eyes had gone hazy and her lips were pink and swollen.

I did that.

His heart pumped faster.

"Yeah." Her fingernails pricked the skin on the back of his neck as she tightened her hold. Then she lifted her other leg and angled her pelvis, rocking against him with more force.

Fuck. He bit the inside of his cheek, willing himself to keep control and not give in to her tempo. It took women more time to warm up, he knew from experience. If he was selfish and moved too fast, he wouldn't be able to give her what she deserved.

She began to lower one of her hands between them, when he caught her wrist.

"What are you doing?"

Her face flushed red. "I, um, I can't…without…"

He caught her mouth in his, relishing the feel of her plump lips. He kissed her until she was breathless putty in his arms, her body languid and loose.

He twined his fingers through hers, pressing her hand back and over her head against the shower wall.

"You can. I'll show you." This time he thrust a little harder, a little faster, building the tempo gradually. With each stroke she gave herself over to him further, letting him take control.

A lump grew in his throat. There was something about the image of smart-mouthed, stubborn-ass Ainsley in his arms letting him take the lead. For a second he felt like his chest might burst.

Don't be stupid.

He focused on their rhythm, the clench and release of her muscles against his penis. Each thrust brought him closer and closer to the spiral, but he had to hold on. He had to show her first.

A second later she was rigid in his arms, her limbs spasmed once, then twice, before she gave a long shudder followed by a sharp groan. She buried her head on his shoulder and he winced as she bit down on the skin.

He followed her, letting himself jerk against her as he emptied himself, giving in as the wall of pleasure crashed over him.

When he was done he collapsed against her, careful to keep his weight propped on his forearms. It took a minute for his frantic breathing to return to normal. Ainsley clung to him, her fingers curled around his shoulders, her body limp beneath his.

She gulped in a few breaths before she lifted her head to grin at him. "You were right. You did show me."

He laughed then, swinging her into his arms and carrying her to the bed in the other room. *Of course I was right.* She'd better get used to it.

CHAPTER EIGHTEEN

Ainsley returned to consciousness slowly. First, there was the weight of an unfamiliar arm around her waist. Then the smell of spicy man. When she cracked her eyelids she saw Ryan, sprawled across the bed beside her.

The mere sight of his naked, muscular back ignited the now familiar throbbing between her legs.

She blew out a shaky breath. Just as she'd expected, her situation was nothing like Glowbugdoodle's. Her time in the shower with Ryan had only left her ravenous for more.

I don't have any makeup. The thought came to her suddenly and she reached to feel her hair. *Knotted. Tangled. Matted.* She didn't even have a hairbrush.

Ryan sighed and rolled onto his back, giving her an unobstructed view of his penis. Her tongue glued itself to the roof of her mouth.

It was a beautiful penis. She'd heard women say that in the past, that a man had a beautiful penis, and she'd never known what they were talking about. Well, now she knew.

She couldn't help herself. She reached down and wrapped her fingers around the smooth skin. His penis jumped and grew harder in her hand. With a grin, she stroked.

Next to her, Ryan stirred, his eyelids fluttering.

A second later they popped wide open and he let out a load groan. "You're insatiable."

He turned toward her, cupping her breast with one hand. His thumb flicked over her nipple, sending a shock of sensation down deep in her belly.

Her mouth fell open and she began to pant, desire building quickly inside of her.

She leaned forward and pulled his lower lip into her mouth, sucking hard.

"Shit," he whispered when she released him.

She fought the urge to chuckle. "Do you need a safe word, Ryan?"

His eyes flashed and his jaw muscles twitched once. A prickle of uncertainty traveled down her spine. Didn't he get the reference to their earlier joke?

He rolled on top of her then, propping himself on his forearms. He kissed her long and hard, then pulled away slowly. "No."

His gaze pierced her. "When we're here together like this, when I'm kissing you," his mouth lowered to hers again. "No more joking."

He trailed a hand down her side, his strong fingers burning a path of sensation along her bare skin.

A shiver shot down her spine. "OK."

Her heartbeat sped. This was different than she'd expected. He was different than what she'd thought he would be.

He reached for his leather bag on the side table and pulled out a condom. She snatched it from his hand.

"No. My turn." Then she lifted up on her elbows, forcing him to roll over. She climbed on top of him and his gaze traveled hungrily over her body. She bent, lowering her nipple into his mouth. His pupils dilated but he complied with her unspoken command and licked. The roughness of his tongue lit all of her nerve endings on fire.

With one hand she rolled the condom onto him, then shimmied down and engulfed his hardness. She used her hands to pin his wrists against the bed. This time she would be in charge.

* * *

Ryan gritted his teeth as he bucked into her. It took all his willpower to keep his wrists pinned to the bed and let her take control.

Pure, unadulterated desire built in his blood and punched through his veins. He jerked up from the bed, sitting as she rode him.

Much better.

He angled himself so that with every stroke she gave a little gasp, a small moan of pleasure. Just as he'd thought. He'd found her G-spot. But that wasn't good enough.

He twined his fingers in her hair, at the nape of her neck, and eased her head backward. When her back was arched, her firm, round breasts staring him in the face, he bent forward and sucked. He used his tongue to circle closer to her nipple. Each time he flicked his tongue over the surface she gave a little shudder. He increased his speed, rocking into her more urgently, licking and sucking in time with the rhythm.

Her breath came in quick bursts, each one spurring him closer to release. His dick throbbed, his body demanding that he let go, but he forced himself to hold on. *Just a few more seconds.*

Then she spiraled, a quick, sharp half scream half pant piercing the air. She clapped a hand over her mouth, muffling the sound. But the noise still ripped through him, unleashing wave after wave of satisfaction and sending it slamming through him.

He pumped a few more times before his body gave one final shudder.

When he slumped back against the headboard, she grinned at him mischievously. The spark in her eyes filled him with happiness.

He lowered her slowly back onto the bed, then collapsed next to her.

He reached with one hand and tangled it in her wild, loose hair. Then he rolled on his side and let his gaze travel over her.

"You're gorgeous when you aren't wearing makeup." He traced a thumb along her cheekbone, down her neck, and over her collarbone. As if instinctively, his dick began to stir again.

He fought the urge to laugh. Would he ever get enough of her? Who would have thought that Ainsley Slone, uptight Princess from the Point, would be the best sex of his life?

She blushed, her face turning pink, but his hand returned to her chin, holding her face so she had to look him in the eye.

"Seriously. Gorgeous. Delicious. I just want to eat you up." He buried his head in her neck, as if pretending to bite her. Ainsley let out a squeal and swatted him away.

She squirmed against him. "It tickles! And I'm hungry. We should see about breakfast. I don't want that poor lady to think we're just in here having sex."

He let himself laugh this time, a deep belly laugh. "If that's what she thinks then she's smart."

Ainsley raised both hands to his chest, as if she'd push him away, but he caught her wrists and pulled her closer instead. Despite her protests, her body relaxed as he curled around her and inhaled her flowery scent.

"But…," she said.

He sighed and released her. To his satisfaction she didn't move away. Instead, she nuzzled closer.

He lowered his head, his lips brushing against her hair. "We definitely need some breakfast, but then I vote we come back up here."

She made a little murmuring sound.

"The roads are flooded out. I don't see a TV around here. What else are we going to do? Besides, if the owner thinks we're up here having wild sex, then we might as well prove her right."

She giggled, then rolled away from him and swung her legs over the edge of the bed. "We should see if she can wash our clothes too."

The blood rushed to his dick, making him hard again. "No clothes?" It took an effort to keep his tone level.

She glanced at him over her shoulder and raised an eyebrow. "Are you objecting?"

"Hell no!" He jumped out of bed and grabbed a robe that was hanging on the bathroom door. He tossed the other robe to her.

* * *

I'm the one who needs a safe word. Ainsley swallowed the thought. Ryan had called her insatiable, but he was the one who seemed to have memorized the *Kama Sutra.* During the twenty-four hours they'd been at the B&B he'd introduced her to positions she never knew existed.

She traced a hand down his chest. When he didn't open his eyes she leaned closer, making sure to press her breasts against him.

Still without opening his eyes, he let out a growl. The next thing she knew, she was on her back with him hovering above her.

She giggled and gripped the strong muscles of his upper arms. "Careful with the noise. We don't want to get kicked out."

Her face heated as she remembered the knowing look the owner had given them at breakfast, before she offered to bring the rest of their meals up on a tray. Apparently the roads were still washed out and might take another day to clear.

She'd tried to call Brett but her phone was dead. *Oh well.*

They were trapped here until they weren't and she was determined to make the most of it.

He kissed her, then growled more loudly. "I can't help myself around you. Besides, we always have the man van."

She tried to frown at him but found she couldn't. It was as if her face muscles were permanently frozen in a grin.

Ryan had already torn another condom off the roll. She glanced at the remainder, sitting on the bedside table, and her stomach clenched. *Ryan took them everywhere. In his overnight bag, which was always in his car.* She willed the thought away.

She'd known who Ryan was when she'd started this. And she had started it. Ryan would never have pushed her if she hadn't wanted it herself.

"Is it always like this?" The words caught in her throat and the minute they were out she wished she could snatch them back.

"Like this?" He had his hand on the curve of her waist now, his thumb stroking across the front of her rib cage.

She swallowed hard. The water would go down eventually. She might as well spit it out and clear her mind. What was the worst that could happen? He hadn't liked when she'd teased about the safe word, but they'd moved past it quickly enough. She thought she had a fair idea of what went on his head by now, but she couldn't be sure. Relationships had always been about commitment for her, but for him it had been about the physical. She couldn't help but wonder if he felt the same way she did.

"For you, Ryan. Is it always like this?"

It had never been like this for her. The electric, insatiable hunger that filled her the minute she woke and saw him or smelled him or even sensed him next to her. The way her entire body tingled the minute he touched her. The longing that resurfaced only seconds after they'd both come.

His jaw tensed. He averted his eyes and swallowed, his Adam's apple bobbing, before he met her gaze again.

Her lungs constricted. All of a sudden she wasn't sure she wanted to know.

Then his gaze softened. "No," he said, managing to be both forceful and gentle at the same time.

He brushed a kiss over her forehead. She relaxed back into the pillows then, her muscles unknotting.

That was all she needed to know, for now.

CHAPTER NINETEEN

The owner knocked softly at the door. "Water is down and the roads are passable! Just thought you all would want to know, but you're welcome to stay as long as you like."

Ryan's stomach sank and he turned to look at Ainsley, who was asleep next to him.

"Thank you!" He made his voice only as loud as necessary for the owner to hear him, trying not to wake Ainsley. She didn't shift or stir next to him and he grinned. She was exhausted. And she should be. He'd lost count of how many times they'd had sex over the day and a half they'd been holed up here. It had easily broken any of his personal records, not that he really kept track of those things.

Disappointment pricked at him. He wasn't ready to leave yet. Here at the B&B they could lose themselves in the moment. But what would happen when they got home?

The muscles in his neck tensed. Once they got back to the real world he'd have to face the problems that had plagued him his entire life. Eventually he was bound to pull a Lawhill, to go AWOL the way his dad had before him. Yet somehow he'd been able to fool himself into thinking otherwise for a few days. His gut told him that he had to see Ainsley tonight and tomorrow and the day after. He didn't want to hide what was happening between them, but he also had to be careful not to take it too far. Not before he got himself figured out.

Truth be told, the very thought of commitment or a relationship still evoked a panicked nausea. And at the same time, he couldn't stand the idea of saying good-bye to her. Was this how it had been for his father in the beginning? Was this how a person got fooled into thinking he was qualified to be a partner and, God forbid, eventually a father? It felt like an impossible hubris, a self-deceit of the greatest magnitude that was inevitably destined to fail.

He glanced at her again, willing himself to commit to his memory the image of her with her tangled hair and no makeup. At the end of the day, Ainsley was still Ainsley. She still wanted things he wasn't capable of giving her. He'd never been able to picture himself with a wife and a house and a white picket fence. Even Ainsley hadn't changed that for him. If anything, the emotions he'd started to feel for her made him even more terrified.

With a heavy sigh, he placed a hand on her shoulder. And just like that, his touch stirred her back to consciousness. She gave him a sleepy grin and rolled toward him. "Who's insatiable now?"

He caught her hand in his and threaded their fingers together. Then he swallowed hard. "The roads are passable. I don't know about you, but my phone died a long time ago, and I'm sure Kate is worried sick."

Correction: Kate was going to murder him. Why hadn't he thought to ask about a landline?

His eyes traveled down to Ainsley's lithe hand. *That was why.* He'd been entirely too busy.

"Oh." The corners of her mouth dropped. Then she rolled away from him, her bare back taunting him with its nakedness. "Yeah, I need to call Brett. And I was supposed to have dinner with my parents last night, so I'm sure I have a voice-mail lecture from my father on manners and my selfishness in failing to prioritize his social arrangements."

Instinctively his nose wrinkled. Any parent would worry about their kid, but her father's specific points of contention made no sense to him. Didn't he see how damn perfect his own daughter was?

He followed her lead, rolling over and sitting up on the edge of the bed. By the time he turned to look at her, she was zipping her jeans back over her hips. His gaze skirted over her, taking in the jeans and the T-shirt. The owner had been kind enough to do their laundry. A sigh came, unbidden, and he dropped his head into his hands.

It really was over. Their perfect weekend had ended, and they had to get back to the cold light of day. He turned back to his own clothes, which were carefully folded on the nightstand. Still, he couldn't force himself to stand and dress.

He heard Ainsley's footsteps on the carpet, then felt her hands twine in his hair when she stepped in front of him. She took one more step forward, bringing the crown of his head to rest against her stomach as her fingers slowly massaged the base of his neck.

"Am I going to see you tomorrow?" Her voice was small.

He wrapped his hands around the back of her thighs and pulled her closer, lifting his head so his face was buried in her stomach. He kissed her softly through the cotton of her T-shirt. "Absolutely."

"Good." She released him and stepped away. "Then we should head out. I need to get back to my car so I can charge my cell phone. I'm supposed to be at work in thirty minutes and Brett is going to lose his shit."

He stood from the bed but grabbed her hand, twining his fingers with hers. He wasn't ready to let go. Not yet.

She moved closer until her face was an inch from his. "And now I have something to look forward to."

Then she kissed him, her lips soft and sweet on his.

He fought the urge to throw her down on the bed and make love to her again. Usually he was climbing the walls, ready to flee a woman's house after twelve hours. He'd spent thirty-six with Ainsley and he needed more.

What the hell was happening to him?

* * *

As soon as she climbed into the driver's seat of her car, Ainsley plugged her cell phone into the travel charger. Then she started the engine and pulled onto the narrow paved road that wound down the rest of the mountain. Only a few minutes later her phone came to life and began to ping in rapid succession.

She deflated at the sound. It really was time to get back to her normal life, and she was going to have a hell of a lot of explaining to do. With a sigh, she pulled over into a private driveway and picked up her phone.

First she texted Brett.

Ainsley: The roads flooded and I got stuck out of town for the weekend. Won't make it in time today. Can you please have someone call and reschedule my appointments?

She could already imagine the steam pouring from his ears, but she clicked send anyway. There wasn't anything she could do about it now.

Then she started to click through the messages.

There were several from Sunday night, when she should have been back and having dinner with her parents. She grinned. Not that she was at all sorry to have missed it.

Dad: You're late.

Dad: Where are you?

Dad: You'd better have a good excuse. Mom went to a lot of trouble to have dinner prepared.

Dad: Since you're apparently not coming, I guess I'll tell you here. The family is going to dinner at Jean Luc's to celebrate your brother-in-law's new promotion next Friday. Please let me know by Tuesday if you would like to bring a date so I can make the proper reservation.

She cringed. Jean Luc's. The restaurant everyone in the Point went to for all of their special occasions. The place where she could've sworn Scott planned to propose to her two months ago.

This was one situation where Ryan's don't-give-a-fuck training was going to come in handy. She hesitated for only a second before she typed.

Ainsley: Sorry, Dad. I have plans, but I hope you all have a great time. Tell Hamilton I said congratulations.

She smirked at the phone when she was finished. God, that felt good. He'd be angry, of course, and he'd ask a million questions, but so what? She was so tired of doing the things everyone else expected her to do. It was time to do what she wanted. And she could imagine a hundred better ways to spend her Friday night, at least ninety-nine of which involved her and Ryan and absolutely no clothing.

Her chest tightened as she scrolled to the next message.

Kate: Ryan texted to say he'd found you on the mountain but his phone was dying. I'm hoping yours still has power. Are you ok? We're all so worried.

Followed by one from James: I hope you're ok and please remember, you don't have to prove anything to anybody. Don't let anyone ever convince you you're not a badass. Whatever happens, we all love you and we support you. You don't have to hike and camp or anything else to prove yourself to us.

She smiled at that. He'd known her almost her entire life. Even in high school at Fallston when she'd been caught up in image and reputation, he'd never allowed her to entirely lose sight of herself.

Tears pricked her eyes as she synced the phone through her navigation system, dialed James, and pulled back onto the road.

He picked up after only one ring.

"Ainsley? Thank God. Please tell me you're alive and all in one piece."

She laughed. "I'm perfectly fine, I promise. And I did make it all the way up the mountain."

There was a long pause.

"Ryan found you? He got you back down?" James's voice carried the low hum of worry.

"He did. I'm totally fine. I was cold and wet and it sucked and I'm never going camping or hiking again."

He chuckled, but it sounded forced. "Yeah, I thought it was craziness you went up there in the first place. I could wring Ryan's neck, but I have a feeling Kate's going to beat me to it."

Her throat tightened. This wasn't Ryan's fault. If anything, he'd been the one who'd come through. Her just-for-one-night knight in shining armor. Although technically they'd spent two nights together, and if she included Kate and James's engagement party and the other three weeks of the Ryan plan...

"So where the hell have you guys been?" he asked.

She swallowed hard. "The roads got rained out. We found this tiny B&B run by a really nice older lady."

She braced herself for the inevitable questions, but she was a big girl. She could handle it.

"What did you guys do at a B&B in the rain for two days?"

There was a long, painful silence as the right words eluded her.

"Oh. My. God." Kate's voice rang through the background on James's end.

Ainsley gripped the steering wheel tighter and kept her eyes on the road. There was no point in finding the right words now.

There was a click, followed by the return of James's voice. "My fiancée is obviously listening in, but I think she expressed my thoughts perfectly."

"Ainsley Slone did you have sex with Ryan Lawhill? Are you concussed? What did the mountain do to you? Somebody tell me what's going on!" The words tumbled over one another as Kate hurried to get them all out.

More than three weeks ago Ryan had dared her to be more unexpected. This was definitely unexpected.

"I did. I definitely slept with him. And before you lecture me or freak out, I have no idea what's going on, and it wasn't a mistake and I don't regret it, so you guys had better not make me feel bad about it." She made sure to keep her voice firm and even.

On the other end, the phone was dead silent.

Then James began to laugh, a deep belly laugh. "Who would've thought?"

"Wow." Kate whispered. "Seriously."

Ainsley began to giggle too. "Absolutely, one hundred percent not me. I have no idea what I'm doing, and I have no idea where to go from here, and I don't want this to be weird for you guys, but I also couldn't keep this from you."

There was a sudden prickle at the back of her neck. Ryan wouldn't mind that she'd told, would he?

"Eh, that's the myth of adulthood. I'm pretty sure none of us knows what the hell we're doing." The confidence in Kate's voice reassured her.

She'd fought like hell over the past few years to build that perfect life, to convince everyone she knew exactly what she was doing, and where had that gotten her? Nowhere.

It was time for a new strategy.

CHAPTER TWENTY

After a quick shower at his loft, Ryan had swung by the studio. Where he'd found it completely impossible to work. No matter what he did or what music he listened to or how loudly he blared it, his mind kept wandering back to Ainsley.

Around four thirty he gave up and headed to Little Ray's. A good shot of espresso usually helped motivate him. Plus, Griffin seemed to have a handle on the whole women and relationships thing. Not that he needed advice. He had everything perfectly under control.

Didn't he?

He couldn't fully quash his anxiety no matter how he tried. He couldn't change who he was, even for Ainsley. He'd still be unpredictable, he was still terrified of commitment. The feelings she'd inspired only caused him to feel an added frustration, without changing his core identity. He tried to reassure himself with the fact that Ainsley knew him. She knew exactly what she was getting herself into and she knew he wasn't Mr. Marriage Material.

They were both adults. Adults who had fantastic sex and wanted to keep seeing each other. There was nothing wrong with that. In fact, as far as he was concerned, there was a whole lot right about it. Maybe she was OK with that. He'd even started to hope that the Lawhill experiment had gotten through to her. Maybe Ainsley wasn't a relationship and marriage and babies person anymore.

He gave a determined shake of his head, then pushed the door and strode into Little Ray's. Enough self-reflection.

"Ryan!" Mabel, Griffin's five-year-old daughter, jumped down from a stool by the counter and raced in his direction. When she reached him she threw her arms around his upper leg and squeezed tight.

"Ouch! Watch it there, Popeye! You're too strong for a little guy like me."

She giggled and he lifted her into the air. Mabel squealed with delight before he set her back on the ground.

She grabbed him by the hand and led him over to the counter, where Griffin was ringing up a customer.

"Daddy! Daddy! Can Ryan babysit me next week?"

He plopped onto a vacant stool and shrugged at Griffin. "If you need a babysitter, I don't mind."

Griffin finished with the register and turned to Ryan with raised eyebrows. "You want to babysit?"

His spine bristled. Why not? He'd offered before. Griffin might as well make the most of it and take Beth out for a night on the town.

One corner of Griffin's mouth quirked upward. "Why don't you ask Ainsley to join you? I hear you two have been getting along well."

He couldn't help the giant grin that overtook his face, stretching his muscles until they ached. So Ainsley had shared the news. And apparently Griffin wasn't mad anymore, thank God. He hadn't kept his promise to Griffin that night at the club and he was glad his friend saw it wasn't out of malice. Ainsley made him happy, which was why he couldn't stop grinning like a damn jackass. He was relieved that his friend seemed to understand, especially since he couldn't discuss any of the details in front of a five-year-old.

"I like Ainsley. She can come too," Mabel announced.

He reached to ruffle her hair, but she stepped away and gave him the side eye. "Beth did my braids. Don't mess them up."

He chuckled. "Sure thing, kiddo. I'll get with Ainsley and Beth and your dad and we'll find a time. Sound OK to you?"

She nodded, her face serious. "OK. I'm going to go help Sarah with the muffins now." Then she skipped underneath the counter and into the back prep area of Little Ray's.

"So," Griffin rested his elbows on the counter, "good weekend, huh?"

Somehow he managed to grin even wider, until it felt like his face would split in two. Just because he didn't need advice didn't mean he couldn't talk about it, especially now that he knew Griffin wouldn't hold it against him.

"She's incredible. Like, once you get below the makeup and the clothes and the manicure..."

"Whoa! Whoa!" Griffin's eyes widened in alarm as he

jerked back and held his hands palm out in front of him. "Too much information."

Ryan glared at him in mock annoyance. It was important that Griffin understand that his intentions were good when it came to Ainsley. "That's not what I was about to say. I was trying to say that she's…I don't know. Once she lets her guard down and stops worrying so much, she's more real. Easier to be with or something."

His face heated and he forced a shrug. Why was he trying to describe it to Griffin anyway?

Because he cared what they thought of him. He wasn't just some irresponsible player, and he had his reasons for the things he did. He reached over the counter and poked his friend in the shoulder. "I do think about more than naked women and sex, you know."

Griffin's eyes glinted mischievously. "Could have fooled me."

Ryan laughed, the momentary tension between them broken. That's what he got for trying to talk about relationships and feelings and shit. The whole screwed-up Dad thing was too complicated to explain. Whoever Ainsley was, and whoever he was, they'd clicked. Did it matter why?

"Hey, Ryan!" Sarah strode from the back, Mabel piggyback on her shoulders. "Don't forget we have that meeting with your mom at two tomorrow to plan the Mid-Atlantic Bully Breeds fund-raiser. Griffin's going to be there, and I enlisted your friend Ainsley to help out with some of the event planning, since she's good at that. I just texted her to check her availability."

His spine stiffened. Ainsley? In a meeting with his mother? How the hell had that happened?

No. Just no. If he couldn't figure out how to stop grinning like a demented clown, his mother would see the truth within seconds, and he wasn't prepared for that.

"Um. I, uh, well, calendar, Ainsley, I don't know." He stopped himself midramble. What was wrong with him? That hadn't even resembled a sentence.

Then he squared his shoulders, took a deep breath, and started again. He'd always managed to figure out these kinds of issues in the past, surely he could do it now. "Yeah. Sure. Whatever."

This was Ainsley they were talking about. Of course she'd be busy. She packed her calendar fuller than Leonardo DiCaprio the night of the Oscars.

Griffin was staring at him now, his expression gleeful. If Mabel hadn't been standing right there, Ryan would have reached out and punched him. But kids learned by example and violence was bad and all that shit.

Sarah's phone chimed and she looked down at it.

"Oh good! Ainsley says she can make it."

The muscles in his jaw twitched as he warred with the dual desires to smile at the mention of her name and grit his teeth at the idea of sitting through a meeting with her and his mother. It would add a whole layer of complications he wasn't ready for, and yet there was a part of him that actually wanted Ainsley to meet his mom.

What the hell is wrong with me? These impulses were digging him deeper and deeper into a hole he wasn't sure he'd be able to get out of. If he wanted out.

Griffin watched him, then shook his head. "Well, this

should be interesting. While we're at it, I'll just text her and ask if the two of you are free to babysit next Tuesday."

Ryan's shoulders slumped and he dropped his head into his hands. Figuring out how to navigate this was going to be a lot harder than he'd expected.

* * *

The next day Ainsley sped down the sidewalk, her strappy sandals slapping against the pavement. She was going to be late for the meeting at Little Ray's and she hated being late, but after her weekend away Brett had insisted she spend the morning at the Meridien "catching up." Which had mostly consisted of him listening in on her phone conversations while she finalized details for next weekend's wedding. She wondered when his anxiety would finally ease up so she could get back to doing her job. Even if she lacked some of her previous enthusiasm, she was still completely competent.

Brett had only let her leave after he'd made the mistake of asking, for what felt like the hundredth time, what she'd been doing all weekend anyway.

She'd finally given up on tact or manners and responded deadpan, "Having incredible sex. Like the best sex of my life. You should really try it sometime."

His jaw had fallen open and he'd stood there, staring at her. She'd chosen that moment to reach for her purse. "Speaking of, I have a meeting. I'll be back when it's over."

Then she'd marched out of the office, leaving Brett alone. And now here she was, running late.

With one hand she twisted her long hair off the back of her neck, giving her skin a chance to breathe, and with the other she yanked open the door to Little Ray's.

Ryan, Griffin, Sarah, and an older woman sat at a table in the corner. She hustled over to them and slid into the only available seat, next to Sarah.

"Sorry I'm late. Work was nuts. Boss is mad I was gone for a few days."

Ryan's face flushed slightly and she fought the urge to laugh. Really? That tiny mention of their weekend had been enough to make him blush? Since when had he become discreet about his conquests?

She held out her hand to the fifty-something woman who sat next to him. "I'm Ainsley. Sarah just asked me to help out a bit."

The woman grasped her hand firmly. "Nicole Parker. I run Mid-Atlantic Bully Breeds."

In preparation for today's meeting she'd spent last night reviewing the rescue's website. They had a lot of damn cute dogs. She'd never been much of a dog person herself, and she'd never given pit bulls much thought, but the rescuers had dressed them up in costumes and bandannas and tiaras. There'd been an especially precious chunky little gray one with a feather boa and a huge smile on her face. If Ainsley was ever going to be a dog person, that was the kind of dog she wanted. One with style.

"Nice to meet you, Nicole. I figured I'd just hang out and listen to what you all have planned and if anything comes up, I'm happy to help."

Next to her, Sarah gripped her pen tightly. Anxiety practically radiated off of her. That was one thing they'd have to work on if Sarah wanted to run more events for Little Ray's. You had to exude confidence and be decisive so the client trusted your decisions.

"Sweetie," Nicole placed a hand on Ryan's shoulder, "be a gentleman and get Ainsley a cup of coffee."

The smile on Ainsley's face froze as her stomach jumped. *Sweetie?*

Ryan's eyes flicked to her. "Sure thing, Mom."

She could feel his attention focused on her as her face grew hot. Why hadn't he told her the client was his mom? That she'd be meeting his mom today?

Without thinking she popped up from her chair. "Thanks. Nicole, but I'll grab it. I'm picky about my coffee."

She rushed from the table as fast as her feet would carry her. His mom? That brought things to a whole new level of weird.

In a daze she ordered her coffee from the male barista at the counter: soy cappuccino, no foam. A second later Ryan's warm hand was on the small of her back as he leaned his mouth close to her ear.

"Sorry. I should have warned you."

She spun on him but worked to keep her face neutral and her tone low. After all, his mom was twenty feet away.

"Why didn't you tell me last night?" He'd stayed at her apartment, and although they hadn't done a whole lot of talking, this was something he should've worked into the conversation.

He shrugged, a wicked grin crossing his face. "I was doing something much more important."

She fought the urge to punch him in the arm.

"A little warning would have been nice. Did you think I wouldn't find out she was your mom or something?"

He dropped his gaze to his shoes. "It was too weird."

She laughed then. *Oh, Ryan.*

She rested a hand on his shoulder. "Look, it's not like I expected to be introduced to your mom or anything like that, I'm just saying a heads-up just would have been nice."

He lifted his eyes and one corner of his mouth quirked upward. "Would it help if I said I'm sorry?"

She gave in then and smiled. Being annoyed wouldn't accomplish anything. Ryan wasn't the type of guy who introduced women to his mother. She knew that. Now she had to accept it. That didn't mean she wasn't going to mess with him though.

The barista slid her coffee across the counter, and she handed him a ten-dollar bill.

She turned away from the counter and leaned closer to Ryan. "Have you ever introduced your mom to a woman you were involved with?"

He made a choking sound and she had to bite the inside of her cheek to keep from laughing. Perhaps she was teaching him something about life after all.

She walked back to the table, Ryan red-faced at her side. When she reached it she slid back into her seat and smiled brightly at Ryan's mom. The only way to combat her anxiety was through friendly professionalism.

"So, Nicole. Tell me what you have in mind for the event." She pulled a pen and notepad from her bag.

Nicole leaned forward, her eyes lit with excitement. She seemed focused. Determined.

Good. Those were the clients Ainsley enjoyed working with. And in this case, the end result would save dogs' lives. She really should help plan charity events more often.

"Heavy hors d'oeuvres," Nicole began.

Ainsley glanced to Griffin. "Did you already decide on a caterer?"

He nodded. "Beth said she'd do it."

"Good." She wrote "catering" on her list and added Beth's name next to it. There was no need for her to stick her nose in there, Beth would have it all under control.

"Alcohol?" She directed the question to Nicole.

"Yes, please." Ryan's mom smiled and Ainsley found herself smiling back. She liked Ryan's mom, which made her heart twinge a little. She doubted they'd be seeing much of each other.

Instead, she shifted her attention farther down the table. "Griffin and Sarah, you guys have a liquor license?"

Sarah raised her eyebrows at Griffin, who shrugged.

Then that was a no. Ainsley pulled out her phone and scrolled until she found a number, which she wrote on a piece of paper and handed to Griffin.

"A one-day liquor license only costs forty-five dollars. Call Steve, tell him I referred you. He'll hook you up with the application and get it pushed through approval. Once you have the license, then call me and I'll give you the number of the distributor we use."

She turned her attention back to Ryan's mom. "Nicole, did you prefer a full bar or just beer and wine?"

A furrow formed between Ryan's mother's eyebrows. "I hadn't really given it much thought. What do you think is best?"

She tapped her pen on the notepad. "I'd recommend a cash bar since this is a charity event. It's easier and less expensive to limit ourselves to beer and wine because we can just have some of Griffin's staff pour the alcohol and we don't need to get a bartender, which would cost more."

Nicole nodded and Ainsley added "cash bar—beer and wine" to her list.

Next to her, Sarah pulled out a pad of paper and hastily scribbled the same.

Mentally, she moved onto the next item of business. "Sarah said this is an auction? Do we know what items we have to auction off?"

Nicole slid a typewritten piece of paper toward her. She turned it around and scanned it. They had a pretty good list of items. The usual sports memorabilia, a few pieces of jewelry. She scrapped her earlier ideas. Nicole had this part under control.

"All the dog-related charity items are listed on the bottom half. Dogsitting, collars, leashes, that kind of thing." Nicole pointed.

"Good. Awesome." Ainsley lifted her eyes from the page and smiled at Nicole. "I think you're going to make some decent money on this thing."

Nicole heaved a big sigh. "Let's hope so. When you specialize in rescuing pit bulls, there's never a shortage of need."

"What can I do to help?" She blurted the words without thinking, then immediately reconsidered. What they needed was money, right? Which was why she was doing all of this. The best thing she could do would be to throw a perfect event.

"Foster homes," Nicole replied evenly.

"Foster homes?"

The older woman gave a quick nod. "Yup. We always need money for vet care, but even with money we need somewhere for the dogs to go. Somewhere they can learn to be part of a family and get some training, to make them more adoptable. They get depressed in the shelters. Lonely. Then the pent-up energy makes them seem hyper and nobody wants to adopt them."

Ainsley frowned. Kate had been a foster parent before. She'd mentioned it a few times, but Ainsley had never really considered what that meant.

"But then you have to give the dog away to someone else?" She chewed on her lip.

Ryan chuckled dryly and shot his mom an affectionate look. "Unless you're my mom. She took Gremlin as a foster five years ago and never adopted her out."

Nicole narrowed her eyes playfully at him. "I've fostered sixty-four other dogs since then. Gremlin was just a special case."

Sixty-four?

He beamed at her, the pride in his eyes apparent. "So you are going to give Hippo away? I'll be sure to let Hank know. We all see the way you look at that dog, Mom."

Nicole crossed her arms, a smile on her lips. "I've only had her a few weeks, thank you very much, and she'll stay until she finds her forever home. In the meantime, weren't you supposed to donate some items to this auction we're discussing?"

He lifted his phone from the table and waved it. "Lee is going to be here any second with CDs, tickets, and T-shirts to donate."

Ainsley picked up her pen again. This wasn't the time to play "meet the mom." She wrote down "Auction Items" and underlined it.

"CDs and T-shirts for which band? And tickets to what? And who's Lee?" She needed all the details for her pad. That was how the system worked.

"You met him at the show the other night. He's in Mustachio the Monkey. Has a beard, doesn't talk a lot," Ryan said.

She jerked her head up to meet his gaze and raised her eyebrows. The guy all in leather? *Met* wasn't the right word for that interaction.

Little Ray's front doorbell tinkled and Ryan's attention shifted. A second later, his face paled, his eyes went wide, and his mouth dropped open.

He stared for a moment before he yelled, "Damn it, Lee! What did you do?"

CHAPTER TWENTY-ONE

As if today wasn't already bad enough. Of course he didn't normally introduce women to his family. Why would he purposely inflict needless pain and suffering on himself? And yes, he should have warned her that the client was his mom, but he'd honestly hoped it wouldn't come up. After all, they were here to work.

Luckily, Ainsley had gone full-fledged Ainsley and taken charge of the meeting immediately. Between her and his mom, they were going to pull this fund-raiser off, no problem. Sarah had been right to ask her.

But this? This was a disaster.

He pushed his chair back and stood from the table, his eyes glued to Lee, who stood just inside the door, freshly shaven, his hair neatly trimmed.

Ryan stalked across the coffee shop and grabbed Lee's elbow, jerking him to a corner. And Lee, who lifted weights with Ryan twice a week, let himself be dragged.

"What the hell did you do to your hair?" It was an essential part of the band's image. They were hairy, unshaven, unkempt, unsociable, and they played angry music. That's why fans loved them.

Lee shrugged. "Seemed like a good time for a change."

The muscles in his neck knotted. "Isn't that something you'd run by your manager ahead of time?"

"Oh. Yeah. Sorry about that."

He pinched the bridge of his nose and willed himself to be cool. Hair grew back. And there was nothing they could do about it now.

"How long do you think it will take to go back to normal? Three months? Maybe four?" He'd never grown the type of grimy, disorderly face shrub preferred by all the members of Mustachio the Monkey, so he wasn't sure.

Lee's eyes shifted to the ground, then to the counter, everywhere but to him.

"Lee?" There was something else Lee wasn't telling him.

Only then did Lee meet his eyes. "They're switching me to the children's section and the kids were scared of me. Well, the ones who didn't think I was related to Santa. Sorry, Ryan, but it had to go."

He sighed loudly. Lee was a walking contradiction: an angry heavy metal musician who worked as a librarian during the day. A fact that Ryan had taken pains to keep off the band's website.

His shoulders slumped. They'd have to find a way around this. Maybe if he asked her nicely Beth could make some kind of strap-on beard for shows.

"It's fine. We'll figure it out." He clapped a hand on Lee's back and directed him toward the table, bracing himself for a lecture from his mom. Or Griffin. Or Ainsley. Yelling "damn it" across a coffee shop was probably frowned upon.

He launched straight into introductions, hoping to delay the inevitable chastising.

"Guys, this is Lee. He's in a band, and he's brought us a bunch of swag we can use for the auction. Lee, this is my mom, Griffin, Sarah, and you remember Ainsley."

Lee's eyes lingered on Sarah for a moment longer than anyone else. Ryan pulled up a chair for him and Lee sat in it. They were here for the auction, not to flirt.

"Thanks, man. I forgot to ask how last weekend's camping trip was." Lee set the box of swag on the table.

Immediately, Ryan's mom's eyes lit. *Shit.* His mom was a smart lady and she was especially fine-tuned to parsing out details of his life, since he was so stingy with them himself. Of course she'd just connected the dots between Ainsley's camping trip and his.

He watched from the corner of his eye as she pressed her lips together, trying to hide the broad smile that threatened to take over her face.

He nearly dropped his head into his hands.

"Fine. It was fine. Lots of rain." He had to work to keep his eyes off of Ainsley.

His mom leaned forward on the table, closer to Ainsley, her eyes sparkling. "Ainsley, what are you doing tonight? Ryan's stepdad and I would love to have you over for cocktails to say thank-you for all the effort you're putting into this. And it'll give you a chance to meet Gremlin and Hippo, actual recipients of your hard work."

Then she reached out and squeezed Ainsley's hand.

Shit. The beans were spilled. Every single last little bean.

CHAPTER TWENTY-TWO

He'd grudgingly agreed to his mom's plan for cocktails. The whole thing made him nervous, a feeling he didn't enjoy, but he'd decided to tough it out. Partly because he knew what she was like when she was determined and partly because he'd promised Claire he would talk Hank into her Bahamas trip. After the way Ainsley had handled everyone at today's meeting, he had a feeling she might be the one to convince his stepfather. She had a gift for managing difficult situations. He comforted himself with the thought that she understood his aversion to relationships and wouldn't read anything into tonight.

"Um, I have a favor to ask you." First, he had to get her on board with the plan.

In the passenger seat, Ainsley brushed her long hair over her shoulder and turned to look at him, then winked. "What kind of favor?"

His blood heated. And he thought he had a dirty mind.

He did his best to frown. "Keep it in your pants, Ms. Slone. This is my mom's house we're going to. And I have an impressionable little sister."

She blushed fire-engine red and he chuckled. He'd never get enough of the back-and-forth between them, which was even more addictive now that he could touch her the ways he most wanted to. He placed his palm on her bare knee, then inched his hand slowly upward, his eyes glued to her tan skin. To his satisfaction she shifted, her legs falling just the slightest bit more open.

"What do you think you're doing?" Her voice was sweet like honey but with an undercurrent of desire.

He lifted his eyes to her face and caught the way her pupils dilated and her lips parted. Bingo. His eyes traveled over the leather interior of his Mustang. They hadn't pulled out of her parking lot yet, and his family didn't expect them for another fifteen minutes. After, the two of them had to be at the restaurant by 8:00 p.m. sharp. The maître d' had made that very, very clear on the phone.

She threw her head back, exposing her long neck, and laughed. "Has anyone ever told you you're completely transparent? It's like everything you think is projected on a giant screen over your head."

"I mean, there's really only one thing I think about…" He waggled his eyebrows.

She swatted his hand away. "I'm a lady. I was promised cocktails and dinner first. Then we can revisit this whole thing you're doing with your hands right now."

Hmm. That still sounded promising. And after she saw the

restaurant where he was taking her for dinner, the rest of their night was inevitable. In spite of himself, he did want to do things right and make Ainsley happy. There was room for them to meet in the middle, and he'd decided to start by taking her to a nice dinner. One that would really make her feel special.

She pushed her knees together and shifted her legs to the other side of the passenger seat. "You better start driving or we won't make it on time. In the meantime, you might as well tell me what this favor involves."

He sighed loudly. Her idea of a favor was so much better than his. But she was teasing him again. And he had to admit he kind of liked it.

"I need you to help me talk my stepdad into something. Well, not really help. I think you have a better shot of convincing him than I do, so if we can make it seem like it's all your idea, that would be best." Between the two of them, she was bound to have more clout with Hank. Mostly because she hadn't gotten arrested in the Bahamas.

"I'm listening."

He'd pulled out of the parking lot and was making short work of the drive. God, it felt good to have his Mustang back.

"It's a favor for my sister, Claire. She wants to go the Bahamas for Senior Week, after graduation, and my stepdad won't let her."

Ainsley frowned. "Why not? It's tradition."

Which was why he had to make it happen for Claire.

He gave a sheepish smile, a little uneasy to tell her the rest. "I'm sure this won't surprise you, but I had some adventures when I was there, and Hank is worried Claire might wind up in trouble."

Ainsley gave a small shake of her head. "You're right. I can't say I'm surprised. Do I want to know what happened at your Senior Week?"

He sighed but resolved to tell her. This was Ainsley, after all, and she wasn't going to judge him. While some things, like never knowing his father, would always be too painful to share, this wasn't one of them.

"I got arrested for trespassing while I was trying to get a glimpse of naked European women on the topless beach."

She laughed. "Well, you're nothing if not predictable."

He smiled. That was one way of looking at it. He'd started to suspect he might have found someone who got him and accepted him exactly the way he was.

* * *

Ainsley took a deep breath and unbuckled her seat belt. "You ready to do this?"

He waggled an eyebrow at her. "Here? Now? In my parents' driveway? I mean it's been a while, but if that's really what you want."

He reached for her seat-belt buckle and she swatted his hand playfully. "Can you be serious for five minutes?"

His lip curled up in distaste. "I really hope not."

With an indignant sigh, she opened the door and climbed out of the car. Typical Ryan. He was back to using humor to deflect emotion, but she was starting to get used to it. Besides, he could be so sweet when it was just the two of them.

Then he was beside her, his arm around her waist, his lips pressed against her cheek.

"Hey, sorry. I'm not trying to be an ass. I just don't take women home to meet my parents. Ever. Really, like ever."

She giggled and melted into him, warmth filling her. It was impossible to stay mad at him.

She jokingly tugged his hand as she set off down the stone pathway. "I guess that makes you kind of a virgin then."

He groaned but fell into step behind her. "That was a terrible joke."

Who was he kidding? He loved it when she joked, the more full of innuendo the better. So she ignored him and lifted the knocker just as the door jerked open.

A beautiful blonde teenager with perfect blue eyes and straight white teeth grinned back at them.

"Hi." Ainsley hesitated on the doorstep, a flicker of nervousness in her gut. They were really doing this. She was really meeting his entire family. Even though this was Ryan, it was hard not to read something into the circumstances.

"Hi! I'm Claire!" The girl threw her arms around Ainsley's neck and Ainsley obligingly squeezed her back. Her tension eased. At least they seemed happy she was here.

At that moment, a large woofing blur shot past her and barreled into Ryan's knees.

He let out a loud *ouf* but managed to stay standing, while the dog ran laps around him.

"That's Gremlin." Claire let her go then and held the door open, motioning her through. "She loves Ryan to death. Like, literally, I think someday she's going to die with happiness when she sees him."

Ainsley grinned and turned back to watch as Ryan crouched and the dog threw herself into his arms, covering his face in kisses. *If only men were more like dogs.* Then she caught herself. Maybe it was too apt a comparison.

Although Kate could be on to something with this whole dog ownership thing. Who wouldn't want that kind of love and devotion? She felt a pang. Everyone. Everyone wanted that in their lives, and she couldn't help but hope things with Ryan might grow into that. Eventually, of course. And gradually. This was Ryan she was thinking about.

Her train of thought was interrupted when she spotted the gray dog from the pictures, sitting perfectly on her fat haunches and grinning at them.

Happiness filled her, chasing away some of her anxiety. One glimpse of that goofy dog was better than a truckload of Prozac. Those issues with Ryan were questions for another day. They'd get there eventually, she just had to trust and wait.

Nicole burst into the hallway, wiping her hands on an apron tied around her waist.

"Ainsley!" Ryan's mom wrapped her in a hug. "I see you've met Gremlin." She smiled bemusedly out the door in the direction of Ryan and the dog, who was still accosting him. "And this is our newest foster, Hippo."

At the sound of her name, the gray dog's tail began to *thunk* rhythmically against the floor. Ainsley found herself grinning wider. It was no surprise this dog had let herself be dressed up for pictures.

Ryan made his way through the front door with Gremlin close on his heels. She couldn't help but watch him, marveling at how relaxed he seemed in his parents' home.

"I see someone loves you," Ainsley joked.

"That's the longest relationship Ryan's had with a girl in his entire life." Claire smirked the minute the words were out of her mouth.

Ryan reached to ruffle her hair. "Ha-ha, very funny. Since you're such an expert on adult relationships and all."

Claire stuck her tongue out at him and Nicole rolled her eyes.

"My children." She waved a hand in their direction. "Anyway, Ainsley, come in and meet Hank. We have Scotch and wine, whichever you prefer."

Ainsley followed her into the kitchen, where a gray-haired man sat at the table. He stood as soon as he saw them and held out a hand.

"Hank."

She shook it. "Ainsley."

Ryan pulled out a chair and waited for her to sit before he flopped into one next to it. On the other side of the table, Claire perched on the edge of her chair, watching them with wide-eyed interest.

Ainsley fought the urge to smirk. Ryan really hadn't been exaggerating when he said he never brought women home.

She shifted her attention back to Hank for a second and scrutinized him. Short steel-gray hair. Barrel-chested. A warm smile. She bet she could get him to agree to the trip, all she needed was an opening.

Hank leaned forward, resting his elbows on the table. "Are you a Scotch person or a wine person?"

"I never say no to wine."

Nicole poured some into a glass and pushed it toward her. Meanwhile, Hank poured Scotch into three tumblers, handing one to Nicole, one to Ryan, and taking a long sip of the last.

"Nicole says you're an event planner?" he asked.

She nodded slowly. "I'm doing mostly weddings right now."

Nicole shook her head. "I don't know how you do it. You came into that meeting today and had everything figured out within minutes. We would be totally lost without you."

Her face grew warm. "It's my pleasure to help. And I hear you have another big event coming up. Claire, you're going to graduate soon?"

Claire fiddled with the glass of soda water that sat in front of her. "Yeah. Six weeks left of school."

"That's awesome. What are you doing to celebrate?" She smiled warmly, but inside she was calculating. *Almost there.* She already had a plan for how to win Hank over.

Claire sighed loudly and slumped back into her chair. "Mom and Dad are having a party. And I'm hoping to go to the Bahamas for my class trip."

Ainsley leaned forward then, making sure to keep her eyes focused on Claire. "The Bahamas? I went there for my senior trip. I don't know if you've ever been snorkeling, but the Exumas are gorgeous. And they say the corral reefs are bleaching with all the environmental changes, so you should definitely see those while you can. Plus there's loads of history, like the old lighthouses and the ruins from the colonial settlements. You can join a tour from practically any of the resorts and a guide will take you out. If you take a dive class in time, you can even go into some of the blue holes to explore. I bet I still have the itinerary I planned somewhere if you want to take a look at it."

Of course she and her friends had also done a lot of drinking and lying around on the beach, but she didn't imagine those would be major selling points for Hank.

Claire glanced nervously at her father. "See, Daddy? There's cultural and nature stuff too. Not everyone has the same priorities as Ryan."

Ainsley squelched a laugh. So much for her attempt at subtlety. Claire didn't have a poker face. She was all in.

Hank leaned back in his chair and crossed his arms over his chest, a bemused expression on his lips. "I'll tell you what. You get that itinerary from Ainsley and I'll think about it."

Ryan drummed his fingers on the tabletop. "I could chaperone. It would be no problem, and then you'd know Claire wasn't getting into any trouble."

She shot him a look. If he shut up now she might still be able to salvage the whole thing. They should have strategized more before their arrival.

"Ainsley could go." Nicole's voice was bright and cheery.

Ainsley froze, then blinked slowly. She? Chaperoning a high-school trip?

"Our treat of course. You'd be doing us a favor. If Ryan's going, then someone has to keep an eye on him too." Nicole rested a hand on her son's forearm.

Ainsley nearly swallowed her own tongue. This wasn't the plan she'd come up with. It wasn't even close.

She drew in a breath, but before she could speak, Claire leapt from her chair, squealing.

"Thankyouthankyouthankyou!" She raced around the table giving them all half hugs.

Ainsley threw back the rest of her glass of wine in one long gulp. Then she reached for her purse. "Ryan, we should go so we won't be late for dinner."

It took effort to keep her smile plastered to her face as they said their good-byes, but she managed it.

Ryan owed her. Big-time.

CHAPTER TWENTY-THREE

As he drove to the restaurant Ryan imagined a free vacation. With Ainsley, on the beach, in a small bikini.

He couldn't keep the grin off his face. This was going to be excellent. His sister and her friends could go off and enjoy themselves while he and Ainsley *really* enjoyed themselves.

And the night was just starting. Wait until she saw what he had planned for dinner. He could definitely meet her in the middle. They'd go on a vacation, with no strings attached. Just some fun in the sun. He'd take her to a nice dinner. It was like all the good parts of a relationship without the scary parts. Like the word *relationship*. That one still gave him hives.

He only had to drive a few blocks before he pulled into the parking lot. Next to him in the passenger seat he saw Ainsley's jaw drop.

"I thought you didn't like French food?" Her voice was shaky.

He grinned and reached for her hand. "You like French food. And beach views and sommeliers and all that fancy shit."

The Lawhill challenge was over. He had to step up his game and take her on dates she'd enjoy, like the trendy new French restaurant she'd mentioned.

Her face lit up and she jumped out of the car before he made it around to her door. Then she clapped her hands, like a child.

"How did you get a reservation?"

He winked at her. "I have connections, remember?"

She grabbed onto his arm, snuggling close to him. "Well, thank you for using your connections for me."

He planted a kiss on the top of her head, letting her flowery scent surround him. Truth be told, he couldn't think of any better way to use them. Besides, it hadn't been anything too impressive. The bass guitarist for one of his bands worked in the kitchen as an assistant chef. He'd been confused but willing to help when Ryan asked to get on the reservation list.

Ainsley practically skipped up the walkway. Anticipation and satisfaction coursed through him. He'd done this. He'd made her this happy. And it had been so damn easy too.

"This would be a great place for Kate's bridal shower, don't you think?" She spun to face him.

He grimaced. "I have no opinion on Kate's bridal shower. Besides, you're the expert on those kinds of things."

She rolled her eyes and fell into step beside him. "But you're the bridesman. You get a say."

"Er, no. I don't get a say, because I don't want a say. And before you ask, I refuse to attend. But I am more than happy to arrange for the male strippers."

She snorted, but they'd reached the door and he pulled it open, holding it for her. Once she stepped inside he walked up to the host's stand and gave his name.

"Right this way." The suit-clad maître d' grabbed two menus off the stand and motioned into the dining room. Ainsley followed him and Ryan brought up the rear.

She gasped when they reached the table, next to floor-to-ceiling glass windows that looked out onto the water. In the far distance they could make out the Belmont lighthouse, which had stood guard since the late 1700s.

He stopped for a moment, watching her. Ainsley's cheeks were tinged pink with pleasure as her blue eyes scanned the restaurant, taking in their surroundings. She sat in the chair the maître d' pulled out for her, then grinned at Ryan when he took the seat opposite.

From across the table she grabbed his hands and squeezed. "Isn't this place amazing? It's so beautiful, so…"

She froze before she finished. *Romantic.* They both knew it was the next word out of her mouth.

Icicles of terror traveled up his spine and he distracted himself by scanning the open menu in front of him.

"So what do people eat on a fancy date at a fancy restaurant like this? A caveman like me needs to be educated."

She fell silent and he could see the disappointment in her face. He cursed himself. Why couldn't he just say it? What was wrong with a little romance? He'd taken her here on purpose, had gotten a thrill seeing her excitement. And yet labeling it threw him into an extreme panic. Ainsley understood, she had to. He'd never hidden who he was from her and she'd jumped in with eyes wide open.

* * *

The look on his face when she'd gotten to the word *romantic* made her heart hurt. But he'd taken her to a restaurant he knew she'd love and had introduced her to his family. They were going to the Bahamas together in a few months. Surely all of that meant something.

The minute the elevator doors pinged shut, Ryan pulled her into his muscular chest and lowered his mouth to hers. The kiss was slow and deep, full of feelings. Or it would have been, if Ryan were capable of feelings. She chided herself. That was mean, unfair. And yet it felt almost true.

Still, she closed her eyes and allowed herself to be swept away by sensation as his tongue languidly circled against hers.

God, he was good. She knew it was coming, knew he would kiss her the minute they got into the elevator and had a second of privacy. And she knew exactly what that kiss would feel like, how his arms would wrap around her, how her palms would brush the stubble on his neck and his chin. But still, the touch of his lips and the feel of his body reduced her knees to jelly. Even if he could be a commitment-phobic ass sometimes. It was what she'd signed on for, and she wasn't ready to give up yet.

The elevator doors pinged open again and he slowly eased her back and away from him, the palm of his hand resting on the small of her back until her feet came to rest firmly on the floor. Then he gave her that melting smile of his.

Her heart thumped rapidly, but she smoothed her hair and stepped out of the elevator into the hall in front of him. "We can stay at your place sometime. If you want."

Truth be told, she was a little curious about his apartment.

He gave a low chuckle. "Why would we go to my place when you have clean sheets and dishes and food in your refrigerator?"

Her nose wrinkled and she shot him a look over her shoulder. Was his loft really that bad? It struck her that he might not be joking about this, and the thought was followed by a needle of concern.

He winked. "Just kidding. But you do have a nicer place. And nicer sheets. Plus I hate cleaning, so yeah. I'm definitely happy to come over here. Anytime you want."

She gave him a wobbly smile, relieved.

He looped an arm around her waist, stopping her in the middle of the hall. Then he tugged her backward into him, until her back pressed into his chest. He buried his head in her hair and nuzzled her neck.

She giggled, a high-pitched sound, as her gaze darted through the hallway. She had neighbors. And they had peepholes.

She turned and kissed him hard on the mouth, then wiggled free and took another few steps in the direction of her apartment door. A few more feet and they'd be inside her apartment, where they could do whatever they wanted without the risk of prying eyes.

She slipped the key into the lock and turned. But before she could open the door, Ryan had a palm on her butt. The heat of his touch unleashed a tumult of need inside of her.

Quickly, she shoved the door open. There was a rustling noise, and she caught a flash of movement out of the corner of her eye. She shrieked involuntarily, jumping back. Her heartbeat surged frantically. Why was someone in her apartment?

Before she could begin to process, Ryan jerked her back and planted himself squarely in front of her. Protecting her, but also blocking her view of the sofa.

"Ryan?" The familiar masculine voice made her stomach drop in shock. Scott? He was supposed to be in Hong Kong… doing whatever it was that kept him working eighty hours a week. She'd never totally figured it out beyond the fact that his job involved stocks and finance and money.

She gripped the back of Ryan's shirt, anxiety flooding her veins, and steadied herself. After a few deep breaths that did nothing to quell her panic, she stepped out from behind him. She needed to find out why he was here. Now that she'd finally moved on, she wasn't about to let him drag her back into his cycle of hoping and waiting. Scott had used her, and she hadn't even been that into him. It was all so clear now, why hadn't she seen it sooner?

"Ainsley." Scott said it like a whisper or a sigh. He waited a beat before he stepped toward her, his hands coming to rest on her upper arms and his lips skimming her cheek.

She froze in confusion and shock. Her pulse thundered in her ears, but she couldn't will her limbs to move. What the hell was he doing here? She swallowed, nearly choked on her anger, and tried again.

Next to her, Ryan stood ramrod straight, his entire body tense. His jaw worked as he stared at her. Anger practically radiated off of him.

She abruptly broke away from Scott and strode into the kitchen, where she poured herself a glass of water. In several greedy gulps she swallowed it all. She tried to collect herself, willing her thoughts to coalesce. How dare her come here, and how dare he look at her that way?

Ryan followed her and stood on the other side of the kitchen island, his arms crossed over his chest, only the counter and her open laptop separating them. His body language was unmistakable: He was giving her enough space to handle Scott on her own, but he also wasn't going anywhere. He leaned forward on the counter, his eyes burning into her as he accidentally bumped an elbow against the laptop's track pad.

Scott slicked a hand over his blond hair, which he always gelled away from his face. Inwardly, Ainsley cringed as she remembered the crunch of his hair beneath her hands and the harsh alcoholic odor of his hair product.

She licked her lips nervously and took a step in his direction. He raised his eyes to hers, hope flashing through them.

"This isn't a good time, Scott." Her voice was strong and clear, in spite of the anxiety tumbling through her.

He shoved his hands into his pockets. "It's important. I promise, you'll want to hear what I have to say."

"Not right now." She was shaking her head. There was nothing he could say that she wanted to hear.

He raised an eyebrow. "Trust me. I know you don't have a reason to, but trust me. I've spent the last twenty-four hours on a plane because I have something I need to ask you."

Her heartbeat raced nervously as she glanced at his hands, still shoved in his pockets. *Something to ask you.* Her mouth went dry, her tongue thick. She'd waited so long for him to say that. This couldn't be it. This was nothing like she'd ever imagined. Plus, she didn't even want him here.

Scott glanced quickly at Ryan, his eyebrows scrunching briefly. "You don't mind, do you, Ry?"

Ryan was staring at the computer screen, his fists clenched at his sides.

His eyes had glazed over, fixed on a single point on the screen, but a muscle in his jaw twitched. Once, then twice.

Ainsley's breathing turned tight and shallow, a new kind of fear coming over her. What was Ryan thinking? What was he looking at?

He turned back to them, his expression suddenly blank. "Not at all. You two have things to talk about."

Her stomach twisted. *No!* She didn't want him to go. She needed him to stay with her.

Scott fidgeted with something in his pocket, and her blood pounded fast and hard. Incredulity lodged in her brain. He'd said he had to ask her a question. She'd waited years for this moment, and now that it might finally be here…

Her head screamed, her temples throbbing. It was wrong, all wrong. She didn't want this.

"I'm going. Good night, Ainsley." Ryan crossed the room and left through the door before she could unglue her tongue from the roof of her mouth, even as she trailed him into the living room. The sense of loss rocked her. She wanted him to stay. Scott was the one who needed to go.

When she turned back to Scott, he was down on one knee. Her heart dropped in trepidation. This was not how things were supposed to happen.

CHAPTER TWENTY-FOUR

Her face heated up as her knees trembled in indignation.

"What are you doing? Get up!" She turned her back to Scott and began to pace through the living room. Her chest was tight, as if all the oxygen had evaporated from the room.

"Ainsley." His voice was pleading, but she refused to face him. If she did, her outrage might become pure rage.

A second later Scott was beside her, tugging at her arm. "I'm sorry. You have every right to be mad. And I know this isn't how you wanted me to do it, so I'll wait, but only if you promise to give me a chance to prove myself."

Anger flashed through her, hot and sharp.

"You want me to give you a chance?" It came out as a squawk.

Scott dropped his gaze to his polished black dress shoes. She pictured Ryan's Converse and her chest began to ache with loss.

"This isn't how it works." She'd set to pacing again, the soft carpet muffling her footsteps. "You don't get to disappear then show up in my apartment and expect everything to go back to normal."

Her eyes burned with frustration. He'd abandoned her and left her to the ridicule of her family, their friends, and everyone else in the Point. What made him think he could propose and everything would be OK?

He spun her to face him and gripped her by the forearms. "Look, Ainsley. I know I broke us when I left. But I made a mistake. Hong Kong was a mistake. I came back for you and I want to make it right."

A sour taste rose in her throat. Their breakup no longer felt like a mistake to her. She'd never loved him, not the way she was supposed to. It had been like a play, a farce she'd somehow convinced herself was true. Now she knew it wasn't real and she wasn't about to make that mistake again. It had taken Ryan for her to understand how she should have felt about Scott from the beginning.

He pulled the box out of his pocket, his fingers wrapped around the dark-blue velvet. Her stomach dropped. She'd imagined that box so many times, but now that it was here?

"I can't." She tore her gaze from his hands and took a long step backward. How was she supposed to tell him how she really felt?

"Why? Is this because of him? Because of Ryan?" His eyebrows furrowed as he gestured to the door.

"No." Her tone was even and measured.

At least, it wasn't exactly because of Ryan. She'd learned things from him and there was no going back now.

Scott's face paled. "You're making a mistake."

White-hot anger coursed through her. She stalked to the door and jerked it open. "I already made a mistake. Our entire relationship was a mistake, one that I refuse to keep making. I want you to leave. And I want my key back."

"Ainsley, I can give you everything you want. The house, the life, the family…" He crossed the living room slowly and stopped in front of her.

Her throat thickened and it took all her effort to keep from crumpling to the floor. She lifted her hand and held the door open. So what if he'd bought her an engagement ring? Coming from Scott, it could never mean what it was supposed to. Of course she still wanted all of those things, she always would. She just didn't want them with him. Not anymore.

He pressed the metal key into her palm.

A tear spilled over, trailing down her cheek. She snatched her hand back and swiped at it furiously with her closed fist. Hadn't she cried enough over him already? Regret lodged in her chest. She'd wasted so much time on him.

"Please leave." She stood painfully still, resolute and determined. He hesitated for a second then stepped through the door. She closed it and locked the dead bolt behind him, dropping the key onto her turquoise console table.

Her hands began to shake violently. She managed to make it across the room and onto the sofa, where she propped her elbows on her knees and dropped her head into her hands. Emotion swirled through her, a jumble of loss and anger and grief.

She wanted the ring and everything it represented. She always had. But she didn't want it to come from Scott. The realization was painful, as acute as she imagined the death of a loved one might feel. And yet at the same time she felt an odd sense of freedom. For the first time in months, maybe years, she knew exactly who she was and what she wanted. And she was tired of settling.

She drew a deep breath into her lungs and held it, slowly exhaling a few seconds later. As she exhaled a rising sense of panic came over her.

She was a relationship person. As hard as she'd tried to fight it and as much as she'd tried to deny it, that was the truth. What was wrong so wrong about that?

Her pulse raced.

The problem was that she was falling for Ryan. She'd known what she was getting into from the beginning, and she'd coached herself to have reasonable expectations, but she couldn't help it.

Tears pricked her eyes. Ryan had never lied to her or deceived her. If anything, she'd been the one fooling herself, but now she realized she couldn't avoid the truth forever. She wanted a relationship, one that carried the possibility of marriage and a family. Not the immediate possibility, but a someday possibility.

In a split second her must-have list narrowed to one, single quality: a man who was so crazy in love with her that he couldn't stand the idea of not being married to her and not having kids with her.

Emotional exhaustion settled over her, bringing a heaviness that permeated her entire body. She curled into a ball on the sofa and pulled the cashmere throw on top of herself.

A lone question rattled through her mind: Was there any way Ryan could want that too?

* * *

The one before the One. The words had practically jumped off the computer screen and clobbered him over the head, triggering a profound feeling of injustice. She'd used him. He'd trusted her and she'd used him.

He pressed his foot harder on the gas pedal and let the wind whip through the car's open windows.

Ainsley's laptop had been open to some website with a background made up almost entirely of hearts, with a title that read "The One Before the One."

His blood had run cold. He was more than familiar with the phrase, plenty of exes had used it to refer jokingly to him in the past. Only it hadn't hurt when they'd said it.

His chest ached. This wasn't what he'd expected from Ainsley. He'd really thought that she had changed, and that he was changing too. While he wasn't ready for all the serious stuff, together they could have handled it.

Frustration at the unfairness of it all overwhelmed him, and he jerked the wheel left, veering sharply in the direction of Diver's. If he was the one before the one, at least he'd done his job. Ainsley would get exactly what she wanted: a ring, a house in the Point, a fancy wedding, a rich husband, perfect little blond doppelgangers. And what had he been expecting? Regret filled him. Whether it was Scott or someone else, Ainsley deserved all of those things. She deserved to be happy.

He gripped the wheel tighter as he gave in to resignation. More than anything, he wanted her to be happy. Trying to hold on to her and keep whatever was going on between them would be selfish.

Still, his throat burned. He reached for the radio and twisted the knob for the bass to full blast. Heavy metal thumped around him, but his muscles remained taut and tense. Fuck. Why was this so hard?

He slowed just enough to turn into the parking lot and carefully angled his Mustang into one of the small spaces. The last thing he needed tonight was a scratched door. He finally had his baby back, and he didn't plan on parting with her again anytime soon.

He stalked into the bar and folded his body onto one of the uncomfortable wooden stools at the far end.

"Whiskey. Neat." He slapped his credit card on the counter and the bartender collected it.

"What about me?" The voice next to him was a purr.

He braced himself and turned his head to the left to smile at Melanie. "Sure. What can I get for you?"

She licked her lips slowly. "Another sex on the beach, please."

To his surprise, her words did nothing for him. Not one thing.

With a sigh, he leaned his forearms on the table. He really needed that whiskey. The sight of Melanie's red lips forming the word *sex* should have been enough to make him rock hard. Instead, all he could picture was Ainsley and the rock in Scott's pants. Because even he knew there was an engagement ring in Scott's pocket.

The bartender placed the glass in front of him, and he threw the drink back, holding a finger up to signal for another. It would take at least three more to dull the sharp edge of the image of that ring.

The one before the One.

His shoulders tensed and he clenched his jaw. Wasn't that exactly the impression he tried to give? He was the fun guy, the fling, and he made sure everybody knew it.

The bartender poured the second shot into his glass, and he threw it back, relishing the burn in his throat. Yup, a few more of these and he'd be a hell of a lot better.

He signaled for a third drink and turned his attention to Melanie, who was staring at him with unnerving intensity.

He forced a smile. "How are things going with you, Melanie?"

She snaked a hand across his forearm, her fingernails clawing at him. "Better now that you're here."

He grunted. Sure. Whatever.

"You used to be good at this." She pouted, puffing out her lower lip.

He carefully extracted his arm from her grip. "Yup."

He had been good at this, the flirting, the foreplay, the chase. Suddenly it all seemed stupid and pointless.

"Is it that blonde chick? In the sparkly dress? Because I can make you forget all about her." She leaned closer and wrapped one hand around his neck, trying to angle his head in her direction.

He frowned and turned back to his drink, swirling the honey-colored liquor in his glass. In spite of himself, it brought back visions of Ainsley, the way her hair fell in messy tangles when they'd been at the B&B.

His lungs tightened. He couldn't do this right now. He should call a ride service and give himself some time to lick his wounds and get back out there. Because he would get back out there. He had to.

He shrugged. "Nah. I'm just having an off week."

"Good. Because I can tell you now, she's not your type."

Annoyance surged inside of him and he quirked an eyebrow at her. "Oh yeah? Then what is my type?"

She smiled wider, apparently immune to sarcasm. "Why me, of course. You might be a giant man slut, but you're my kind of giant man slut."

Her hand darted underneath the bar, in the direction of his crotch. He grabbed it, stopping her in midair.

"Did you just call me a giant man slut?" Recognition sliced through him. The whiskey had brought a nice haze to things, but he was nowhere close to drunk.

Her mouth fell open, but no words came.

He dropped her hand as if it were burning hot. "You attacked my car."

She grimaced. "I don't know what you're talking about."

He threw a few bills on the counter and stood abruptly, knocking the stool flat onto the floor. Other guests turned to stare at them, but he didn't care.

"You. Smashed. My. Car." He ground the words out.

She glared.

"Melanie, why would you do that to my car?"

"Why did you pick her?" She stood and faced him, planting her hands on her hips.

His heart punched against his ribs. Had he picked Ainsley? What had happened between them was only supposed to be for fun. He couldn't give her the things she wanted, not like Scott could.

Melanie was right, though. In spite of himself, he'd fallen for Ainsley. He'd picked her.

With a sharp shake of his head, he spun on his heel and walked out of the bar. He'd call for a ride outside.

When it came to Ainsley he had only one option now. He had to get over it and move on.

CHAPTER TWENTY-FIVE

Ainsley had fallen asleep staring at the phone, desperately hoping for Ryan to call her back.

The chime of her phone jerked her back to consciousness. Her eyes scanned the living room as she stretched stiffly, trying to work out the kinks she'd developed sleeping on the sofa.

Slowly, the events from the night before came filtering back to her. With them came a dull throbbing in her sternum and a vague sense of nausea. For a second she was tempted to bury her head in the throw pillow and cocoon herself in the cashmere throw, but she forced herself to reach for the phone. Whoever it was, Scott or Ryan or her job or her friends, it was time she started owning her decisions. The only way she'd ever really be happy was if she dug deep, figured out what it was she wanted, and went for it.

Momentarily filled with determination, she glanced at the screen of the phone, then frowned at the unfamiliar number. The area code was Belmont, but she didn't have it programmed as a contact.

Unknown: Hey, Ainsley. This is Brigitte. I know you don't have to go in to work until ten, but I have something really important I need to talk to you about. Anyway, can you meet me for coffee?

In spite of herself, her heart squeezed a little in disappointment. Not Ryan. And she really needed to talk to him.

With a sigh, she pushed herself into a sitting position and typed.

Ainsley: Sure. Just need to take a shower. Java Java in the Point ok?

She wasn't ready to face everyone at Little Ray's. Not before she had a chance to talk to Ryan. The thought of him brought a fresh wave of pain. Why wouldn't he return her call? She was aching to talk to him even though she wasn't entirely sure what she'd say yet.

Brigitte: Sure. See you in 45 minutes.

Instead of getting up and heading for the shower, she stared at the phone. She had to tell Ryan what had happened with Scott, that she'd realized she didn't love him and maybe never had. Although she'd avoid the word *love*. She had a feeling that might put Ryan into panic mode.

It rang six times, her anxiety ratcheting with each ring, before it clicked over to voice mail. She swallowed, trying to clear the lump from her throat.

"I, uh, just wanted to tell you that right after you left I asked

Scott to leave and got my key back. I know last night was awkward, and I'd really like to talk to you."

Before she could ramble any further, she punched the off button and took a bracing breath. There. She'd opened the door to communication. Now all Ryan had to do was step through.

Her stomach twisted. She had to tell him how she felt. At least then, whether he wanted her or not, she'd know. The casual hookup thing wasn't going to work for her, and she owed it to herself to admit that.

The phone in her hand chirped, making her jump. She looked at the screen.

Ryan: Sorry, tied up at work. Everything ok?

Her anger flamed hotter. After everything, the least he could do was call her back. And yet underneath her indignation was a flicker of hope. She just couldn't help it.

Ainsley: Last night was weird and now I'm not sure what to say to you. I don't want things to be weird between us too. I asked Scott to leave, he gave my key back, we're not getting back together.

Her heart thudded in her chest as she waited. Please let him understand how much she wanted him.

Ryan: Not because of me, I hope. I want you to be happy.

Her face heated in outrage. What the hell was that supposed to mean?

She typed, then stared at the words.

Ainsley: What if you make me happy?

Before she could press send, she backtracked, erasing one letter at a time. Her palms began to sweat. She couldn't just put it out there like that. She needed to broach it carefully, give the words some finesse.

Ainsley: Can I talk to you in person?

She stared at the screen anxiously as the seconds ticked by.

Ryan: I'm in recording sessions all day, but I'll see you tonight, right? At Griffin and Beth's? I know Mabel is looking forward to it.

A bitter taste flooded her mouth. Babysitting. Not exactly the place for a real conversation. How dare he avoid her?

Indignation flared inside of her.

Ainsley: Before that. Text me after your meetings and I'll meet you.

She wasn't letting him off the hook that easily. This was something they both had to face, whether he wanted to or not. She deserved that much from him.

Ryan: K.

She stared at the one letter for a long moment, her stomach churning. *Fine. Be that way.*

Ryan was awful when it came to feelings, and they both knew it, but she couldn't just let go of him without trying. She had a feeling she'd regret that forever. In spite of everything they'd been happy. She wanted to believe they still could be.

As she attempted to fight the sense of foreboding, Ainsley pushed herself off the sofa and headed for the shower. She'd be anxious and sick to her stomach all day, but she still had a bride to meet.

Forty minutes later she entered the coffeehouse, corporate and sterile compared to the lively bustle of Little

Ray's. Brigitte sat at a corner table with two cups in front of her.

Ainsley wound her way through the tables and slid into the seat across from her old high-school classmate. The dark circles under Brigitte's eyes spawned a pinprick of worry.

"Are you OK?"

Brigitte slid one of the coffee mugs over to her. She took a deep breath. "Thanks for meeting me. I was just wondering, how did you do it?"

Confusion crept up on her. "Do what?"

Brigitte pressed her lips together in a tight, anxious line. "How did you ignore everyone's judgment and do what you wanted to do? How did you decide not to get married?"

A bark of laughter burst out of her before she clapped a hand over her mouth, immediately regretting it. The question had caught her completely off guard and was more or less untrue. Their breakup had hardly been her choice. Scott had announced his move to Hong Kong and then gotten on the plane, without her.

She frowned thoughtfully. Although, as of last night, it had become her choice. "I guess it kind of happened?"

She reached for the coffee, taking care to blow on the surface of the steaming liquid, making an effort to compose herself. "Why do you ask?"

Brigitte didn't need to know she was a muddle of turmoil today.

"I don't know if I want to get married." Brigitte's voice was barely louder than a whisper.

Ainsley startled. "You don't know?"

"Actually, I'm pretty sure I don't want to get married." Brigitte mustered a wan smile.

Ainsley froze, her hands wrapped around her coffee cup. She was filled with sympathy for Brigitte. "You don't want to get married."

She repeated the words slowly, taking care to make sure she was really hearing what Brigitte was saying, not just projecting her own issues.

Brigitte stared at the tabletop and tucked a strand of hair behind her ear. "No. I don't."

"OK." But why was Brigitte telling her this? She felt for the other woman, but what could she do about it?

Brigitte's shoulders slumped as she relaxed back against her seat. "I had a feeling you'd understand. I just can't figure out how I'm supposed to tell everyone."

Her spine prickled in apprehension. Did that make her the Point's expert on jilting and being jilted?

She managed a shrug. "I'd start by telling your fiancé. Then your parents." This was Belmont, the news would spread quickly.

Brigitte blew out a long breath. "Yeah. I need to get up the courage to do it though."

"I don't know that it's one of those things you ever feel ready for. I think you just have to get in there and do it." She knew what it was to be ghosted on. Scott hadn't had the balls to tell her where they stood, and she'd been too scared to press. The memory of her own complacency angered her. Well, she wasn't making that mistake again.

The tight lines on Brigitte's face eased slightly. "I didn't know who else to ask and I knew you wouldn't judge me, not like other people would. I feel like we grew up thinking that we'd get married and settle in the Point, but now that I'm actually an adult and right on the verge of that, it doesn't seem so exciting anymore. I don't want that to be the only thing I've accomplished when I reach the age of thirty."

Ainsley gave a cautious nod. She knew that feeling. Post-Scott, her life had felt oddly empty and inadequate. She'd spent the last few years planning weddings for other people and waiting for her own turn. Now she realized that wasn't enough. It was time for her to get her own life.

Brigitte reached across the table and squeezed her hand. "So you'll help me not get married?"

"Absolutely." She found herself grinning at Brigitte. Brett would kill her, but she needed a new job anyway. With or without Ryan, her reinvention must continue.

* * *

"I don't understand you." Kate glared at him from her side of the sofa.

Ryan shrugged. "So what else is new?"

She gripped him by both shoulders and shook him gently. "I'm not blind. I can see that you're feeling something. Why don't you just tell me what it is?"

He eased out of her grasp and stood, fighting the dejection that threatened to consume him. "I promise you, I'm fine. This was inevitable, and I think it's for the best that we're pulling the plug now."

She gave a groan of exasperation and chucked a pillow in his direction. "Don't be such a bullheaded man-child. Sit. Talk about your feelings."

He pretended to wretch, careful not to show her just how miserable he felt. This wasn't what he wanted at all, but it had to be done.

"If Ainsley told you she doesn't want to marry Scott, she doesn't want to marry Scott. As her friend I think it's very obvious that she wasn't happy with him and that she is happy with you. There's a real possibility here."

He squared his shoulders and looked her right in the eye, ignoring the painful clenching of his stomach. "But Ainsley does want to get married, right? Someday?"

Kate hesitated.

"Exactly. We all know Ainsley wants to get married and have kids, the whole shebang."

Kate threw her hands up in the air. "So what? That's what a lot of people want. It's not weird! You act like she just told you she wants to have a threesome with a unicorn."

He couldn't help it, he laughed. So hard he nearly choked. It was a relief to feel something other than despair.

"See?" Kate stood and crossed her living room to poke him in the shoulder. "Marriage is not unicorn sex. Doesn't that help put it in context? You might actually want to get married and have a family one day."

He blew out a breath. It wasn't that he thought marriage was weird or forbidden or gross or a fate worse than death.

He just knew that it wasn't for him. Or he was scared that it would turn out not to be for him and that wasn't a risk he could take, not when he cared about someone. His gut twisted. And he really did care about her. Which was why he had to do this now, before his Lawhill side came raring to life and he screwed things up. He knew what it was to be abandoned and he wouldn't put anyone else through that.

"You're right. Marriage is not unicorn sex. You want it and James wants it and Ainsley wants it. I don't think there's anything wrong with that. I just know that it isn't for me, not now and not ever."

She stared at him for a moment, her mouth hanging open.

"But how do you know?" she finally asked.

He couldn't even begin to explain to Kate. It was all too raw, especially now.

He looped an arm around her shoulder and guided her back to the sofa. "Trust me, I know."

He thought he'd come to terms with that, but for the first time he was starting to wonder. No, he told himself. This would be hard, but it was for the best. He had to be strong, not selfish.

Kate rested her head on his shoulder. "What are you going to do about babysitting for Mabel?"

His stomach twisted. Just thinking about it brought fresh pangs of worry.

"I'm going. I promised Mabel and Griffin. Plus it's better if we all get back to normal as soon as possible."

Maybe if he said it enough times, it would come true. Because he was trying to ignore the part of himself that was desperate to see Ainsley.

"Does this mean you don't care if you're being a stubborn idiot and I don't understand you at all?"

"Exactly." He reached with his free hand to pat her on the head. "That's exactly what it means. Don't worry, in a few weeks it will be like this never happened at all."

And just like that he descended back into hopelessness. Not that he'd ever let his friends catch on.

CHAPTER TWENTY-SIX

Ainsley had pulled up to Griffin's thirty minutes earlier, at the time she and Ryan had agreed. She'd sat there, biting her nails and fuming. She deserved more than this, a ten-minute chat in a car before they were expected to entertain a five-year-old. Why was Ryan treating her this way? What she wanted more than anything was for them both to come clean about their feelings and reach some sort of understanding. And yet she was starting to believe Ryan would be incapable of that.

When he finally pulled up ten minutes late, she slammed her own driver-side door and climbed into his passenger seat.

Then she sat in the passenger seat of Ryan's Mustang with her gaze fixed forward. Anxiety paralyzed her. She couldn't think where to begin.

He cleared his throat, causing her stomach to jump.

"I'm sorry," he murmured despondently.

She bit her lip and willed the tears to stay away. Instead she wrung her hands. If he was sad too, then why was he doing this?

"I think you're the best. Really, the best. If I could be in a relationship with anyone, I would want it to be you. But it's because I care about you that I know we can't keep moving forward. Last night kind of snapped me back to reality and made me realize that we're fooling ourselves. I know you and I know that you can't do casual forever. That wouldn't be fair to you, you deserve more." He paused and sucked in a ragged breath.

She reluctantly peeked at him then and found that he'd tilted his head back against the headrest, a pained look on his face. That reduced her back to pure sadness, the anger boiling off in a mere second.

In a flash his eyes were open and he was staring straight at her, his gaze intense. "If we keep doing this I'm going to fall in love with you. I can't fall in love with you, because I know that the things you want for your future aren't in the cards for me. I'll want to be able to give them to you, but I won't be able to, and seeing how that hurts you will rip me apart."

Her breath caught in her throat, anguish tearing through her. *Why?* It wasn't like she was asking for a promise of a guarantee for the future, just the chance to see where things took them.

"How do you know that you'll never want those things?" Her voice cracked.

He closed his eyes and pinched the bridge of his nose, as if in physical pain. "I just do."

It felt like her heart was ripping in two. She couldn't get out of the car and away from the conversation fast enough.

"Fine." It was all she could say without her voice quaking. She yanked the door handle open and practically tumbled out of the car. It took a second for her to regain her balance and then she was booking it in the direction of the front door.

She clenched her fists at her side and took a deep breath before she knocked on the door. She'd promised Beth and Griffin she'd babysit Ryan while he babysat Mabel. Hard as it might be, she couldn't back out now.

* * *

Beth and Griffin had left twenty minutes before, but Ainsley still hadn't come out of the bathroom. He could hear her sniffling inside, which made his chest ache.

Fuck. He'd made her cry. Crying women were bad enough, but crying Ainsley? Every muscle in his body tensed with the desire to burst in there and hold her, soothe her. It had been so much worse than he expected, so much more agonizing. Why was doing the right thing so hard?

"Ryan, do you want to share my blue play dough?" He and Mabel sat at the kitchen table, several mounds of colored play dough sitting in front of her. Beth had made it from scratch, of course.

He pasted a grin to his face and forced his attention to Mabel. "Thanks, May, blue is my favorite color."

She broke off a piece and handed it to him. "I thought so."

"Oh yeah?"

She nodded. "Yup. Cuz you're a boy and boys like blue."

The door to the bathroom creaked open and he found himself clenching the ball of play dough tightly in his fist. His heart hammered in his chest.

Ainsley walked carefully into the kitchen and took the seat at the table farthest from him.

"Hi, Ainsley!" Mabel smashed a fist down on top of her play-dough pile, flattening it.

"Hi, sweetie." Ainsley's expression was tender and wistful as she watched Mabel play.

This. This was why he couldn't press forward blindly, as if the future didn't matter.

Mabel leaned over and kissed Ainsley on the cheek. "You smell good."

"Thank you, May. That's very nice of you to say." Ainsley gingerly picked up a piece of play dough and began to roll it into little balls.

"That's why you shouldn't be sad. 'Cuz you look just like a princess, and princesses shouldn't be sad because they meet Prince Charming and live happily ever after."

His breath caught in his throat. *Shit.* Leave it to a five-year-old to twist the knife.

Ainsley went silent, and he was painfully aware of the seconds as they ticked by.

"I think maybe princesses are just princesses and they don't need a prince charming. Maybe they can rescue themselves and live happily ever after anyway." Ainsley stacked the little balls on top of each other, carefully keeping her eyes away from him.

His throat was raw and painful. Did she really believe that? Or did she just want Mabel to believe?

Mabel gave a serious nod. "Probably."

And that one word brought the chaos of his emotions into sharp contrast. Ainsley was going to be one hell of a mom. If he really cared about her, he wouldn't stand in her way.

* * *

Ainsley stood outside the door to Mabel's room and cautiously peeked inside. For the most part she'd stayed out of the way and let the two of them interact, but she felt obligated to check in on occasion. As painful as it was to see him, she'd made a promise to Griffin and Beth.

Ryan sat cross-legged on the floor, decked out in a feather boa and a rhinestone tiara. Mabel held a mirror up to his face, giving Ainsley a glimpse of his reflection.

"See how pretty you look?" Mabel crooned.

Blue eye shadow was smeared above his eyelids and all along his forehead, while his cheeks were striped magenta with blush. The sight should have made her laugh, but instead her stomach just ached.

"Very beautiful. How did you do that?" Ryan's deep voice carried into the hallway.

"I used magic. I'm your fairy godmother."

"Oh, well, thank you. I'm lucky to have such a talented fairy godmother," Ryan said.

Curiosity got the best of her and she ducked her head around the corner one more time. Ryan sat in the middle of the room with his back to the open door and Mabel curled onto his lap. Her heart squeezed and she retreated back into the hallway, where they couldn't see her.

She sunk to sitting, gathered her knees closer to her chest and fought the tears that threatened to spill over. Why couldn't he see it? Underneath his sarcasm and his jokes and pranks, Ryan was sweet. He was more than capable of watching Mabel, even without her here. He just preferred to let them all think he was irresponsible. Why?

She took a deep breath and pushed herself up onto her feet. It was time to get control of herself. He'd made his decision and there was nothing she could do about it. She squared her shoulders and headed to the bathroom.

To her dismay, splashing her face with cold water did nothing to alleviate the hard pit that had formed in her stomach.

Stupid, stubborn asshole. *I'll want to be able to give them to you, but I won't be able to.* The only person he was fooling was himself. He might be determined to cling to this idea that he was someone other people couldn't rely on, but she was sick of perpetuating the myth. She was done enabling his Peter Pan complex. Whether he wanted marriage and kids and commitment wasn't her problem anymore. Hanging around and watching him with May was like a slow kind of torture. She had to get out of here.

Determination rose in her chest, and before she could change her mind she threw open the door from the bathroom to the hallway and marched into Mabel's room. "I just got a call from work and there's an emergency. A wedding emergency. I need to go immediately."

Ryan's eyes went wide. "But..."

"You've got this."

Mabel twisted in his lap and reached to pat his cheek. "Yeah, Princess Ryan. You got this."

His mouth hung open.

Ainsley's jaw clenched. "Yeah, Princess Ryan. You got this."

His cheeks seemed to redden underneath the makeup Mabel had applied, but she couldn't be entirely sure. "But Griffin and Beth…"

She waved a hand dismissively. "Don't worry. I'll text them and explain. And I'll tell them what a good job you're doing. Just remember, Mabel needs to brush her teeth and change into her pj's before eight thirty. She can choose three stories before bed. Then lights out, and her night-light is right next to the bed."

His eyes darted wildly around the room.

"Ryan."

His gaze snapped back to her face.

"I'm not messing with you. You can do this." She tried to soften the hard edge to her voice. It was time for some tough love. What he wanted in his life was for him to decide, but she couldn't sit here and watch him interact with Mabel. It filled her with a delusional mixture of hope and longing.

He grimaced. "I guess I don't really have a choice, do I?"

"Exactly."

She turned then so he wouldn't see the pain etched on her face. Getting out of there wouldn't erase her misery, but it might help her stop imagining the future. From now on, she had to remember that Ryan's place in her life was as a friend and nothing else.

CHAPTER TWENTY-SEVEN

Ryan bounced his leg and tried to focus on the music pulsing from the sound stage in the studio.

The sound engineer shot him a glare, making him freeze. Yeah, he was driving himself crazy today too.

From the other side of the glass partition, Lee slung the guitar strap off of his shoulder. "It doesn't sound right."

Ryan leaned to the microphone and pressed the button so the band members could hear him. "What are you talking about? It sounds great from here."

Lee trudged to the door dividing them and yanked it open. "Nope. It sounds like shit. Not enough pent-up emotion, too much anger without the angst underlying it."

Angst. Ryan swallowed a sigh. These last few days he'd felt like the king of angst and it made him want to punch himself in the face.

Damon, the band member with the face tattoos, stalked

out behind Lee, jostling him as he forced his way through the doorway.

"Everything's off today. This sucks."

A sudden burst of energy hit Ryan, causing him to bolt up from his chair. "Stop being a bunch of fucking whiners and get your shit together."

Lee blinked at him in shock.

Damon pointed a finger right at his chest. "If anyone's moping it's you. You're bringing the mood down, man."

His shoulders slumped. That was true. No matter how hard he tried he couldn't get Ainsley out of his mind. It was like a slide show of torture, starting with Ainsley in her sparkly dress and strappy heels, then with ruffled bed-head at the bed and breakfast, followed by her ass in yoga pants, and ending with her back as she darted down the stairs at Griffin and Beth's. It had been nearly a week and he hadn't seen her since the babysitting gig.

Nervous energy coursed through him. He wanted to do something, anything, to fix things with Ainsley. But he also knew he couldn't. No matter how much the separation sucked for him, he couldn't do that to her.

He shrugged and held his hands up, palms out, in a gesture of surrender. "You're right, guys. I'm an unfocused dick and you deserve better. I promise I'm trying to get my head right, it's just proving to be more challenging than I expected."

To his surprise, Damon clapped a hand on his shoulder. "Female problems?"

He nodded, not trusting himself to speak.

"It took me a long time to learn that my mama was right

when she advised me to just say yes and do whatever my old lady wants. I keep her happy and she keeps me happy, you know what I mean?" He winked.

The hair on the back of his neck stood on end. It wasn't all about sex for him, no matter what other people thought. The truth of it was, he didn't have what it would take to keep Ainsley happy.

"Um, yeah. Sure. Thanks for the advice." He glanced at his watch. It was 1:00 p.m. "Why don't you guys take a break and come back in an hour?"

They paid for the studio by the day, so as much as he wanted to cut bait and go home to relax with a beer, they couldn't afford that. Plus, his mom's benefit was tomorrow, which gave them slightly more than twenty-four hours to lay down three tracks. They had to stay on schedule.

The drummer wandered into the sound booth, looking dazed and stoned as usual. "What's up?"

"We're going to lunch while Ryan pulls his head of his ass." Lee stepped toward the door that led into the main office and propped it open. "Hurry up."

Ryan squared his shoulders. He wasn't quite sure how to do it, but Lee was right. He needed to get his head of his ass.

* * *

Ainsley clicked another window on the desktop and glanced nervously at the door. Somehow she'd managed to avoid Brett all morning, but that luck couldn't continue forever.

She skimmed the bullet points on the web page. After requirements it listed a bachelor's degree, three to five years of work experience, and a passion for success.

Passion for success? Check. Maybe applying to MBA programs wouldn't be as daunting as she'd expected.

Then she saw it. Impressive GRE scores. Her heart sank. A test? She hated taking tests and always had. Which, come to think of it, she'd probably have to do a lot of in graduate school.

She sighed and clicked the browser window closed, then picked up the legal pad sitting next to her keyboard.

She'd spent a good hour this morning researching jobs. So far the only three that had appealed to her were Realtor, blogger, and home staging. She tapped the desk with her pen. None of those felt right. For the first time in her life she felt compelled to do something to make the world a better place. The problem was she had absolutely no qualifying skills or experience for that kind of gig. An employer would take one look at her event-planning résumé and laugh her out of the office.

From behind her, the doorknob clicked and she braced herself. Avoiding Brett forever was impossible.

She pasted a smile on her face and spun in the desk chair.

He was red-faced and waved a piece of paper in the air.

"Did you know about this?" Spit flew from his mouth and she tried not to flinch.

"About what?"

"Brigitte Meyer is canceling her wedding!" His cheeks grew redder by the minute.

She crossed her legs. "I did."

For a second, it looked like his eyes would bug out of his head. "What? When? How could you not tell me this?"

A vein in his throat pulsed.

She smoothed a hand over her skirt. "It was her news to tell. I wanted her to have a chance to discuss it with her family and her fiancé. It would have been indiscreet of me to go around sharing that information before she was prepared to talk about it."

"Unbelievable." He threw his hands up in the air. "What kind of a reputation is that for the Meridien? We might as well start referring to you as the un-wedding planner."

The Un-Wedding Planner. Considering the past few months of her life, that probably was the right job for her. Too bad it didn't actually exist.

She forced the corners of her mouth upward. "It sounds like we have a space on our calendar, and we get to keep the deposit as well as the food and beverage minimums."

The hotel wouldn't lose that much money from the cancellation, not if they played their cards right. "Maybe we should consider throwing a charity event in its place."

She clasped her hands on her lap and waited for his response.

Go big or go home. It was time to pursue the new priorities in her life.

CHAPTER TWENTY-EIGHT

Ryan let himself through the front door and was immediately greeted by wagging pit bulls. Hippo leaned on him hard enough to make him stumble for a second. Then she turned her head up to him, a giant grin plastered across her face.

"All right, chunky lady." He patted her a few times, while Gremlin wiggled circles around him.

"Ryan?" His mom called from the kitchen.

"Coming!" Both dogs followed him through the hallway and into the kitchen, where they sat and looked at him expectantly.

He gaped as he took in the state of the kitchen. Large plastic containers covered every available surface.

His mom's face was flushed and she pushed her bangs off of her forehead. "Great. You can load these up and get them over to Little Ray's for me."

His gaze scanned the boxes in the kitchen. No way they

would all fit in his Mustang. "Mom, you know I don't have the man van anymore, right?"

Her mouth fell open. "Shit. I didn't even think about that."

"Don't worry. I'll figure it out. You don't mind if I borrow your car, do you?" He reached for her keys on the peg by the back door. The boxes would fit in her SUV, saving him multiple trips.

"When you get there, find Ainsley and ask her where she wants you to put all the auction items. I have them labeled by section and I can lay them out on the tables when I get there, or she can do it if she prefers. I know how she has a specific image in her mind when it comes to this kind of thing."

He gulped, the sound of her name like a slap. Ainsley. He'd known she'd be there tonight, he just hadn't planned on running into her yet.

His mom's eyes narrowed as she examined him. "What happened?"

He dropped his gaze to his feet and lifted one hand to rub the back of his neck. It was impossible to hide his misery from his mom. She was tuned in to that kind of thing.

She stepped closer and put a finger under his chin, tilting his head until he was looking straight at her. His face heated and he sidestepped her. He couldn't help but feel ashamed.

"You know what happened, don't make me talk about it," he muttered.

She planted her hands on her hips and spoke gently but firmly. "You're not getting away from me that easily."

His throat grew tighter and he let out a sound that was half moan, half growl. It felt like he would split open, and he could hardly stand it anymore.

"I can't date Ainsley, I can't date anybody. I'm damaged goods."

She sucked in a breath, as if he'd slapped her. Then she stepped forward and wrapped her arms around him.

"Of course you're not damaged goods, why would you ever think that?"

He tried to laugh, but instead the anguish garbled it into a choking sound. "Because of Dad, mom. He left you and he left me. He wasn't meant to be a husband or a father, and I don't think I am either."

"Oh, honey!" He could hear her crying now, which hurt his heart. "Your father's issues are not your issues. Trust me, you are so very different from your father."

He sniffled. She was just saying that to make him feel better.

She squeezed harder. "It's true. I see you all the time and wonder how such a wonderful boy came from the two of us. You think you're tough and you are strong, I see it, but underneath you have such a big heart. Is that why you've kept women at arm's length? You were worried you'd love someone and they'd abandon you the way your father did?"

Her words pierced him like an arrow, creating a gaping hole in his soul. *Holy shit.* All this time he thought he'd been protecting other people, but had it really been about protecting himself?

"But what if I do that too? What if I think I love someone

or I want to get married or have a kid…" He trailed off. He'd never discussed any of this with her before, too scared it would reopen her old wounds.

She gave a dry chuckle and patted him on the back. "Trust me, sweetie. Your dad never thought he wanted to get married or have a child. It all just kind of happened, and then when it did, he still didn't want those things. It wasn't about you or me, it was about him."

But how could someone decide they just didn't want their child?

And then it hit him. His mom was right. That was the very thing that made him so different from his father.

"Wow." It was all he could manage. Everything was so different from what he'd always thought.

She rested her head on his shoulder, her mom-scent reassuring him. "I'm so sorry. I should have known this is what you were thinking or how you were feeling. I just figured…"

"It's OK, Mom." And it was. They'd both dealt with things the best way they knew how. It was time for him to grow up and take responsibility for his own emotions, his future, and his happiness. He'd thought that was what he was doing all along, but now he finally saw the truth.

A single shred of hope lodged inside of him and began to sprout.

He had to talk to Ainsley, now. There was no more time to waste.

* * *

Ainsley hustled through the kitchen of Little Ray's with her clipboard firmly in hand. "How are you doing with the food prep?"

She knew Beth didn't actually need any help, but she needed to make sure her time line was up to date.

Beth looked up from the cutting board in front of her. A lock of her short, curly hair fell over her forehead and she grinned. "Doing great! Cold hors d'oeuvres are all prepared and in the refrigerator. Next up is the cheese tray."

Cheese. Ainsley nearly drooled at the mention.

Beth lifted one eyebrow. "How about you? How are you doing?"

Ainsley's skin prickled under the scrutiny of Beth's concerned glance. "Great. Just great. Went to spin class this morning, had my green smoothie, and I've already put away three cups of espresso."

It was only 4:00 p.m. and they had a long night in front of them, which meant she'd resorted to the big guns caffeinewise.

Beth's forehead furrowed. "Do you want a snack? I could whip something up."

"No, no. Don't worry about me." She waved a hand. She was far too busy, and her stomach tied in too many knots, to eat. Tonight was a big night, for Nicole and Hippo and MABB. After a lot of arm-twisting, Brett had agreed to her idea of a charity dinner at the Meridien, and tonight was an important step in her learning process. She was good at what she did and she wanted to do more useful work, give back. This might be her chance to combine the two.

Her heart lurched. Plus, it would be the first time she'd seen

Ryan since last week. An uneasy kind of panic settled over her.

"Are you sure? You look kind of…I don't know, off." Beth had put down the knife and taken a few steps closer to her.

"Off?" Her voice was sharp with alarm. She couldn't afford to look off, not tonight.

Beth gave a wan smile. "I didn't mean it like you look bad, you just seem tired? Nervous? I'm worried about you."

Her heart filled. No matter what, she had friends who cared about her and she'd never take that for granted.

She closed the few steps between them and grabbed Beth into a hug, ignoring the bits of food that dotted the front of her friend's apron. She'd have to change for the party anyway, and this dress was already slated for the dry cleaner's.

"I love you."

Beth squeezed her in return. "I love you too. I hope you know that Griffin and I see all the work you've done here for this event and we're so impressed. Everyone who knows what you've put into this is so proud of you."

Her spine tingled. Did that everyone include Ryan?

She stepped away from Beth and straightened the belt of her dress. There was too much work to be done.

CHAPTER TWENTY-NINE

Ainsley reached out and steadied herself on the banquet table with one hand. Her head was spinning, the stupid result of too much caffeine and not enough food, but she didn't have time to stop now. The guests would start arriving in thirty minutes, and while the food and the auction items and the flowers were all laid out perfectly, she knew from experience that anything could happen. Just when you let your guard down disaster would strike.

Across the room, Kate leaned out from the kitchen and shot her a thumbs-up sign. She wore a white apron over her cocktail dress. The minute she'd walked through the door she and James had volunteered to help Beth in the kitchen. He was back there too, white apron over his button-down shirt and suit slacks.

Her mouth stretched into a grin and she gave Kate a thumbs-up in return. Still, it took her a moment to push herself up from the table.

Maybe she did need a snack. As she was pivoting on her heel, the bell attached to the front door rang. She peeked over her shoulder and caught sight of Ryan, looking mouthwatering in a dark, slim-cut suit.

Her mouth went dry with a combination of panic, pain, and longing. God, he was handsome. Why did he have to be so handsome? She turned her back on him, determined to keep herself busy with something until the rest of the crowd arrived. It was too hard to look at him, it caused too much regret and doubt to swirl through her mind.

She reminded herself for the hundredth time that there was nothing else she could have done. She'd been herself and she'd asked for what she wanted. It was natural to be disappointed, but this was out of her hands. That realization had to be enough. Somehow she would learn to accept it.

Suddenly, she was dizzy again, the room spinning in front of her eyes. Before she could grab the table the room went dark.

The first thing that came to her was the smell. Ryan's strong, clean scent filled her nose. Her heart soared hopefully, then crashed back down again, all in the span of a second. She was probably imagining it. She tried to open her eyes, but her eyelids were too heavy. There was heat on her cheek, along with a slight pressure.

"Ainsley? Are you OK?" Her head was tilted, her body at an angle. Under her back was a strong barrier.

It took effort to force her eyes open and she found herself looking directly into Ryan's face. In spite of herself, the hope revived.

His mouth relaxed into a grin and he let out a whoosh of breath. "Thank God."

She tried to lift her head, to sit up, but the wooziness returned.

Ryan brought his other hand to her cheek, holding her face in his hands. "Don't move, OK? Beth's getting you a snack and Kate's getting you some water."

Griffin, James, Nicole, Sarah, and a few other people hovered only two or three feet behind him, forming a circle around them. She realized then that she was sitting on his lap, propped against him.

Her face heated and she wiggled, trying to right herself. She couldn't be sitting on his lap in front of all these people. His nearness was bliss, but they'd broken up. Fresh disappointment filled her stomach at the memory.

"Hey." He stroked her cheek with the back of his hand. "Stay still, OK? You fell pretty hard."

He peered at her intently. She swallowed, fighting the sadness. He couldn't keep looking at her like this. Not if she was supposed to move on and get over him.

Then he leaned closer, his breath warm against her ear. "You're not pregnant, are you?"

She stiffened, then raised her arm to shove him. Was he freaking nuts? He had no business asking her that, especially not here in front of all these people.

He caught her hand in midair and squeezed it in his larger one, the gesture unexpectedly tender.

"No. Are you insane?" she hissed, warring between anger and affection. She glanced around wildly but found that everyone continued staring at her anxiously. Good. Then they couldn't hear the whispered conversation.

"Um, if you guys don't mind finishing the setup? I'll be fine in a few, and the show must go on!" She managed her cheeriest tone. The way this conversation with Ryan was going, she was half tempted to punch him and didn't need a handful of rapt witnesses.

"What's wrong with you?" she demanded.

His face blanched, then his mouth twisted in grim determination. "Sorry, I'm not good at this whole baring my soul thing. Um. OK. So maybe you guessed this, but I realized I have some baggage. My dad left my mom when I was little, left me, and I never talk about it with anybody because it sucks and there's nothing I can do to change it. I don't need people psychoanalyzing me and reading into things."

Sympathy consumed her. Ryan seemed so assured, so confident. She'd thought he was happy.

She lifted her hand to his cheek. "I'm so sorry, Ryan."

He nuzzled lightly into her hand before he continued. "Well, maybe I did need people psychoanalyzing me. All this time I figured I'd just stay away from women so I didn't hurt them the way my dad hurt my mom, but I think it's probably more complicated than that. And I'd be lying if I told you I had it all figured out, but at least now I recognize it. And I want to work on it."

She stared at him, speechless and shocked. As much as she'd hoped he would change his mind and come to his senses, she knew things like that didn't happen in real life. Yet here he was.

He gave a heartfelt smile before he leaned forward and

rested his forehead against hers. "I realized that marriage and kids aren't unicorn sex. I think maybe I want them, I just never let myself think about it all before because I didn't think it would happen for me. I didn't want to take all of that away from you, the chance to get married and have kids if you wanted them."

"Yeah, I do want them. Someday." Her heartbeat fluttered happily, catching in her throat. She tilted her chin up and kissed him gently on the mouth. Ryan Lawhill would never be a true fairy-tale prince, but damn if he wasn't perfect for her.

A thought came to her, making her body go cold. "Not now, though, right? Like not...immediately."

He reared back in panic, his eyes going wide. "No. Definitely, no. I was thinking we could start with a dog or something first."

She kissed him again, melding her body to his chest, her tongue caressing his. Good. They finally were on the same page.

He pulled back abruptly. "Wait, wait. I forgot the most important part. I love you."

Warmth flooded her. "I love you too."

He grinned then. "See, I told you I'm no good at this relationship thing. Do you think you can teach me?"

She sighed and relaxed against him. She had a feeling that wouldn't be a problem.

EPILOGUE

One month later, in the Bahamas

Ryan stretched out in the beach chair and let the sun heat his skin.

Next to him, he heard the squeak of the rubber slats as Ainsley shifted again. He kept his eyes closed.

"Ryan?" she whispered.

He opened one eye. "Mhmm?"

She bit her lip. "Do you think Hippo's doing OK? With your mom?"

He reached to rest his hand on hers. "Absolutely, babe. She lived there for months. Plus, Hippo's happy everywhere there's food and people to snuggle her."

Ainsley sighed. "I just don't want her to think we abandoned her."

He rolled onto his side and smiled indulgently at her. "She won't think that."

"OK." Ainsley settled back against her chair reluctantly and closed her eyes. Seconds later, as he was about to roll onto his back, she jolted upright. "Do you think Claire's OK? That scuba instructor seemed kind of flaky. Should we check on her and her friends?"

"Definitely not." This time he sat up and leaned toward her, then rested a hand on each of her shoulders and gently pushed her until she was reclining.

His heart thudded in his chest. Her blonde hair was wild and wind-tossed, not a stitch of makeup graced her tan face. God, he loved her.

"Do I need to teach you how to relax, too?"

She quirked an eyebrow at him. "Maybe. What does this teaching involve?"

He flopped onto his back and crossed his arms behind his head. "Here, I'll show you."

Satisfaction coursed through his body. They still had so much to teach each other, and he was loving every second of it.

James Abell desperately needs a date to his sister's wedding. So when he runs into Kate Massie, his high school crush, he asks her a favor: come to the wedding with him and pretend that they're together. But soon one little lie turns into a full-blown fake relationship. Only the toe-curling kisses and electricity between them feels pretty real. Will the two fall for their own white lie?

Turn the page for a free excerpt from Kelly Eadon's THE WEDDING DATE.

CHAPTER ONE

Music blasted through the elevator. Its low, thumping bass line and bouncing beat made Kate Massie itch to dance.

"Yeah, girl, shake that booty." She could barely make out the muffled lyrics.

Kate couldn't help but grin as she glanced around the elevator. Three men stared back at her, their suits and ties as somber as their expressions. *Whose ring tone is it?* It wasn't the type of thing she expected to hear blaring from the briefcase of a fifty-something lawyer.

"She's a slut and she knows it. Just like that, uh, uh." The song transitioned to sexual grunting. Kate would have giggled, but all three men continued to stare at her.

That's when she realized.

Holy shit. It must be her phone.

Ryan, one of her best friends, must have changed her ring tone again. That was it, she officially needed to kill him.

Kate glanced at her cavernous bag, which was stuffed to the

brim with her laptop, sunglasses, makeup, granola bars, business cards, and God knew what else, and began to dig through, frantically searching for her kelly-green phone case. All of a sudden she felt like Mary freaking Poppins. The X-rated version.

Her cheeks flamed. The song had played for so long it had to be over. *Please let it be over.* By the time Kate found the phone the call had rolled to voice mail.

Stay calm. Kate straightened her shoulders and met each man's gaze, one at a time. All three continued to stare back coldly. She choked back the laughter that bubbled frantically inside her.

"So, uh, do you gentlemen have any big plans this weekend?"

One of them grunted something unintelligible, and a bead of sweat formed on the back of her neck.

As the elevator came to a halt on the ground floor, the song began to play again. Her stomach dropped.

You've got to be kidding me.

She'd just started this job. She'd see these men every day for the next year, and she refused to let them think she was…well, she wasn't sure what. She had to prove she was poised and in control. *That's what the Notorious RBG would do, right?*

Kate gave a little shimmy and danced her way out of the elevator and into the hall, keeping time with the beat. Then she booked it to her parking space. She never turned to see their faces.

In the safety of her beat-up Toyota sedan, Kate finally allowed herself to dissolve into laughter. When she regained control of herself, she checked her phone. Two missed calls. One from her sister, Rachel, and the second from Ryan. She wouldn't give him the satisfaction of a response yet.

Kate put on her Bluetooth headset, autodialed her sister, and pulled out of the parking garage.

Rachel answered on the first ring. "Hey! What're you doing?"

"I'm on my way to the gym. You'll never guess what happened." Kate filled her in on the most recent humiliation.

Rachel snorted.

"I know. Ryan got me this time." She'd already begun to plan her revenge. Something involving his beloved Ford Mustang and Silly String. Or maybe penis-shaped glitter. She still had some left from a bachelorette party.

"At least the lawyers know who you are." Her sister's voice was bright.

She flipped on her turn signal and merged onto the highway. Belmont, the beach town where she'd grown up, was only a fifteen-minute drive from the city.

"That's one way of looking at it. I may not have made a good impression, but at least I made an impression."

Rachel laughed again. "Other than your choice of elevator music, how's work?"

She bit her lip. "Mmm, OK, I guess. Kinda boring."

Thanks to the anemic legal job market, Kate had accepted a one-year clerkship for a federal judge. It was prestigious but not what she'd pictured herself doing after law school.

"The economy will pick up, and you'll get a job prosecuting. I know it."

Kate couldn't help but grin at her sister's optimism.

"What are you doing tonight?" Rachel asked.

She found a spot in the line of cars headed for Belmont and flipped on her cruise control. "Not sure yet. Gym, then something."

Her sister sighed loudly. "Kate. It's the weekend. Have fun. I need to live vicariously through you 'cuz I'm an old married fuddy-duddy."

"You'll never be a fuddy-duddy."

Her sister chuckled.

"I'll find something fun to do, I promise."

Rachel's voice turned soft with concern. "I just don't want you to be lonely."

"I know." She'd agonized over her decision to move back to Belmont. Yes, the beach was gorgeous and she had her best friends Ryan and Beth to keep her company, but this wasn't where she'd pictured herself. She'd always dreamed of a glamorous career prosecuting in a big city like New York or Philadelphia.

"What about guys? Have you met any guys?"

Her breath hitched. "There's a ridiculously sexy guy at the gym. Right now I'm content to ogle him."

In fact he'd seduced her in a dream the night before. Imaginary relationships were so much easier than real ones.

There was a long pause. "I want you to be happy again."

Her heart twisted. "I know. And I am happy, Rach. At least I'm as happy as I can be under the circumstances. I'm trying really hard. I promise."

Of all people, her sister understood why she couldn't put down roots here.

"I know you are. I'm proud of you and…"

On her sister's end of the line there was shrieking in the background.

"Ummm, the kids are destroying something. Shit, I gotta go."

"Love you!"

"Love you more!"

Her chest ached as her sister's end of the line went silent. Ever since college she'd had big plans for herself: go to law school, prosecute, and live in a big city near her sister. The plans hadn't worked out. Yet. She resolved to go to the gym and kick, punch, and sweat her way to a better mood, then grab some ice cream for dinner. The two would balance each other out.

When she reached the gym, she parked her car, slung her bag over her shoulder, and jogged to the front door. Only five minutes until kickboxing class, which didn't leave her much time to change. She began to dig through her Mary Poppins bag as she used her hip to push the gym door open. She was still searching for her membership card when she slammed into something solid. A large hand reached out to grip her elbow and kept her balanced.

Someone solid. And delicious smelling. Kate caught the scent of sandalwood, apple, and woods. She tore her attention from the contents of her bag.

"I'm so sorry." She met the man's vivid light-gray eyes.

Her stomach did a flip, and the intensity of his gaze sucked the breath from her lungs.

She'd run straight into the headlining star of last night's dream.

"Are you OK?" James couldn't believe his luck. He'd given up hope of seeing her today and had been leaving the gym when *bam*, there she was.

His pulse pounded. Of course he'd known her the moment he first saw her. Kate Massie. His date from junior prom. He'd have recognized her long legs and sparkling brown eyes anywhere.

"I'm sorry. I wasn't paying attention." A flush of pink spread across her cheeks. Her forehead furrowed as she stared at him, but she didn't remove her elbow from his grasp. The feel of her soft skin under his fingertips sent a surge of heat through him.

A woman's singsong voice called his name, jerking him back to the present. His jaw tensed and he stepped out of the doorway, pulling Kate with him. Ainsley would recognize her immediately, and their brief moment alone would end before it had even started.

Ainsley was out of breath when the woman rushed up to him. "Thank goodness you haven't left yet. I just remembered I left my lipstick in your car."

She froze, her jaw dropping as her attention shifted to Kate. "Ohmygawd!" she squealed. "Katie?"

Kate's eyes narrowed, as if she was trying to place her. So she didn't recognize Ainsley, either.

Then Ainsley enveloped her in a hug. "I can't believe it's you! What are you doing here? Did you finish law school? Did you move back? Where are you working? Where are you living?" The rapid-fire speed of her questions seemed to trigger Kate's memory and she broke into a grin.

God, I love her smile. She was one of those people who smiled with her eyes, not just her lips. Although her lips were equally appealing. He caught himself staring at her mouth and forced his eyes away.

"Ainsley! It's great to see you. Things are pretty good. I finished law school, I moved back, and I'm working for a judge." Her attention flicked back to him, and her pupils dilated slightly.

And suddenly his night just got a lot more interesting.

Ainsley placed a hand on his shoulder. "You remember my friend James, right? James Abell, you went to our junior prom with him?"

A smile spread across her face, stoking the fire inside him. Kate hadn't gone to their high school, but she had played soccer with Ainsley. When he'd needed a date at the last minute, Ainsley had recruited her.

"Hey." She reached out to grasp his hand.

Her fingers fit perfectly in his, and he waited a long moment before he released them.

"Hey, Kate, it's good to see you again." He'd recognized her the other day and had been working on a plan to reintroduce himself ever since. *Problem solved.*

"Are you going to kickboxing class?" Ainsley motioned down the hall toward the group fitness room.

Kate untangled her gaze from his. "Yeah, it's my first time. I need to change first."

"Yay!" Ainsley clapped her hands. "I'm going, too. We can go together."

This was his chance. He had to act fast.

"We're getting drinks with some friends after this. You should come, Kate."

He and Ainsley met a group of fellow Fallston Prep School graduates for happy hour every Friday night.

Ainsley tugged Kate in the direction of the women's locker room. "Oh, you should come! I'll give you the details."

She shot him another smile. "I'd love to. See you later."

Adrenaline coursed through him. He'd see her later.

CHAPTER TWO

She smoothed back a few sweaty strands of hair and glanced at her reflection in the rearview mirror. At least she'd run into him before her workout and not after.

No way is that James Abell. Absolutely no way.

Her junior prom date had been tall, gangly, and awkward, with bushy hair. Ainsley had practically begged Kate to go with him because he was too shy to ask anyone. He wasn't the least bit awkward anymore. Her face heated all over again as she recalled his tall, well-sculpted body and the way his faded T-shirt outlined his chest muscles.

I bet he has no problem getting dates anymore.

The mere memory of his body launched a primal flutter in her stomach. How ironic that this man, the man from her dream, was the same bumbling boy who'd been too scared to dance with her ten years before.

She took a steadying breath and let herself through the front door of her apartment. Wally threw himself at her, covering her workout clothes with a fine layer of black dog fur. He woofed and wiggled in circles around her legs as she struggled in the direction of her bedroom.

Her childhood best friend and roommate, Beth, sat cross-legged on the living room floor, with fabric and googly eyes strewn around her.

"What are you doing, bunny?" Kate flopped onto the floor next to Beth. She dislodged a piece of felt that had attached itself to her running shoe and handed it back to her friend.

Creative chaos, Beth called it. She was always working on a new project, each one weirder than the last. Her creations littered parts of their dining room table and the living room floor.

Beth dabbed hot glue onto the felt. "Making rat costumes for *The Pied Piper*."

As one of her many part-time jobs, Beth managed Belmont's children's theater.

Kate snickered. "You couldn't find a way to recycle the costumes for *The Three Little Pigs*?"

Last year Kate had spent her spring break constructing pig heads from papier mâché, and she still couldn't look at anything pink without having flashbacks.

Beth wrinkled her nose. "Very funny. Do you want to help? I have an extra glue gun around here somewhere."

The invitation gave her the warm fuzzies. The highlight of moving back to Belmont had been the chance to live with Beth.

She fiddled with a piece of felt. "I, um, kind of made plans."

"Oh, yeah?" Beth's eyes brightened as she lowered the glue gun. "Do these plans involve a cute guy?"

Kate shot her a look. Why did everyone keep asking that question? Beth, Rachel. They knew she was in Belmont only temporarily. They knew she needed to focus on finding a job as a prosecutor. And they knew how she felt about relationships.

"Well, what does he look like?" Beth was, as usual, impervious to Kate's snarky attitude.

Tall. Handsome. Magnetically sexy and charismatic.

Beth's face lit up as she grabbed Kate's hands. "Is this a date tonight?"

She rolled her eyes. "Of course not. It's like a group thing. Ainsley and her boyfriend will be there, too."

Beth's eyebrows rose at the mention of Ainsley's name, but she said nothing. For the most part they'd hung out with their own public school crowd in high school.

"Does that mean you want me to make you a rat costume to wear?" Beth held up a square of brown felt.

Kate grimaced at the mental image of walking into one of the preppiest bars in town wearing head-to-toe felt and googly eyes.

Beth giggled. "I'm going to take that as a no. Which is a good thing, because I do have a date later, and I don't know if I have time to turn you into a rat."

"A date, huh? Who's the lucky guy?" It was her turn to raise an eyebrow.

Beth shrugged. "A guy I met the other week at an art show. He seemed nice."

Oh, Beth. She honestly believed the universe would drop the perfect guy in her lap and it would all work out. Plus she was too nice to turn down dates.

Kate stood from her spot on the floor. She needed to take a shower before going out in public.

"Don't get kidnapped," she called over her shoulder. She closed the bathroom door behind her and turned the shower on full blast.

Tonight was the perfect chance to get out and be social, just as she'd promised Rachel. While she was at it, she might as well harvest some more mental images of James for her late-night fantasies.

* * *

James sidled up to the wooden bar, took the spot next to Ainsley, caught the bartender's eye, and pointed to a local beer on tap.

"Scott's meeting us on his way from work. Who else is coming?" she asked.

"Just us." A lot of their regular group had bowed out for one reason or another: work, family obligations, that kind of thing. Not that he was sorry it would be only the four of them.

"Can you believe Kate Massie is back in Belmont?" Ainsley should have been a social anthropologist. She was obsessed with interpreting social situations and homing in on unspoken social cues.

He took a swig of the beer the bartender plopped in front of him. "Why? She's from here, isn't she?"

He knew Ainsley. If she got any inkling of the way Kate made his blood pound she'd spiral into matchmaker mode. She meant well, but he wasn't in the mood for her meddling.

His mom did enough meddling on the subject of his love life.

Ainsley fiddled with the paper napkin beneath her drink. "I guess. I tried to catch up with her in college, but she said she never came back here anymore."

He was careful to keep his expression neutral. He'd lost track of Kate after junior prom. He should've asked her for her number, but he'd been too shy and tongue-tied in her presence.

That was a long time ago.

It was better not to dwell on what could have happened in the past. He'd turned over a new leaf when he broke up with Brooke, and he'd spent the past six months making up for lost time. Literally running into Kate at the gym must have been a sign.

He took another swig of beer and tapped his thumb impatiently against the wooden bar. What time had Ainsley told Kate to arrive? He was ready for her to meet the new James Abell.

9 781455 594016